Provocation

DAVID GLEDHILL

This book is dedicated to the servicemen and women who fought and won the Cold War on the ground and in the air.

DeeGee Media Ltd.

http://deegee-media.webnode.com/

First Published 2015.

CONTENTS

PROLOGUE

RAF WILDENRATH, WEST GERMANY, MARCH 1983

Carl Pocklington rested his heels on the balcony rail and kicked back in his chair. Wassenberg was quiet at this late hour and, as he watched, a car made its way down the gentle incline into the centre of town its cold engine pushing out a cloud of exhaust smoke. Their lovemaking had been urgent and unfamiliar feelings were stirring which had been dormant for too long. He nursed the bottle of Grolsch lager, its presence more a comfort than a necessity.

In the bedroom Anneliese Kolber was sleeping soundly. It had been a whirlwind since he had met her four months ago and he realised that he was head-over-heels in love. There could be no disguising the depth of his feelings for the attractive young German girl despite the age gap but he could not have anticipated the turn of events which had unfolded that evening. Sitting at a quiet table in the local restaurant, the wine flowing, she had at first coaxed but, increasingly, cajoled. From the outset her story had gripped him. She was born and raised in Ismaning, a small suburb of Munich, or so she had said, and her strong Bavarian accent seemed to back up the story. Tonight, however, she had ended the subterfuge. Her family's roots were indeed in Bavaria but, towards the end of World War 2 they had headed north to avoid the devastating attacks on the city and become trapped between the Allies advancing from the west and the Russians pushing from the east. Their flight had stalled in Magdeburg where they had, reluctantly, settled. When the Inner German Border finally split the two halves of her country, the family was trapped on the wrong side of the fence. Life for her parents had been hard for the following years but there was a reluctant gratitude towards the occupying Soviet forces who allowed them to rebuild their shattered lives, albeit in the austere concrete jungle of the shattered city. The young Anneliese had known only a life under occupation and the drab concrete blocks of flats were what she called home but she had always borne hopes that one day she could return to her family roots in the south of her divided country. Whether it was a good thing or a bad thing for the ambitious young girl, her good looks and sharp intellect had singled her out and she attracted the attention of the local Stasi representative who had cultivated her. She had flourished and, when she was offered a chance to train as an agent with the prospect of working in the West, she had taken the chance willingly. With no doctrinal loyalty to the puppet Government in East Berlin she hid her overwhelming desire to escape despite intensive scrutiny during training and indoctrination. Treading the fine line had become a driving motivation in her life and she had, finally, seen a potential route out. Nevertheless, if she was ever to flee to the West and remain there permanently she would need money. Her new role was hardly lucrative and her freedom was limited by the latitude her handler allowed. If he suspected even a hint of treachery she would be recalled to East Germany leaving Carl and his embryonic hopes and desires behind. In the meantime she plotted.

For Carl with his right wing views and his unadventurous upbringing in an expensive boarding school in Surrey, the contrast could not have been starker. He felt immense sympathy for her plight and an overwhelming urge to give her the money she had asked for. After all, it was sitting in the local bank doing very little other than earn a few Deutschmarks in interest. The earth-shaking revelation had been Anneliese's admission that she worked for the Stasi which would mean that his hard-earned cash would be bankrolling the very people he was supposed to be fighting against. If the Station Provost Marshal at Wildenrath picked up the slightest hint of his links with her, he would be removed from his post within hours. She asked a lot. His job on 60 Squadron seemed to an outsider to be a nice little backwater ferrying VIPs around Germany and, occasionally, back to the UK. The aging Percival Pembroke commuter plane was slow and the job undemanding; well, at least on the face of it. It was a far cry from the mayhem of a Buccaneer cockpit where he had learned his trade before losing his ejection seat category a few years ago. The reality was that whenever the small plane flew on its regular trips into Berlin, either he or a fellow navigator sat in the small cabin armed with the latest photographic equipment and his role was somewhat more clandestine. At least once a week the Pembroke made its way down one of the corridors into RAF Gatow in West Berlin and the cameras snapped away as it went. The pictures taken during the sorties provided a significant piece in the jigsaw puzzle identifying the military intent of the Group of Soviet Forces in Germany which were ranged across Eastern Europe. One of the first indications of the outbreak of World War 3 would be military manoeuvres, probably captured on film by a Pembroke crew or maybe by the BRIXMIS Military Liaison Mission, as Soviet forces massed on the border. He was the instrument for collecting that intelligence but was, suddenly, intricately involved as a piece of the intelligence jigsaw.

The revelations stunned him. He had an irresistible desire to help his pretty German girlfriend but what would he do? Could he betray his country even for love? He took another long draught of beer. The coming months would tell.

CHAPTER 1

THE CENTRAL BERLIN CORRIDOR, EAST GERMANY

The Pan American Airlines Boeing 727 descended to 10,000 feet overhead the radio beacon at Wolfsburg and turned onto east. John Peterson cross checked his VOR radio navigation system, the figures "270" staring back at him from the small dial, the steering bars rock steady, reassuring the former fighter pilot that he had set the correct heading. His Air Force callsign "Shooter" seemed truly redundant in the cockpit of his new machine. Flying around Europe he could afford to be more casual with the accuracy of his navigation but along these 20 mile wide corridors that converged on Berlin, precision was paramount. The warnings on his navigation chart were stark:

"Aircraft deviating from the corridors may be intercepted and fired upon without warning."

The view through the windows from the confined cockpit of the jetliner was limited and he stared blankly at the featureless terrain, hankering for the days when he flew the F4 Phantom from Ramstein Air Force base near Frankfurt. Although the operational pace had been hectic and the hours wearing a gas mask tedious, the rewards were enormous and fond memories were still fresh. His new life as an airline pilot was comfortable and predictable but, arguably, less fulfilling.

It was some time yet before he would initiate the pre-landing checks and begin the let down into Berlin Tempelhof. Alongside him, the co-pilot scribbled a few notes on his chart oblivious to the world outside despite their precarious situation. There was a gulf between the pace of life in this cockpit and that of his Phantom, Peterson reflected. The radio crackled into life.

"Clipper 324, Berlin Centre, you have converging traffic, northwest range five miles closing, showing similar level."

He screwed his head around but the intrusive bulkhead behind the cockpit window blocked his view. In his Phantom he would already be manoeuvring to spot the approaching track but, if he did so now, he would spill those precious gins and tonic down the back and antagonise his passengers.

"Roger Berlin Centre, no tally," he responded, reverting unintentionally to "fighter speak". "Keep talking."

"Northwest range two, closing rapidly, showing 10,000 feet."

He glanced at the altimeter which showed precisely the same height. Whatever it was, it was a collision risk and he stared intently, straining for a pick up. His wait was short.

The increased chatter from the air traffic controller was both redundant and distracting. The pilot needed no prompting. He had a problem. Far from being a collision risk, the burnished, silver Mig-21 Fishbed, which had slotted onto his wing and moved into tight close formation, was a clear and present threat of a different type. What he could not see was the wingman who had slotted into position one mile behind, well inside weapons parameters for the AA-2 Atoll infra red guided air-to-air missiles which hung beneath the delta wing.

The Mig dropped from view and his heartbeat quickened. So far there had been no interception signals from the other cockpit but the wait was brief as the fighter pulled up ahead of the wing line of the Boeing and slotted alongside, agonisingly close. The dark visor of the Mig pilot hid the face behind, his white flying helmet framed against the blue sky. The Mig jockeyed for position his presence affecting the airflow around the larger airliner. Behind him Peterson heard the click of a shutter as the co-pilot snapped a shot of the aggressor, apparently oblivious to the severity of the situation. The Mig pilot attempted a few ungainly hand signals but he was too close and his hand quickly returned inside the cockpit as the Mig gyrated alarmingly coming very close to colliding. The American pilot disengaged the autopilot fighting the urge to draw away despite fearing imminent contact. The radio was quiet as the controller lapsed into silence, presumably in frantic discussion with his Soviet counterpart in Berlin. The standoff continued for what seemed like hours but, in reality was only minutes before the Mig eased out into a loose formation alongside. Far from improving the mood, the manoeuvre raised the tension in the cockpit.

Without warning, the second Mig which until now had been invisible, appeared from under the nose and pulled up, entering a vigorous climb as the afterburner lit, filling the windscreen with its delta wing planform. The dramatic image was transitory as it separated at high speed, disappearing from view. The airliner rocked in the wake turbulence and Peterson clicked on the seat belt signs in the cabin only now realising his omission.

As quickly as the incident had begun, it was over. No shots had been fired but the message had been clear. The ordered routine of life in the airspace over East Germany had been suspended.

"Clipper 324, Berlin Centre, radio check". . . . .

As Peterson engaged the nosewheel steering after completing his landing roll at Tempelhof airport and eased the airliner onto the fast access track, sweat glistened on his forehead. The incident had unsettled his normally robust demeanour. He was relieved to be on the ground at his destination rather than at an East German military airfield. He suspected that the extensive reports he was about to file would delay the flight back to Frankfurt. He had been party to what might be the opening gambit of World War 3.

CHAPTER 2

RAF WATTISHAM, SUFFOLK

Roy South wandered down the corridor and knocked on the office door. The Boss could be a prickly old git but the muffled response from inside sounded vaguely positive for a change so he pushed open the door and walked in.

"Roy, take a pew."

The perfunctory wave directed him to the seat on the other side of the desk, the Boss's head still buried in a file.

"You know "Flash" Gordon from your time as an instructor on the Conversion Unit, don't you?" Didn't he go through the conversion course with you?"

"He did Boss, why?" he replied with a slight feeling of trepidation. His mind slipped back to his short conversion course onto the Phantom at RAF Coningsby in Lincolnshire where he had endured the pain with the young navigator as they had grappled with learning the foibles of the F4 Phantom. His time on the Operational Conversion Unit had not been plain sailing and the occasional stumble had caused more than a few sleepless nights as he had traded the cockpit of a Vulcan bomber for the tighter confines of his new jet. His young navigator had fought to come to terms with the complex and unpredictable radar but his own progress had also slowed during the air combat phase when faced with the three dimensional challenge of basic fighter manoeuvres. He struggled to link events on the course with his new role as Flight Commander on the Squadron but the conversation moved on swiftly solving his quandary.

"Because it looks like it's got you a detachment to Wildenrath."

His spirits rose rapidly. Wildenrath was the RAF fighter base located on the border between West Germany and the Netherlands. Belgium lay a few kilometres to the south and it was a superb location for a detachment. With its two squadrons of Phantoms, squadrons of Rapier and Bloodhound surface-to-air missiles and a communications squadron flying Pembrokes, Wildenrath was a bustling Station. The social life amongst the population of isolated Brits was second to none and the flying, which was predominantly low level over the North German countryside, was exhilarating.

"He's the planner for an exercise that's coming up and when I heard his name, yours sprang to mind. You owe him a beer because this one will be popular. I want you to lead a detachment to Wildenrath. Bold Challenge is a Berlin Corridor reinforcement exercise and this year it'll be hosted by 92 Squadron but we've been tasked to provide two jets to bolster their numbers. They have a detachment to Decimomannu coming up and they can't handle the full commitment. It seemed like a good deal so I jumped at the chance."

"Good idea Boss, who are the key players?"

"The Americans are sending Phantoms from Ramstein and the French will provide four Mirage IIIs from Dijon. It's a tri-partite commitment that dates back to the post war agreements which is why the Germans are not playing. The new F-15As from Bitburg were due to take part but the unit is on TACEVAL during that week so they can't play."

"Can I take any support with me?"

"No, the resident squadron will handle all the turn-rounds on the jets and any rectification that's needed. They're grateful for the extra airframes to let them prepare for their upcoming detachment. You'll operate from Delta Dispersal at Wildenrath alongside 92 Squadron. I'll give you a spare crew but they'll have to get over there on the ferry unless you can scrounge two spare seats on the trooper flight from Luton. I'll leave that to you and you can decide who you take with you."

"When is it?"

"Thought you might ask. It's a short fuse and the exercise begins next Monday so you'll have to fly out on Friday to be in place and ready to go on the first wave on Monday morning."

"No pressure then," he replied, running through an imaginary checklist in his head.

"You need to be in the same fit as the Wildenrath jets so liaise with SENGO and have the guns fitted. Two jets and a spare in case you have a problem on start up. Here are the details of the project officer at HQ RAF Germany. Get in touch with him and introduce yourself but let 92 Squadron do all the planning. Here's Flash's number at Wildenrath. Enjoy the exercise."

South grasped the proffered tasking signal but the Wing Commander held his grip on the flimsy paper and met his gaze.

"Oh I should have added. The stakes were raised yesterday. The Sovs intercepted a 727 inbound to Tempelhof. A couple of Fishbeds targeted the midday flight inside the central corridor. No shots were fired but they gave the crew a fright. If I was to guess I'd say HQ RAF Germany might want to send a message back to the Sovs so expect some aggressive exercise play."

South withdrew, his mind in overdrive. It was already Wednesday and with only the briefest details he had much to do to catch up. They would have to fly out on Friday morning to bed down the jets before the exercise. Between now and then he had a raft of things to arrange. The thought that the exercise might be a flashpoint had not yet fully registered. Maybe the Cold War was warming up.

CHAPTER 3

THE KREMLIN, MOSCOW

Colonel General Artur Portnov had endured another tiresome meeting in the Supreme Soviet and his frustration bubbled below the surface. He threw his service dress hat onto the desk and dropped heavily into his chair, his medals clattering against the lip as he picked up a glass and drew heavily on the contents. It was early for vodka but he needed the relief it offered. Flicking open the buttons on his tunic easing the ever-growing tension on his dress uniform, he rolled back in the chair. His prominent gut was testament to the quality of the fillet steak, his secret passion at the Guards Club in Frunzeskaya. The buzz from the vodka slowly eased the tension but an incipient migraine threatened to ruin his morning. If he had to listen to any more drivel from that pipsqueak Gorbachev he swore he would arrange for the idiot to be arrested even if he had to do it himself. All the talk of appeasement was folly and it was time Andropov took a firmer grip. In the past even the Party Chairman had been removed for such suggestions of weakness. Another slug of vodka helped and his thoughts became less emotional and more pragmatic.

What to do about it, he mused. He had a number of protégés amongst the leadership of the 16th Tactical Air Army in East Germany who knew that their compliance would guarantee sponsorship when it came time for them to bid for political status. He would begin to call in a few favours but he needed a vehicle for his plans. This week's incident in the Berlin Corridor had helped. The upcoming NATO air exercise should provide another opportunity and it was time to stoke up a few old rivalries in the military hierarchy. The annual event was always interesting and the intelligence reports amused him for days. If Soviet troops found working with their East German brethren difficult, he could see that NATO was not immune, particularly when the maverick French pilots were thrown into the mix. As always, the Americans would dominate. They may allow the British to lead a few sorties but he doubted if the concession would be extended to the French. The fact that France had opted out of the NATO command structure would be offered as the excuse but the real reasons were clear. Even so, with the exercise planned to run in the northern airspace this year he would need to target the decision makers in the 2nd Allied Tactical Air Force Headquarters at Rheindahlen, known as TWOATAF, who would command the forces. For that he might need help. He felt sure that with the additional air traffic in the border area it would not be too difficult to provoke a hasty response. There had been another incident some months before when a military transport aircraft flying into Berlin had strayed from the transit corridor and infringed East German airspace. The controllers had been way too lax and had allowed the western air traffic controllers to steer it back on course without intervention. The idiots had even confessed openly that the weather was too bad to launch the alert aircraft from Zerbst. What an admission. Maybe an increase in the alert state was called for? That was always a good way to get the claxons blaring across the bases in West Germany and would compensate. A few tank regiments moved into the forward holding areas always generated a predictable response from the western politicians. With carefully chosen confrontations he could guarantee a few more early morning call outs along the border. Give them a week and they will be lulled into a false complacency; if they still had the energy to think clearly.

He would make contact with his man in Berlin who was highly placed at the Stasi Headquarters. It was time for a long chat. He might even take a few days out to visit the former capital and take a break from the cauldron of daily politics in Moscow. With his military privileges he could take a journey into the Western Sector through Checkpoint Charlie and then he would sample some delights, and he was not thinking of culinary options.

His mind snapped back to the present. He would not be part of this lunacy in the Presidium. The Soviet Union had grown strong by assembling the most formidable Army in history. There were three armies, massive standing formations of troops, ranged along the Inner German Border from the Baltic Sea in the north to the Czechoslovakian border in the south and their presence was no mistake. They were there to implement the grand plan should it ever be necessary and their aim was simple: to roll across West Germany and the Low Countries and to capture the channel ports. Without a toehold in Europe, the Americans would be unable to reinforce and he doubted they really had the stomach for nuclear or chemical warfare. They would be relegated to sniping from the UK. What was abundantly clear was that if the Soviet Union showed the West any hint of compliance, the gains made by the Warsaw Pact since the end of the Great Patriotic War would be rolled back and all would be lost. The satellite states might even consider democracy for heaven's sake.

It was time to rattle a few cages.

CHAPTER 4

RAF WILDENRATH ON THE DUTCH BORDER

RAF Wildenrath, one of the so called "Clutch" airfields, was clustered together with its sister stations on the Dutch border set between the towns of Mönchen Gladbach in Germany and Roermond in Holland. Along with the bomber bases at Laarbruch and Brüggen it provided the air defence contribution to the NATO Second Allied Tactical Air Force or TWOATAF. Much further east, RAF Gutersloh was the fourth RAF airfield closer to the Inner German Border and only a few minutes flying time from East Germany.

The east/west runway split the forest of Nordrhein Westphalia with the airfield lying south of the village from which it took its name. Built in the immediate aftermath of World War 2 the first commander was a wartime flying ace and it had been home to many illustrious fighter squadrons over the years. Five dispersals clustered around the runway with normal flying operations taking place from the south side. No. 19 Squadron operated from one of the these, known as Bravo Dispersal, which also housed two hardened shelters for Battle Flight, the Quick Reaction Alert facility. No. 92 Squadron flew from Delta Dispersal at the western end of the airfield with the southern taxiway running parallel to the main runway linking the fighter dispersals. A redundant dispersal, known as Charlie Dispersal, sat between the two occupied by the squadrons.

On the opposite side of Wildenrath airfield to the north, Alpha Dispersal was home to No. 25 Squadron with its Bloodhound surface-to-air missiles, the launchers set in revetments pointing menacingly eastwards. A separate hangar housed a large Army contingent which provided a battle damage repair squadron and a signals regiment deploying into the field, regularly, to support Army units and the RAF Harrier force. Large hangars set alongside the aircraft servicing platform housed No. 60 Squadron, the communications squadron, equipped with the Pembroke communications aircraft. In addition to their usual task ferrying passengers and priority freight around Germany and to the UK, the Pembrokes regularly plied the Berlin air corridors landing at RAF Gatow in the British controlled sector. During these missions specially adapted versions of the innocent looking communications plane would photograph Soviet installations as it made its way eastwards. On approach to RAF Gatow the crew would switch off the surveillance equipment and close the curtains in the cabin. After landing the Pembroke would park with the cabin door next to the hangar to ensure that East German Guards in the adjacent watch towers in the Soviet sector could not see into the aircraft. Tight operational security became the norm and crews avoided indiscrete conversation to foil the directional microphones which were trained on them from the watchtowers. Invariably, a fictitious 'snag' on the aircraft would develop that would require an air test in the local airspace after rectification. Depending on the workload back on the Squadron, the airtest would be scheduled for later in the day or, if the crew was fortunate and the weather intervened, on the following day. The flight would take full advantage of the 20 mile Berlin Control Zone and the Pembroke would skirt the edges of the Zone with its cameras snapping away. With the "snag" miraculously cleared the crew would return to Wildenrath via a different air corridor and return their haul to the intelligence analysts. Few of the regular personnel at Wildenrath had any inkling of the task but were often frustrated when requests to accompany the crews to Berlin were denied.

Set between the two main dispersals on the south side, "Charlie Dispersal" was normally unoccupied but occasionally was brought into use during reinforcement exercises. It had been some time since an Air National Guard Phantom squadron had flown in from the United States to take part in the annual NATO Exercise "Cold Fire". For a brief two weeks the dispersal had been a hive of activity as the American visitors had been challenged by the changeable weather conditions of Autumn in Northern Germany. Since then the dispersal had lain idle, opened up occasionally to allow infrequent NATO visitors to experience the unusual first generation hardened shelters which ringed the taxiways. For the next week it would become the temporary home for the visitors for Exercise Bold Challenge. With the impending exercise, the pilots briefing facility, or PBF, had been opened up along with the shelters and technicians were busily checking communications and services ready for the arrival of the aircraft at the end of the week. The shelters would be the temporary home for the Phantoms of the United States Air Force and the Mirage IIIs of the French Air Force.

A short way down the taxiway in Delta Dispersal, Jim "Flash" Gordon sat in a small communal office and flicked through a file, the pink paper cover of which was marked prominently with SECRET, over-stamped in red at the header and footer. Having signed out the classified folder from the Squadron Registry he was taking good care of it whilst it was in his care. He had been planning Exercise Bold Challenge for six months and all the details of how the exercise would evolve were contained in the loose leaf entries in the file and firmly imprinted in his mind. With the arrival of the jets the following day, his planning skills would be put to the test and his efforts would turn towards executing the plan. He felt a buzz of anticipation at the culmination of his efforts.

The exercise was a stark reminder of the divisions of the Cold War. With the setting up of the opposing power blocks, NATO and the Warsaw Pact, the former wartime allies were now overtly hostile towards each other. Post war agreements allowed for the western powers to gain access to the capital Berlin in the Soviet Sector via road, rail and air links. As the Soviets had tightened their grip in the years immediately after the war, the closure of the road and rail links had left air corridors as the only means to access the beleaguered city. The infamous Berlin Airlift of 1948 had seen aircraft of the allied nations resupply the entire needs of the West Berliners by air for nearly twelve months. During that time, a steady flow of transport aircraft flew into Berlin and over 200,000 sorties were flown. Only aircraft operated by the three wartime allies, America, France and Great Britain could fly down the specially designated air corridors which converged on West Berlin. The northerly corridor started near Hamburg, the central corridor near Hannover and the southerly corridor near Kassel, all converging on the former capital city. Before 1952, the IGB could be crossed at almost any point along its length but with the reinforcement of the border in the early 60s, hundreds of rail, road, river and even cart tracks were cut by the most comprehensive defences ever devised. A four metre high fence was backed up by anti vehicle ditches, tripwires, claymore mines, searchlights and dog runs. Watchtowers set a few kilometres apart allowed the border guards to monitor activity along the fence. The sobering aspect was that the defences were to keep the East German population in, not the NATO forces out.

Exercise Bold Challenge was the legacy of division. Mounted by three of the wartime allies it was designed to ensure that the right of access to West Berlin could be assured. The fourth wartime ally had become the aggressor. Once a year, flights of fighter jets gathered at one of the West German airbases and flew missions escorting transport aircraft along simulated corridors designed to represent the dimensions of the Berlin Corridors precisely. Opposed by "Red Air", the mission leader's task was to ensure that the friendly transport was protected as it made its way to its famous destination. The scenarios were designed to escalate after a rise in tensions, all the way through to a full blown shooting war. Each of the allies would be given the opportunity to lead a mission and the outcomes would be carefully analysed and dissected.

As Flash drew the simulated "Berlin Corridor" on the low flying chart his pilot, Mark "Razor" Keene peered over his shoulder catching him unawares.

"Is that where we're working next week?"

"Yes, they've put us over in the airspace above Low Flying Area 3 to the east. Some of the play area butts right onto the Buffer Zone and the Air Defence Interception Zone. It's going to be quite interesting working so close."

Razor pulled up a chair and pored over the chart picking up the details from Flash's scribblings.

"Impressive."

"Isn't it? What you see is two of the most powerful military power blocks ever created facing off across a narrow fortified strip of land. NATO has thousands of combat aircraft ranged against the Warsaw Pact. Over the

Inner German Border the Soviet 16th Tactical Air Army provides air support to the Group of Soviet Forces Germany with about 1,300 aircraft. It's reinforced by the Polish, East German and Czechoslovakian Air Forces all along the boundary. They operate from different air bases but work together on exercises but you can be certain, the Soviets call the shots and run all the command and control networks. Some of the bases you'll recognise from the intelligence briefings. They have a lot of aging kit ranging from old marks of Mig-21 Fishbed such as the Deltas which have only two stern hemisphere AA-2 Atoll infra-red guided missiles, to some of the later Lima models which have four, including a semi-active version of the Atoll. The Mig-23 Floggers are more modern and much more capable and carry four AA-7 Apex semi-active missiles and four AA-8 Aphid infra-red guided missiles. They have a much better radar. There are also Delta model Floggers which carry out the ground attack mission alongside a number of other types. The older Su-7 Fitters are being supplemented by the Su-24 Fencer and they say it can carry out deep strike into the rear areas. It may even be able to reach UK from East German bases. Don't forget the Mil-24 Hind helicopters. They have transport and attack versions which operate close to the front line."

"Let's hope they stay on their side. How come the exercise area is so close to the IGB?"

"The hierarchy want the Sovs to see it. There are radar sites and listening posts all the way up the border. The orientation and dimensions of the corridor have been planned to replicate the southern corridor from Kassel up to Berlin. When we get the daily tasking signal we'll be able to practice the actual timings as if it was real. I've been checking the intelligence books and there's a Ramona site right here," he said stabbing his finger at a point a few miles behind "The Iron Curtain."

"They'll be monitoring us but we'll be under radar control from the Loneship GCI site so they'll be keeping a close watch for anyone getting too close. Stand by for a "Brass Monkey" call if anyone infringes the zone."

"That could be tense. Anyone who gets that close to the IGB might be on a quick trip home. What's that site you've marked on their side of the border?"

"Are you familiar with the Ramona equipment?"

"Never heard of it, fill me in."

"It's a Czech-built passive detection, electronic support measures system. A series of sensitive receivers listen to our frequencies and track any emissions. They can triangulate our location and work out exactly which platform is transmitting. It's not only radio frequencies they can track. They can detect your IFF and TACAN and if you're transmitting they can track your position. It's nearly as good as radar if you give it the chance. That's why it's not good to witter too much on the radio. The rumour is that they have an even better system called Tamara being tested right now."

"Nice. Have we got the same capability?"

"Yes we have. The Army signals unit on base has some clever kit and they're always deploying up into the border area when the exercises are running. I'm sure they'll be out next week to listen in to our chat frequencies."

"Bloody hell, is nothing private around here?"

"Nope, get used to it. Big brother is watching . . . . . and listening."

"Where are the main air bases?"

"Probably the ones which will affect us most are Zerbst here, Brandenburg here and Juterbog, Altes Laage here," he said jabbing a finger on the map.

"So what's the plan? Who's providing the opposing Red Air?"

"The Tactical Weapons Unit from Brawdy has been tasked to send a couple of Hawks over to simulate Russian Migs. They're flying in tomorrow with the rest of the "Blue" players and they'll work out of Charlie Dispersal with the rest of the guys."

"Should be good. I'm looking forward to seeing how this develops. This is a first for me. It'll make a change from the normal low flying sorties."

"I'm giving an exercise briefing on Friday once all the external players are here. They'll be arriving on Friday morning and the briefing's at 1500 in the main briefing room on Charlie. We're only putting two jets into it and 56 Squadron are sending a pair from Wattisham. We're allocating three crews so that we all get a chance to try each of the scenarios. The Americans are sending four Phantoms; E models, and the French have some Mirage IIIs. Should be an interesting mix."

"Sounds good. Do the Americans have pulse-Doppler radars?"

"No, the E model only has a pulse set. They'll be OK for the medium level stuff but they'll struggle when we take it down to low level. The maximum height in the real corridors is 10,000 feet so some of the runs will be 5,000 feet and below. That'll sort the men from the boys. Mind you, they have TISEO which is a long range electro-optical identification system so they will identify the bad guy well before we do. If they can get a radar lock, that is."

"Outstanding. Let me know if you need any help. I'm a dab hand with low flying charts."

The navigator grimaced.

"Maybe you should leave the clever stuff to me Biggles!"

CHAPTER 5

STASI HEADQUARTERS, EAST BERLIN

Dieter Meier flicked through the intelligence report on his desk and pushed it tiredly aside turning to the more interesting reports from his network of agents spread around West Germany. From his drab office in the Ministerium für Staatssicherheit Headquarters, more commonly known as the Stasi, on the Ruschestraße in the Lichtenberg district of Berlin, he controlled a network which spread out across Europe. It had been a lean few months but he hoped for a turnaround in fortunes once a few of his recent initiatives came to fruition. There was the usual diet of low grade material but nothing to set his pulse racing. Even his star pupil in the Chancellor's Office in Bonn, the West German Capital, had been remarkably quiet.

Born in Magdeburg shortly after the War he had suffered the backlash from the hard right policies of the war years. As a young boy he remembered the strikes of 1953 that led to the transformation of the German Democratic Republic into a socialist state. Despite the excesses of the socialist party and the communist Government it had not taken much to shift his thinking towards the doctrine of the left. With the division of his country in 1961, initially with a wall in Berlin but followed soon after by a reinforcement of the whole border, he decided to act. As he worked through University he realised that the only way to progress in the new hierarchy was to be part of the apparatus and he made moves to join the secret service. His attitudes hardened and he surprised even himself with his ruthless streak. Since he had joined the organisation as a young 21 year old he had risen through the ranks quickly becoming the youngest controller of a network of agents in the Ministry's history. If he was to keep the momentum going he would need to continue the success of his networks.

There was one agent who showed particular promise and he had shown a good deal of courage to place her under cover. Relatively untested and only recently graduated from the training school, Anneliese Kolber was from his own home town and had come to his notice after an incident at the Magdeburg University. Since then he had recognised her promise and followed her progress carefully. She was now undercover in the Wegberg area in West Germany close to a number of British airbases and the major NATO headquarters at Rheindahlen. Communications had been difficult recently but there were signs that her effort to cultivate a member of the Royal Air Force was beginning to pay off. Stunningly attractive, he had little doubt that most red-blooded males would be hard pressed to reject her advances. Although not a member of one of the fighter squadrons, the navigator she was nurturing had easy access to the operational plans which was where Meier's interest lay. If he could lay his hands on a copy of "Supplan Mike", the NATO battle plan, it would be the coup of the decade.

He glanced at the last report she had sent. Carl Pocklington was a middle aged navigator serving with 60 Squadron, the communications squadron flying aging Pembroke commuter planes from RAF Wildenrath. He had been at the base for well over a year sent to Germany to recover from a messy divorce. There was no suggestion of any communist leanings or sympathies so the only tactic which could possibly work was entrapment or seduction. With a relatively comfortable lifestyle and no financial pressures, despite the divorce settlement, it was unlikely that he could be bought off. Anneliese seemed like the strongest option and, if she was to be trusted, she was making progress.

With a carefully nurtured contact in the vetting office at the Rheindahlen HQ he would have early warning if the RAF Police took any interest in his new target. Unlike the navigator this local German civilian had been easily recruited and a regular flow of Deutschmarks guaranteed his cooperation. He made a note to chase up the latest activity in the office. It was better to be forewarned if an investigation took an unexpected turn.

As he closed the file, the door opened and Heinrich Gartner, the section chief walked in and dropped into the chair on the other side of the desk. What Dieter could not know was that the older man had endured a torrid discussion with an old mentor in Moscow. The General had given him instructions which would be difficult to misinterpret. Toe caps appeared from behind the desk and arranged themselves neatly along the edge. The intelligence chief rocked back on the chair legs, teetering, and latched his fingers together, his hands cupping his neck, elbows outstretched. Make yourself at home, Meier thought irreverently.

"Dieter, update me on your contacts in West Germany. The Commissar has been asking pointed questions again and I want to be up to speed. Who are you running at the minute?"

CHAPTER 6

IN THE COLOGNE/BONN AIR TRAFFIC CONTROL ZONE

"RAFAIR 5645, Clutch Radar, descend to 3,000 feet on the Wildenrath QNH 1015 and contact Wildenrath Zone on Stud 3."

"Roger to Wildenrath on Stud 3, good day Sir............ Stud 3, Stud 3, Go!"

"RAFAIR 5645, check."

"5646."

"Wildenrath, RAFAIR 5645 Flight with you descending to 3,000 feet, 1015 set."

"RAFAIR 5645 Flight good morning, cleared further descent to 1,500 feet, set the Wildenrath QFE 1012. Are you familiar with Wildenrath Sir?"

"Affirmative, 5645."

"Roger, clear further descent at your discretion. Call me initials. Runway 27 in use, colour state Blue. Recovery state, visual approaches, 2500 lbs on the ground with Brüggen as crash diversion. Request intentions."

"Roger copied, 5645 Flight for visual run in and break."

The Phantoms made their final descent overhead the NATO Headquarters at Rheindahlen, all four sets of eyes straining to see the airfield at Wildenrath. RAF Brüggen sat just four miles north of the field with a parallel east/west runway and the embarrassment factor would be high if they misidentified the airfield. With the TACAN needles pointing firmly to the southwest there could be no excuse for such a basic error. Even so, some crews still managed to do it. The runway began to appear from the German haze, the stark concrete standing out from the surrounding forest. To the north side the large servicing hangar with its broad hard standing stood out, a white VC10 transport jet stark against the toned-down surroundings.

RAFAIR 5645 Flight, field in sight to Stud 1..... Stud 1, Stud 1, Go!"

The formation switched frequencies checking in with the Local Controller and turning onto a westerly heading towards the airfield. The range wound down rapidly through three miles as both pilots pushed the throttles up and the Phantoms accelerated to 450 knots for the join. Unseen from the air the Local Controller trained his binoculars on the pair as they dropped down to 500 feet for the break into the circuit, the Rolls Royce Speys sending out a smoke trail as the speed increased. As they crossed the runway threshold in perfect battle formation, tightly separated by a few hundred yards, the leader cranked on 90 degrees of bank and broke hard downwind into the circuit. Two seconds later the wingman followed with a slightly gentler manoeuvre arcing around behind his leader the speed washing off in the turn. As the leader steadied up on the reciprocal heading the speed had reduced considerably helped by the massive speedbrakes which had been deployed from under the wings during the break manoeuvre. With the speed falling below 250 knots the sturdy undercarriage dropped from the wheel wells and extended into the airflow followed by the landing flaps. From the ground, the intensity of the engine noise rose again as the pilot eased the throttles back up to approach power settings to counteract the drag of the flaps. Behind him his wingman had picked up a comfortable spacing and was following the identical sequence configuring his own jet for the landing. The leader turned finals descending slowly towards the piano keys, the throttles surging to ensure the jet touched down at the end of the runway. As the tyres thumped onto the concrete threshold the pilot popped the brake chute which streamed from the tail cone and deployed into the turbulent air behind the jet. With the sudden retardation the Phantom began to slow down and, with the leader holding to one side of the runway, his navigator watched in his mirrors as the wingman touched down. Any problems with the brake chute and they could expect the second crew to "bolt" and set up for a further landing. As it was, the wingman settled down firmly onto the runway and his chute popped out slowing the jet in concert.

"RAFAIR 5645 Flight, turn left at the end and drop your chutes on the ORP. You're parking in Delta Dispersal, HAS's 60 and 61. Enter the loop on your left and follow the taxiway around. Your marshallers are waiting."

"5645 roger, entering the loop and switching to Cobra."

"Roger, good day."

"Cobra, RAFAIR 5645 and 5646 entering the loop, understand we're for HAS 60 and 61?"

"5645 and 5646, loud and clear and welcome to Wildenrath. That's affirmative. Clear taxy in and call me when contact the marshaller. Confirm your state?"

"Both serviceable."

"Outstanding! The engineers will be happy. See you inside."

The Phantoms taxied into the dispersal entrance immediately shielded from a casual observer on the airfield as the trees which ringed the dispersal enveloped the grey airframes. The jets taxied past a number of hardened aircraft shelters nestling in the trees, the massive clamshell doors open, the turnround crews inside the gloomy structures preparing the jets for the next sortie. As they rounded the turn in the taxiway the pilot's briefing facility came into view, the squat green single storey building exposed in its position next to the taxiway. A green-suited pilot waved as they taxied past as he made his way into the building. At the next turn a marshaller brandishing a pair of wands directed them to continue around the loop to the last HASs each side of the narrow taxiway. The leader acknowledged the gesture with a flash of his taxi light bright on the nosewheel door before hitting the nosewheel steering button and stamping on the left rudder pedal to bring the reluctant Phantom around the tight corner. A welcome breeze washed over him as they had opened the canopies as soon as they were clear of the runway. Still sweaty inside the restrictive rubberised immersion suit the cool air was refreshing. Holding to the left of the narrow revetment he swung the huge jet in a right hand arc his navigator offering reassuring words that the wingtip was clear of the revetment wall and the concrete face of the shelter. As he steadied up pointing back towards the taxiway his wingman made a turn into the neck in front of the HAS opposite blowing a strong draught of AVTUR-laden fumes into his face as its jet pipes passed across the cockpit. Ignoring his wingman's progress the pilot returned his attention to the flight line mechanic in front of his jet as the wands came together over his head prompting him to push hard on the brakes bringing the Phantom to a hesitant stop. The see-in crew disappeared underneath checking for leaks and undoing panels before reappearing. A tractor pulled into the neck ahead of them and move purposefully into position under the radome as a towing arm was removed and quickly attached to the nosewheel. After another signal, the pilot released the brakes and the Phantom began its slow journey backwards into the shelter where it would be turned around for its next sortie.

*

As they made their way across the taxiway towards the squadron complex the crews chatted amiably. It had been a low key sortie and, after a couple of practice interceptions between the two Phantoms, the intercept controller at the Sector Operations Centre at Neatishead in Norfolk had passed them off directly to "Dutch Mil" the military air traffic control agency. After a brief spell with "Clutch Radar" they had broken into the circuit at Wildenrath barely having raised a sweat. As they dumped flying equipment into the flying clothing section adjacent to operations they took in the workmanlike atmosphere of the Cold War flying station. Everything was naturally green, toned down or painted green to blend in with the countryside. Their white flying helmets which had been dumped on the baize covered counter stood out from the green-painted helmets of the local crews. Having stowed their kit they threaded their way down the maze of corridors to squadron operations where they were greeted by the duty authoriser. The ops room sat alongside engineering control divided by a thin transparent partition. Boards on every wall recorded the daily activity as well as the obligatory statistics around which a fighter squadron revolved. To the layman the codes and annotations would be unintelligible. To the crews, used to the need to record every intercept, every identification, each single engine approach *ad-nauseum*, it was crystal clear.

"Gents, welcome aboard and thanks for helping out next week. As your jets are serviceable how do you feel about flying a familiarisation sortie this afternoon? I know some of you have been stationed here and flown on detachments before but the air staff at HQ RAF Germany insist that all visitors fly a familiarisation sortie in-theatre before doing any real flying. It would get us ahead of the game for next week as we'll have to fly familiarisation rides with the French on Monday. The Americans are from Bitburg so at least we don't have to show them around."

"Sounds good to me," said Ray South as he looked up at the flying programme on the wall behind the authoriser. "What time did you have in mind to launch?"

"How about I give you time to catch a quick sandwich in the feeder and we'll plan to brief in 30 minutes. I take it you don't need to debrief the transit sortie?"

"No it was straight forward and nothing to say about it," he replied. "Thirty minutes sounds good. Who's leading the sortie?"

"If it's OK with you we'll get Razor and Flash to lead and we can fly it as a 3-ship. Any of the areas you'd prefer to visit?"

"Where are we working next week?"

"Over in Low Flying Area 3 east of Cologne and up towards the ADIZ. Should be exciting working that close to the bad guys! I can get Flash to plan a circular route out to the buffer zone and north past Gutersloh coming back down through areas 1 and 2. How does that sound?"

"Perfect. Can we get some low flying maps from you? Mine are a bit dog-eared these days."

"No trouble. I'll get the Ops Clerk to dig some out and they'll be in the briefing room for you. You'll be allocated some Mike Lima callsigns while you're working with us. Your airframe "Charlie" will take Mike Lima 65 and "Delta" will take Mike Lima 73. Those callsigns will stay with the jets for the duration of the exercise. Confirm your jets are carrying guns?"

"Yes, a Suu-23 on each."

He picked up the handset for the public address system and hit the transmit button.

"Razor and Flash to the ops room."

The message rang out across the site prompting the newly assigned crew to seek out the good news.

"Have a chat with the lead crew and then you can hit the feeder for an early lunch."

CHAPTER 7

DELTA DISPERSAL, RAF WILDENRATH

The squat grey and green camouflaged Puma helicopter set down gently onto the runway threshold and the clatter of the rotors subsided as the engines spooled down to idle. The massive disc tilted noticeably as it turned through 90 degrees and headed towards Delta Dispersal at a walking pace. Off to the side of the taxiway the operational readiness platform stretched out along the side of the asphalt surface used occasionally for visiting aircraft which required "last chance checks" before takeoff. The lead vehicle in a group of green camouflaged Land Rovers clustered at the far end of the dispersal flashed its headlights and received an answering flash of the taxilight from the helicopter pilot. Unbidden, a knot of aircrew climbed from the rear of each vehicle and formed up, hats removed and heads bowed against the downdraught.

The helicopter slewed around through 180 degrees and came to a halt as the loadmaster climbed out and made his way to the waiting group. With the rotors still turning he shouted a few instructions behind a cupped hand gesturing at the rotors overhead and pointing back towards the square cabin hatch. With nodded acknowledgement the aircrew set off in single file directly towards the waiting helicopter.

With the passengers aboard the loadmaster reattached his strop to the cabin wall and took up his position in the door watching around the lumbering helicopter as it taxied back towards the runway. As it crossed the slick, white piano keys at the threshold the note of the engines increased and the helicopter nodded forward as it lifted into the air and flew off at low level down the runway. Making its way north eastwards towards the border crossing at Helmstedt it would stop briefly at RAF Gutersloh. Onboard was one of the 92 Squadron flight commanders who would be checking out the Quick Reaction Alert facilities at the old Lightning base. Now used by the Harriers, the alert sheds were not used on a day-to-day basis but could be brought back into use should tensions rise and a forward operating base be needed. He had been given the nod that such a deployment might come soon.

In addition to the familiar RAF green flying suits, the passengers sported a number of other shades of green from a variety of nations. The brightly coloured squadron patches fixed to the arms identified two American aircrew and two French pilots, the advanced guard for the forthcoming detachment, who had been invited along for the visit. Even though the Cold War touched everyone's lives opportunities to get close to the wire were limited. To be able to hug the border in a helicopter was almost unheard of.

*

As the helicopter dropped him on the large aircraft servicing platform, Peter Fleming, the 92 Squadron flight commander, ducked low, the rotors above his head intimidating as they chopped through the air forcing the blast down and along the ground around his feet. A movements NCO beckoned from the doorway of the air terminal and he made his way over turning to watch briefly as the Puma lifted back into the air and hover taxied over towards the nearby runway. He ducked inside and the clatter of the rotors faded into the background.

*

The Puma pilot headed northeast from Gutersloh hugging the ground following the main highway towards Bielefeld and onwards before turning east to Wolfsburg where the TACAN beacon would give him a comforting point on which to home. Navigating in the Air Defence Interception Zone was an activity which required consummate skill. He would be talking to a controller from the local control and reporting centre but any errors would result in swift and punitive action. That assumed he stayed to the western side of the Inner German Border. To stray further east would exact retribution of a different type. He listened to the occasional commentary from the controller who punctuated his chat with frequent changes of heading. Any pilot operating this close to the border was under strict radar control. Once visual he may be allowed a little more latitude to follow the scar across the landscape. His brief was strict and had been carefully rehearsed before takeoff at Gutersloh. A few miles short of Wolfsburg he turned east following the line of the A2 autobahn and on towards the border crossing point at Helmstedt. Slowly, the watchtowers appear from the haze and he called to his controller who replied with his authority to continue visually. Rising 50 feet above the ground the towers stood stark against the horizon clearly delineating the line of the border on the ground. It was impossible to miss. The small helicopter site at which they would meet the guides from the West German Bundesgrenzschutz lay to the south of the town. Crossing the boundary of the landing site he flared the approach checking the forward motion and drifted slowly over the white "H" marked on the ground. Cleared to alight by the control tower, in reality a small hut, he touched down gently and closed down.

As the rotors slowed to a stop and the door was pulled back the passengers disembarked. A German border guard stood some way distant from the landing site restraining a large German Shepherd dog which seemed happy to devour the visitors if provoked. Alongside, a rather more welcoming guide beckoned the group over and made his introductions. As they walked the short distance to the observation platform set up close to the wire, a Bundesgrenzschutz Hueycobra clattered over the fence and alighted on an adjacent spot temporarily drowning out the conversation. With calm restored the guide launched into his carefully prepared script.

The Inner German Border stretched from the Baltic Sea in the north to Czechoslovakia in the south and was heavily fortified along all 858 miles of its length. On the East German side, the signal, or hinterland fence, divided the Restricted Area, which stretched 5 Km from the fence, from the heavily guarded cleared strip which marked the actual border. Any escape attempt would be impossible without first crossing this "No Man's Land" giving the guards an early warning. Built on high ground where feasible, the fence itself was only two metres high but by no means an easy obstacle. In its exposed location anyone crossing the cleared area was easily visible against the horizon. Strands of electrified barbed wire built into the structure acted as a visible deterrent. Cutting the wires or pulling them out of place set off alarms in the adjacent watch towers alerting the guards to a possible breach of the fence. Claymore mines triggered by vibration were strategically placed along the whole length to catch anyone who managed to scale the wire. Even before braving these defences dog runs were built into the structure and often guard dogs would roam freely.

A network of command bunkers, watch towers and observation posts spanned the fence. The command tower was a short squat tower that provided the command centre for a sector of the border. Inside, equipment allowed border gates to be opened and closed remotely and the fence lights to be turned on and off. Any vibration on the wire would trigger sensors which would flash an alert to the border guards who could control massive searchlights to illuminate the perimeter. The bunkers were connected to other units in the network by long range radios.

The BT-11 observation towers standing 11 metres high were easily identifiable by the octagonal observation deck which topped the concrete structure. Each face of the deck contained a firing port below the windows from which guards could target any prospective escapee. Interspersed with the more common BT-9 square tower they were supplemented by a thousand observation bunkers known as an "earth bunker" sunk into a depression in the ground. With this combination of defences there was nowhere along the border fence that was not in view of a tower or post. A patrol strip ran between the watch towers and the cleared strip to allow the border guards easy access to the fence in the event of an incident. Solid enough to take a vehicle the track linked each command tower along the length of the IGB.

The actual border was less intrusive. Small square granite stones with "DDR" marked on the western face marked the border line. More impressive concrete posts painted vividly in the red, black and gold of the German Democratic Republic and known as barbers poles, were spaced about 500 feet apart as a more visible reminder to the unwary.

Having delivered the chilling description of the border, the guard loaded the visitors onto a waiting bus which drove a few miles down the fence to a point where a road led to an East German village. Red and white barriers prevented local civilians from approaching the border but with the border guards in tow, the barriers were raised and the bus moved up to a small clearing alongside the fence. The village was 500 yards across the border and within a stone's throw. At this point the stark concrete-panelled section of the fence was topped by a roller mechanism which prevented anyone making sufficient purchase to scale the top. In the immediate distance a section of protected wire fence separated the village from the border ensuring that an over-enthusiastic villager was dissuaded from joining family in the West. The West German border sign was equally stark with its warning "Halt, Hier Grenze" or "Stop, Border". Although the road still existed, a thoroughfare it was not. The enforced isolation was not lost on the visitors and muted conversations reflected the sombre mood.

It was across this most heavily defended border that anyone wishing to escape to The West would have to pass.

*

Back at RAF Gutersloh, Peter Fleming chatted amiably to John Stone, his old colleague from his days as an instructor at the Tactical Weapons Unit at RAF Chivenor. They pulled up in the Land Rover outside the former Lightning Quick Reaction Alert sheds on the dispersal. Since their days instructing, the pair had gone their separate ways, him to a flying tour at Wildenrath and his unfortunate colleague to a ground appointment as Squadron Leader Operations at Gutersloh. The compromise was that if he had to undertake his penance on the ground there were far worse places to suffer than at the busy base in the scenic Harz Mountains. The challenge for the frustrated Harrier pilot was that every few months, his whole operation loaded their entire world into a fleet of vehicles and decamped into the local forests where the Harriers would operate from "hides". Unlike their other fixed wing compatriots, the Harriers would hope to survive by concealing themselves in the woods away from the prying eyes of the Soviet electronic reconnaissance satellites. So close to the Inner German Border it was likely that their tenancy of such a vulnerable forward operating site would be short. The Soviet hordes were expected to roll through the Harz Mountains rapidly in the initial push for territory. As if this was not a sufficient challenge, he was also responsible for the QRA sheds on the south eastern side of the airfield. The large square metal buildings, empty now, shared the dispersal with concrete hardened aircraft shelters normally occupied by the Harrier squadron. Every so often the Phantoms from Wildenrath would deploy forwards and operate from the vacated facility, for a few short days within striking distance of the "Iron Curtain".

Fleming's spirits fell as they approached the slightly jaded hangars, the paint peeling and weeds peeking through gaps in the concrete taxyway. Vehicles littered the access track in marked bays alongside the grass and more vehicles had been crammed into the large bays formerly occupied by the Lightning fighters. With such an enormous fleet needed to deploy the Harrier Force into the field no spare hangar space was wasted in keeping the trucks safe from the harsh German climate.

They walked into the small annex alongside the alert sheds which in earlier years had acted as the crewroom and sleeping area for the QRA crews. A corporal dressed in oil-stained overalls whipped his boots from the low coffee table and jumped to his feet, surprised at the arrival of the unannounced visitors.

"Will these guys have a problem being displaced for the duration of our detachment," Fleming asked.

"We've identified a compound over the other side of the airfield where we can store the vehicles for a short time," Stone explained. "The guys will be absorbed by their unit for the few days you're here. I suspect quite a few of them will take the chance to squeeze in some well-earned leave. They rarely get that opportunity with the pace of life around here."

"I hope no one at the Headquarters decides it would be clever to throw an exercise while we're in residence. It would be good to think that we could concentrate on live operations for a few days. After all, the whole point of scheduling this "Early Jet" is because of the disruption that Bold Challenge will cause at Wildenrath. "Their Airships" at JHQ are concerned that with so many movements, Battle Flight might be affected during the exercise period. Moving up here temporarily seems to kill two birds with one stone."

"Way too logical old chap. What do you bet the hooter goes off at "O Dark Early" during your detachment?"

"I'd almost bet on it!"

He began picking through a pile of old documents mentally starting a checklist of actions. It might not be long before the Phantoms flew in.

CHAPTER 8

HOHENSCHÖNHAUSEN PRISON, EAST BERLIN

Meier waited patiently in the dark and dingy interview room. The atmosphere in the Stasi jail was depressing even for visitors and he could only imagine the trauma of being incarcerated in this hell hole. He had seen the conditions in the cells during previous visits and had no real desire to see them again. For the man he had come to see, this was his life. A former Colonel in the NVA, the East German Army, he had been convicted of spying for the West and, after a brief show trial, had been sent to Hohenschönhausen to serve his sentence. He had swapped the relative luxury of an Army married quarter for a small prison cell with a slatted wooden bunk, a slop bucket and no window. Austerity somehow seemed too grand a description.

The door creaked as it opened and the man was led in, his hands secured behind his back with handcuffs. After a brief exchange with the guard, Meier assured the concerned-looking conscript that the prisoner would be no trouble and shooed him from the room. The man dressed in the gaudy prison garb looked apprehensive, remaining quiet, anticipating the encounter.

"Kurt, it's good of you to see me," said Meier in a feeble attempt at sincerity.

"I had little choice," the man replied curtly.

"True but thank you all the same. I have a request and I think you may be able to help me."

"What's in it for me," he shot back a little too quickly.

"We can come to that but I wouldn't want to raise any false hopes. I don't have the authority to release you. But we run ahead of ourselves. Let me pose the questions first and then we can discuss compensation. I'm sure a few extra privileges would be a good start."

The man looked down avoiding eye contact. He had been a soldier from a proud Prussian background. His misfortune had been for his family to be trapped on the wrong side of the Inner German Border when the "Iron Curtain" had been built. Faced with the tide of left wing indoctrination it had only been a question of time before he had been persuaded to pass operational secrets to his contacts in the West German Secret Service. His role had been compromised when a high profile spy in MI6 had defected in the late 70s. Since his arrest he had languished in the dingy cells with no hope of release. The key had been thrown away.

"Let me start," said Meier, probing gently. "You won't be aware but there have been a number of incidents in the air corridors over our airspace recently. Our Soviet friends have become increasingly upset at the arrogance of the West Berliners and want to show some strength. We have made our presence known but, so far, we have stopped short of direct intervention. What I need to know is whether our moves will be taken seriously by the British and American politicians and, more importantly, how the decision-making chain operates in the Western capitals."

"I'm not sure if I can help. All my contacts were in Bonn, not London or Washington."

"Of course but I know you were well connected in the Bundestag. I'm sure the mechanisms are similar. I need to know how much power the military commanders hold in the decision chain."

"But my handler was an intelligence operative not military or political."

"I suspect you must have talked about such things, particularly when you thought you may have to flee to the West."

"I suppose we did. He often spoke of who he would have to persuade if I was to escape. The names were all political never military. Unlike our Soviet cousins, in a democracy, the military commanders answer to political masters. The tactical decisions are taken in the field but strategy is decided in the Foreign Office in the Ministries of State."

"So you would expect a lengthy decision-making chain? Let's say we forced down an aircraft, how long before action would be taken?"

"Hard to say but I would think days not hours. To send someone into our territory would take some time to agree and if NATO became involved consensus might never be reached."

Meier contemplated the information which confirmed his suspicions. There was little to gain from pushing too hard at this stage. He would return with more specific questions later. After all, his contact was hardly likely to move house any time soon. As he pressed the buzzer to recall the guard he felt an unexpected hint of compassion and came to a compromise.

"I'll make sure you are moved to a more comfortable cell and I'll have your rations increased. I think it might be useful for us to continue this conversation at some stage. Perhaps you could think over our discussion and let me know if you have any more information that I might find helpful. It could be mutually beneficial."

As the man was led out Meier pondered his next move.

CHAPTER 9

CHARLIE DISPERSAL, RAF WILDENRATH

Razor looked back at the camouflaged bulk of the American F-4E Phantom as they moved around the revetment walls which separated the dispersals dominating the skyline. Externally the American airframe looked very similar to his own, although fitting the Spey engines to the British version had added to the girth. The main difference was the re-profiled nose. The radome was longer and slimmer but underneath, a large housing held the internal Vulcan M61 Gatling gun. After experience in Vietnam the Americans had realised that the day of the gun was not over and a hasty modification had reinstalled the weapon into the streamlined, internal fairing, albeit at the expense of installing a smaller radar scanner. The other obvious difference was the engines. Fitted with the General Electric J79, the afterburner cans were ridged, earning the nickname the "turkey feather" afterburner for obvious reasons. The J79 was a good engine but the British Phantoms had been fitted with the Rolls Royce Spey in a bid to offer workshare to a beleaguered British aircraft industry to offset the order for combat aircraft lost to the Americans. The American engine was a pure jet so it worked more efficiently in the upper air, accelerating quicker and taking the Phantom to a higher Mach number. It was, however, thirstier and a Spey powered Phantom could travel quite a bit farther on a single tank of fuel. On the wings the leading-edge flaps had been replaced with slats. Extending into the airflow at slower speeds, these manoeuvre devices improved the handling of the Phantom in air combat. It would never make the Phantom an agile dogfighter but gave it a big advantage over its "hard wing" brethren. There had been no major surprises in the cockpit layout, although the "pit", as the rear seat was affectionately known, had sprouted some additional controls and displays for the extra equipment. His own front cockpit was remarkably similar and he would have been perfectly happy to take the F-4E for a spin. It was the radar where the British version won out. With its look-down, shoot down AN/AWG 12 the British FGR2 was far superior compared to the old pulse-only AN/APG120 which soldiered on in the F-4E. In order to refit the gun the compromise was to fit the APG120 with its smaller scanner but at the cost of capability. Looking down against a target flying at ultra low level, the US weapon systems operator or "whizzo" was hopelessly compromised. The mass of ground clutter which flooded the screen made it impossible to pick out targets from the noise. It explained why American crews favoured the higher levels.

It was the next stop that interested Razor most and it would be his first opportunity to take a look at the Mirage III flown by the French visitors. As they approached the squat but sleek jet he could not fail to be impressed. Experts joked that if a jet looked right it was right and the Mirage looked every bit the fighter. With its tailless delta wing configuration it had the looks of a sports car when set against the brute force functionality of the Phantom. The tactical disruptive pattern camouflage which had replaced the burnished silver of earlier years looked in keeping with the drab concrete surroundings of the dispersal but it had undoubtedly taken away from the image. The neat engine intakes seemed impossibly small for the task of feeding air to the single Atar 09 turbojet engine. Slim external fuel tanks had been fitted for the exercise onto the inboard underwing pylons breaking up the clean lines and looking out of place. Razor knew however, that this was its biggest weakness. With its slim profile and razor sharp wings it lacked internal fuel being more similar in endurance to the Lightning than his own Phantom. With tanks fitted, only two external pylons remained free under the wings to carry the Matra Magic infra-red guided missiles. A single Matra 530 semi active missile would complement the short range missiles but fitted under the fuselage. Twin 30 mm DEFA cannons fitted in the belly could only be identified by the small sections of the gun barrels peeking from the gun ports under the air intakes. Carrying this "draggy" external load, the Mirage would be "bugging out" from any fight early leaving the Phantoms to carry the burden. When compared to the complexity of the Phantom avionics the Mirage systems were rudimentary and with the added workload of a single pilot at low level, it was apparent that the French pilots would be working hard in the coming days.

The French pilot began to explain the characteristics of his aircraft in his heavily accented English. Despite the cruel jokes around the squadron, Razor acknowledged that his English was far better than Razor's schoolboy French and he was obviously proud of his jet. As the small group worked around the jet, the pilot pointed out small, esoteric aspects to the rapt audience. Such detail could only ever be of interest to aircrew. Suddenly, the tannoy rang out ending the impromptu briefing.

"All Bold Challenge personnel to the main briefing room. Exercise briefing in one zero minutes. I say again . . . . ."

The message echoed around the austere dispersal as the small group broke up, drifting back towards the hardened briefing facility.

*

As they walked into the room it was already packed to the limits. The seats were full and bodies were by now spread around the aisles, squeezed into every inch of spare space. The new arrivals found a small nook still unoccupied and shuffled around to fit four bodies into the tiny gap.

As the RAF Wildenrath Station Commander entered, the room was called to attention but he quickly beckoned them back into their seats worried that the manoeuvre may risk physical injury in the confined space. The buzz quickly stilled.

"Gentlemen," he began. "Welcome to Wildenrath and I hope your tight schedule will allow us to offer some traditional hospitality before you depart. In the meantime you have a lot to do and we've prepared some briefings to set the scene. Make no mistake; the timing of this exercise is fortunate. I've received a number of briefings over the last few weeks which make me think that the "Cold War" is hotting up. Normally this exercise allows us to dust off the Exercise Operation Order and refine a few procedures but, more importantly, the chance to fly together. This time, world events lead me to think that, at some stage in the near future, we might actually be called upon to execute the plan. The Soviets have been particularly aggressive around the corridors recently and the exercise, underway in the Letzlinger Heide Training Area, is already involving units that we haven't seen deployed into the forward area for some time. Your intelligence briefing will give some ideas as to why that might be but give it some serious thought. The Warsaw Pact force levels in the Group of Soviet Forces in Germany are at unprecedented levels since the end of the Second World War. There must be a reason for that. On a happier note, I'm particularly pleased to see our French allies here and a hearty welcome. We don't get many opportunities to work together so we should take maximum benefit. That's enough from me; now please stay seated before someone is injured in the crush."

"Thank you Sir," replied the Boss of 92 Squadron as the senior officer departed. He waited for the ripple of conversation to die before pressing on.

"Gents, let's get down to it. It'll get hot in here quite soon with this many bodies so we'll try to be brief. This is what we have for you. We'll start with an intelligence briefing and pick up the points the Station Commander just made. We'll have a quick orientation briefing to cover the Station and the local area. Flash Gordon will then give an overall exercise briefing and cover the flying schedule. He'll finish up with an operations briefing which will give the key points for operating out of Wildenrath and, particularly, out of Charlie Dispersal. There's a lot to cover so can we hold questions until the end of each briefing. OK let's start with intelligence."

As he scanned the attentive audience Flash felt the familiar nerves in the pit of his stomach. He had about five minutes before he would be called to the podium and he hoped his preparation had been thorough. This audience would not take prisoners if he got it wrong. The overpowering atmosphere and the rapidly rising temperature in the room, as the noisy extractor fans in the adjacent plant room tried in vain to equalise the temperature, merely added to his psychological pressure. His attention wandered as he rehearsed his opening lines, the words of the intelligence officer fading into the background.

CHAPTER 10

HEADQUARTERS ROYAL AIR FORCE GERMANY, RAF RHEINDAHLEN

The Commander-in-Chief Royal Air Force Germany walked into the office prompting the startled occupants to their feet. It was rare to see even the CINC's Personal Staff Officer but the big man himself was unprecedented. The surprise was quickly replaced by an unnerving sense of foreboding or perhaps a feeling of guilt. What had they done wrong?

"Sit down Gentlemen, relax please," the Four Star officer said as he slumped into one of the chairs.

"I'm on my way to see the counter-intelligence chaps but I wanted to speak to you first. Have we seen anything on the ground across the IGB that gives us any concerns at the minute? And before you reply, I heard what the briefer said at the morning briefing. I want the un-sanitised version. Are there any warnings and indicators that suggest anything other than routine exercises are afoot?"

"Well Sir," said the Warrant Officer who headed up the small team, " We normally keep a very close eye on those and . . . . . "

"Do you chaps task the Wildenrath Pembrokes?" he interrupted diving off at a tangent.

"Yes Sir we do."

"Tell me how you go about it. Who identifies things that we should be looking at?"

"We take inputs from all sources Sir. Mostly from Defence Intelligence in London but not exclusively. BRIXMIS have teams on the ground and if they see something that we can overfly and they haven't managed to get close enough on the ground, they tip us off. We also collate reports from the other liaison teams, the French and Americans, and compile a potential target list. The Secret Intelligence Services sometimes have tip offs from agents in Berlin and Russia and we get word through Defence Intelligence. It really is a mix."

"So who actually decides the collection plan for the Squadron?"

"Normally that's us Sir. We're the only agency with the links and the detail who can compile the flight plan. Obviously our biggest constraint is the structure of the corridors. We can only go where we're allowed, although it's not unknown to run flights up and down the IGB looking into the western regions of the GDR. Battle Flight is often tasked to run border patrols and the crews carry cameras."

"What are the typical targets?"

"For the Pembrokes, they're a mix of permanent fixed sites and temporary operating locations. Some, like the missile batteries and airfields are photographed on every flight unless there's a higher priority. We look for new equipment and changes to installations, particularly if any mobile kit is rolled in. The training areas are always important, chiefly during exercise season, as this might be a cover for larger manoeuvres or even an operational build up. A full scale exercise deploys massive numbers of troops, tanks and aircraft into the forward area."

"That's a good link back to the warnings and indicators. What do you have?"

"We have seen a few things that don't add up recently. Incidents inside the corridor are rare and, generally, the Sovs allow us to go about our business unhindered. There was an incident last week where a civilian airliner inbound to Tempelhof was intercepted. The airliner was flying at the upper limit at 10,000 feet and the Mig-21 moved in to close proximity. It was all carefully controlled but they normally stay just above the upper limit of the corridor. This pilot came alongside. There was no attempt to intervene but it scared the airline pilot and, more importantly, the airline risk managers."

"So no weapons fired?"

"No Sir. The Fishbed moved into close formation and shadowed the airliner for about 15 miles staying at the upper height limit of the corridor before it broke off. His wingman was much more aggressive."

"What else?"

"There was a Division-level exercise last week and units came, mainly by rail from the eastern half of the country. Thankfully, they all packed up after the event but I must admit, they haven't gone back to barracks yet. A lot of them are still holed up in the marshalling areas. The air assets flew back to their respective bases but they can be repositioned at a few hours notice so not really a good indicator. The Sovs practice both forward deployment and operating from highway strips on a regular basis so these movements are not uncommon."

"So nothing that suggests a change in normal business? The reason for my question is that the 16th Tactical Air Army staff has been particularly belligerent at a couple of the recent liaison meetings in Berlin. Some of the sabre rattling is worthy of the dark days of the Cuban Missile Crisis. I wonder why the sudden increase in hostility. There's no immediately obvious reason to me."

"Nothing on that scale Sir but we have been getting a few hits from signals intelligence suggesting that a new weapons system is about to be tested. They normally do that in the rear areas where only the satellites can see them. If they decide to push anything forward it might be seen as provocative."

"Anything else?"

"Well yes, but it's probably nothing that you'd worry about Sir. We had a tip that they were showing undue interest in our operational plans. As you know, Supplan Mike details everything about how TWOATAF would go to war. If they get access to that, all hell would break loose. In the event of a border incursion, we'd be starting a chess match with all our moves pre-notified to the Grand Master. It would be little short of suicide given their numerical superiority."

"Thank you. Keep it under your hat for the time being but I think it's time to deploy QRA forward to RAF Gutersloh. The normal posture is to fly from home base at Wildenrath but that's 20 minutes flying time to the border and difficult to react to unforeseen circumstances. I want them closer to the action. Time for a little sabre rattling of my own I think."

CHAPTER 11

WALDSTUBE RESTAURANT, DAHLHEIM VILLAGE

Pocklington made his way across the crowded restaurant towards the booth in the corner. Anneliese Kolbe flicked distractedly through the menu pushing her hair over her ear. The gesture made his heart flip. Sensing his approach she looked up smiling broadly, jumping to her feet and hugging him. Her scent magnified his emotions and he was taken back to his schooldays, experiencing his first schoolboy crush all over again. They sat opposite each other, his hand darting across the table covering hers.

"I ordered wine, liebchen."

"Perfect, thank you."

"How was your day," she asked in a vain attempt to lighten the mood, the earlier discussions still fresh in both their minds.

"Oh not too busy," he replied. "Pretty much an average day. We had one sortie back to the UK to take the Deputy CinC to a Conference at Strike Command. I had an airtest which was mind numbingly boring. The aircraft has just come out of servicing and we needed a shakedown before the Berlin trip. I spent most of the hour reading out checks and going round in circles in the circuit. Not the most exciting profile we fly I'm afraid."

"But it's still flying, my love, and it's what you enjoy."

There was a pregnant pause.

"Look about the discussion we had this morning. . . . ."

"I know, it was wrong of me to ask."

"It's only money but there's still a principle involved. . . . ."

She cut in.

"There are people who will recall me in an instant if they think that I have betrayed them. They have no scruples."

Her harsh pronunciation of the final word emphasised the rift in their backgrounds.

"I don't want to go back. It's that simple," she sighed, her eyes dropping to the napkin which she played with, nervously. Her eyes were damp and the emotions raw.

"If only there was some other way but surely, those same people would not allow you to disappear. They would track you down if you came over to the West. They have long memories from what you've told me."

"It's not easy. Although the Stasi. . . . ."

Pocklington winced and looked around nervously checking the adjacent booths to see if their hushed conversation had been overheard. Their fellow diners continued eating, seemingly oblivious. As he paused the waitress placed a carafe of house wine and two green-stemmed wine glasses on the table.

"Möchten Sie essen; would you like to eat?" she asked unaware of the tension between the couple.

"Noch fünf minuten bitte," replied Anneliese and the girl nodded and withdrew. She lowered her voice and moved closer.

"There is another way you know. If I could supply a little information to them it might keep them happy long enough to come up with a plan to disappear."

"But how is that possible? I live and work on a military base in Germany. It might be secure inside the wire but I have to come outside the wire every evening and even an amateur would track me down without too much effort. You've already said your contact has many well connected Russian friends."

"It wouldn't need to be much liebchen, enough to keep them happy. If they think I have a source they will be patient."

"How much is a little? Once I make that first move I'm complicit. Anything of value is not anonymous. Every secret document is marked and each one is strictly controlled. We have to sign them out of the Registry every time we read them. We have one of those new photocopiers but every scan has to be logged and accounted for. I can't copy documents without being found out immediately."

"There are other ways you know and I could help. Sometimes the old techniques are the best."

Pocklington felt vaguely uneasy at the way she had become so workmanlike, so swiftly, particularly given that she was describing a blatant act of espionage.

"If I do that, you realise that you're asking me to betray everything that's important to me."

"But unless you do there can be no future for us."

The waitress reappeared unseen and stood poised with her notepad. They fussed nervously with their menus, distracted.

CHAPTER 12

DELTA DISPERSAL, RAF WILDENRATH

Razor pushed the toe brakes and brought his Phantom to a halt at the exit to the dispersal. They had briefed a navigation route around the airspace to give the UK-based crews a refamiliarisation of the airspace. Both crews had flown in Germany before so it would be an easy sortie and they would take the opportunity to have a go at any other tactical aircraft that happened to be sharing the low flying areas with them. Looking in his mirrors he watched for the other Phantoms to emerge from their shelters and enter the taxiway behind him. As they joined the loop taxiway he chopped the formation across to the Tower frequency and checked in. With takeoff clearance granted the formation lined up in a "vic" formation on Runway 09 and rolled down the runway with a mere 15 seconds spacing between the jets. Safely airborne, the formation chopped across to a quiet frequency and headed east towards the low level departure point in the Dormagen Gap hugging the ground, 500 feet above the rolling German countryside.

Crossing the broad River Rhine Razor felt slightly vulnerable sitting alone at the head of the formation, however, with a pair of Phantoms sitting only a mile behind him in a tight line abreast battle formation, he was as safe from attack from behind as it was possible to be. Flash had dropped the turning points for the route into the inertial navigation system or INAS. With the range and bearing to the first turn showing on the instruments in both cockpits there was little navigation to do at this stage as, only a few minutes after takeoff, the INAS would be accurate. Only later in the sortie would the present position drift off. At that stage he would "fix" the system giving it a gentle reminder of its location but, in the meantime, Razor would keep them on track. Should they find any" trade", the nickname for targets, the line on the map would become irrelevant as they manoeuvred around the low level airspace looking for simulated weapons shots on a hapless passer-by. Air defence navigation was rarely precise providing they stayed within the confines of the low flying area, stayed out of restricted airspace and knew where they were flying.

Flash shared his time between the AWG12 radar which scanned the presently empty airspace around them, the radar warning receiver or RWR which flashed the occasional threat vector on the small display screen buried in the left hand side of his back cockpit, and the real world outside. With his ejection seat straps loosened he twisted around in his seat looking for the Phantoms which he knew were only a mile behind. He could see their radars flashing on the RWR as they made their own scan of the airspace and hoped that they were paying as much attention to the area behind the formation as he was. Being intercepted by another roving formation without reacting was an accolade he didn't need. The Möhne Dam, made famous during a wartime raid by Lancasters of No. 617 Squadron during World War 2 slipped past as they turned north eastwards towards the Buffer Zone. Their route would take them under the restricted airspace but they would remain clear of the thin strip known as the Air Defence Interception Zone or ADIZ which abutted the actual border. The deconfliction zone was designed to prevent inadvertent penetration of East German airspace and they had no wish to become a report on a staff officer's desk at the Joint Headquarters. The RWR continued to ping its warning of the Phantoms behind but the radar stayed frustratingly clear of targets.

As the formation, still in a perfect arrow, headed north past Gutersloh airfield the first sign of activity appeared on the radar. The blips popped up on the scope and Flash called a snap vector towards to begin an intercept. Showing a speed of about 400 knots the radar contacts were obviously fast jets and were fair game. Checking the mirrors, he could see that the Phantoms behind had followed his opening move. The game was on.

In the cockpit of the leading Harrier which Flash had just detected, the pilot checked his wingman who sat in tight battle formation a mile away. They were hugging the foothills their mission drawing to a close. Airborne for 35 minutes the fuel was already working down towards minimums but they had a few minutes combat margin. The AN/ARI8223 radar warner in the cockpit was quiet but with its simple technology it would only alert him in the event of a lock from a threat system. He began to run through his recovery checks as the range on the TACAN display wound down. Gutersloh was less than 30 miles to the south and he was about to call his wingman into fighting wing for the recovery when the radar warner bleeped.

After Flash's radio call the Phantom formation had turned in place and were now diverging from their planned track. In the front cockpits, eyes were scanning the rolling landscape ahead for signs of the approaching contacts. In this part of the low flying area close to Gutersloh the likelihood was that they would encounter a formation of Harriers recovering to their base after a simulated bombing mission.

"Bogeys bearing 350."

"Contact," he heard from the trailing pair.

The navigators were tracking the contacts in pulse Doppler, as yet in search mode to avoid alerting the prey of their interest. In the lead Phantom it was Flash's prerogative as to when he would lock, if at all, at which time the radar warning receivers in the targets would rattle a warning.

"It's a pair, 450 knots," the calls short and clipped. This close to the border their transmissions would be intercepted by the listening posts in East Germany. For real, long transmissions would attract attention and possibly be jammed electronically and there was no way the Phantom crews were allowing that to happen.

"Targets heading 180, low, fast," he intoned.

The tension heightened. At this height the radar horizon extended out to a mere 27 miles so the time from contact to intercept would be short. If Flash chose to fire a Sparrow missile the shot would come in the heart of the engagement envelope at about five miles about the same time as the front-seaters would visually acquire the targets. In order to be able to shoot, the pilot would have to see his prey and visually identify it. Too late and the shot could not be taken.

"Go Sidewinder," Flash ordered perfunctorily. "Coming heads-in for the ident."

He moved the acquisition markers around the contact on the radar display between his knees and squeezed the trigger on his hand controller. The first pressure froze the radar scanner in the nose and pointed the radar energy directly at the approaching contact closest to his nose. With the radar target bright on his display he squeezed the trigger fully and the radar locked onto the green blip. The display jittered briefly and then the symbology changed bringing up the additional tracking information on the small screen.

"Your dot, centre the target," Flash called as his eye moved across to the telescope protruding from the left hand quarter light in his cockpit. Razor eased the jet around bringing the lively steering dot towards the centre of his radar scope under his gunsight. He glanced at the radio altimeter the needle hovering around the 300 foot mark, as he played the dot. In the back Flash pressed his eye to the rubber boot around the eyepiece of the telescope sighting system and tensed. This brief operation was extremely disorientating as the world oscillated in the small scope. If the device was accurately boresighted he would be rewarded with the sight of a fast jet in the viewfinder. At first the scope was void but as he watched, the distinctive shape of a Harrier jump jet danced across his vision.

"Hostile, hostile, hostile, he called urgently, rewarded by an instant response from the trailing Phantoms.

"Locked on the westerly."

"Locked on the easterly."

Each navigator had selected his own target.

"Fox 1 on the westerly."

"Fox 1 on the easterly."

If this had been real, two "smoking telegraph poles" would have flashed past the leading Phantom inbound towards their targets at close to Mach 3.

Flash watched the Harrier dance around the sighting scope checking for signs of evasion but none came. The Harriers trekked inexorably closer and their pilots were either indifferent or were not equipped with radar warning receivers. Behind him the navigators would be mentally counting down the missile time of flight towards a simulated impact; three seconds per mile for each mile of range. The radars would have to remain locked to their targets for about 15 seconds if the missiles were to be successful.

"Tally Ho," he heard from his front cockpit as the Phantom reefed into a hard turn the onset of G instant. Razor had seen the leading Harrier and manoeuvred instantaneously for a close aboard pass. With its legendary turning performance, a well flown Harrier was a match for any opponent and Razor had no wish to give any turning room. The pass would be within feet of the rapidly approaching fast jet that would pass the cockpit at a combined closing speed of 900 knots. Flash braced himself for the merge.

In the cockpit of the trailing Phantom, Roy South had watched the blip track down the scope sharing his attention between the radar, the horizon and the ground only feet below. Like Razor ahead, he wanted an early visual pick up and he and listened to the commentary from his back seat as the target grew ever closer. As the missile timed out and the radar broke lock he saw a brief flicker against the background and spotted the Harrier hugging the contours, it popped up briefly against a ridgeline before dropping back into the obscurity of the terrain. His eyes fixed on the spot where it had disappeared and he began to see the movement of the camouflaged jet against its surroundings. He eased the stick over and the Phantom banked towards before he checked the turn. Too much and he would put the approaching target into the gunsight. That might risk a collision but it would certainly mean he would lose sight of the elusive contact behind the armoured windscreen. He held a slight offset and the shape of the Harrier grew.

Razor tensed involuntarily as the Harrier flashed past his canopy about 500 feet away already reefing into a turn towards him and pulling up and away from the ground.

"Bogeys now," he called alerting the trailing pair that he was passing the prey. "Bogey's in a left hand turn pulling up. Extending."

He pushed the throttles forward to the firewall and the Speys, after a short delay, surged in thrust delivering 20,000 lbs each and rapidly accelerating the Phantom. He checked his turn, eased the stick back right and pushed towards the ground accelerating rapidly. His manoeuvre would drag the Harrier around behind him, hopefully setting it up for a follow on shot for the wingmen flying a few miles behind. In the back, Flash pulled hard against the straps of his ejection seat and bent his body in a bizarre position to look over his shoulder. As Razor concentrated on avoiding the ground and dropping back to the safety of low level where he would be immune from a missile shot, his navigator's commentary gave a mental picture of his opponent's reaction. The intense concentration was not needed for long because, as the Harrier dropped into his 6 o'clock by now well over a mile behind, the radio call announced its fate.

"Fox 2 on the Harrier heading north, disengaging."

Within seconds they had fired Sparrow and Sidewinder missiles each of which would have destroyed the target before it had even employed its own weapons. As the Harrier pilot registered his fate the Phantom formation settled back on track and continued north.

CHAPTER 13

THE HARZ MOUNTAINS CLOSE TO THE INNER GERMAN BORDER

Johann Horst had taken off from the small airfield close to the Inner German Border. His Cessna 172 in its bright red livery belonged to the local flying club and with only 80 hours in his log book Johann considered himself to be a very fortunate young man. His father paid little attention to his exploits in the air and was happy to fund what he thought to be a good way to keep his son focussed on his studies. Edging slowly towards his 2nd Class degree his attention was often diverted from his legal studies into the far more inviting areas of Aviation Law and Air Navigation. If he had his way, he would be pursuing a career in aviation rather than a courtroom. Before today was finished he would wish his attention to both those topics had been more thorough.

He had climbed up through the military low flying belt and was level at 3,000 feet heading north. Passing over the undulating terrain he looked down at the line drawn on his aviation chart on his knee. Approaching his next turning point his planned route would take him northwest towards the small village which he had nominated as a turning point from where he would return back southerly to the small grass airfield from where he had departed. The next leg would take about 20 minutes at about two miles per minute providing he pegged his speed at 120 knots as he had flight planned. His hand played the throttle watching the airspeed indicator settle on the magic number. The north westerly breeze would slow his groundspeed a little so maybe 23 minutes would be closer. He was feeling confident as he identified the small town ahead. The river came in from the southwest and cut through the centre of town. A small railway line tracked up the eastern boundary and headed north towards the town of Hannover many miles distant but, most significantly, a bright white chimney stack from an industrial plant in the suburbs identified it without any doubt.

He was feeling slightly over confident when he made his first error of the day. Dialling the heading bug on the compass around to the new heading he made the most basic of mistakes. Misreading the new heading of 305 degrees he set the bug at 035 degrees on the instrument. His now inaccurate course was almost 90 degrees away from the one which would take him on a safe vector away from the border. Many clues should have alerted him to his error but his embryonic skills were lacking. The turn onto northwest should have been to the left and the fact he came right did not seem unduly concerning. That East Germany was only a short distance to the east should have alerted his senses to the fact he was now drawing ever closer to the heavily defended strip of territory. He was also only vaguely aware of the radio transmission which to a more seasoned aviator would have set alarm bells ringing at maximum volume.

"Brass Monkey, Brass Monkey, Brass Monkey. Aircraft in the Air Defence Interception Zone in the vicinity of Nordhausen, heading 035 degrees come up on 121.5 and identify yourself."

The call should have instigated an instant turn onto a westerly heading and all around him military aircraft flying under visual flight rules executed the emergency procedure. Missions were thrown away as worried aviators consulted low flying charts to make sure it was not they who had penetrated the Air Defence Interception Zone. Johann pressed on in splendid ignorance.

*

Flash watched over his shoulder as the trailing element of Phantoms pulled hard onto a westerly heading, the sound of the "Brass Monkey" call on Guard raising an instant chill. In both cockpits he and Flash rapidly checked their position breathing a sigh of relief that they were innocent of the transgression.

*

The hooter sounded in the QRA shed at RAF Gutersloh and the air and groundcrew tumbled out of the door of the annex squeezing through the gap in the huge doors as they automatically responded. The crews had barely settled in since arriving from Wildenrath and already they had been scrambled. The flight line mechanic was first to reach the Houchin external power set as the aircrew sprinted up the ladders and dropped into the cockpits. Within seconds all other sounds were drowned out by the whine of the Rolls Royce Spey jet engines as both Phantoms powered up. Aircrew were helped to strap in before the groundcrew disappeared back down the ladders donning ear defenders to protect against the din. Within seconds the crews had checked in with Wing Operations and were briefed on the apparently suicidal course being set by the Cessna light aircraft only a few miles from their present position. Had they been at Wildenrath it would already have been too late. With their deployed location only 30 miles from the Inner German Border there might still be time to prevent the ill-fated pilot from penetrating the "Iron Curtain". The left hand engines on both jets spooled up as the groundcrew beneath the jets closed up the panels and pulled the chocks. Only minutes after the hooter had sounded the Phantoms rolled from the hangar making their way towards the active runway.

*

In a final act of self denial, the intense scar across the landscape which represented the Inner German Border did not register as the impenetrable barrier that it should have. He pressed on, following his erroneous heading of 035 and penetrated East German airspace. Many miles behind him, the pilots of two American F-15A Eagles from the US base at Bitburg knew of his fate before he did as the intercept controller hauled them off and positioned the fighters on a holding CAP in the Buffer Zone. As he passed over a stark concrete watch tower Johann would never see the East German Border Guard pick up the telephone and dial his Watch Commander. He could also not be aware of the incessant scan of the Bar Lock surveillance radar which had already detected the slow moving track penetrating its air defence zone.

*

Twenty miles behind, the pair of Phantoms accelerated to just below the

Mach holding the height down at 3,000 feet. The increasingly urgent calls from the fighter controller in the control and reporting centre at "Loneship" were redundant. The crew needed no additional motivation with the tension in the cockpit palpable.

Making rapid plots on his map on to his kneeboard, the Phantom navigator quickly realised that there would be no way they would overhaul the light aircraft before it crossed the border unless, miraculously, it reversed its course. Twenty miles ahead with the Phantom in a long tailchase the Cessna was invisible on radar and the scope remained frustratingly blank as they powered towards the border. Suddenly, a tell tale smear appeared on the pulse Doppler display and the navigator called the contact locking the radar to the blip.

"Bogey, 070 range 35, high speed, low level."

"Roger, I hold that. Contact showing in hostile airspace," replied the controller. "You are not, repeat not, cleared hot pursuit."

The Cessna had company. The navigator slapped his hand controller in frustration as his pilot cursed and nudged the throttles up holding the speed; barely subsonic. The countryside was sparsely populated below the jet but he had no desire to drop a sonic boom on the few people who populated the beautiful mountainous region. Nervousness was setting in as they closed down the range towards border penetration. At this speed they would arrive at the wire in minutes. Already their provocative course was attracting attention and the radar warning receiver began to pulse with vectors, all firmly arranged around their 12 o'clock in the eastern sector. A selection of increasingly urgent audio tones began to sound in their headsets each one originating from a Soviet surface-to-air missile tracking radar.

"I think I see the puddle jumper," said the pilot in the front seat. "Ahh jeez, I can also see watch towers."

It was impossible. With the border only a few miles ahead the Phantoms entered an inwards turn reversing their own course back towards the west. They would hold their position on combat air patrol awaiting instructions. Whatever fate awaited the pilot of the light aircraft it was to be dealt by a high speed fighter but the Phantom crew suspected that it may be one wearing a Red Star.

*

Johann Horst was stunned as a dark green Mig-21 Fishbed wearing the colours of the East German Air Force flew over the top of his light aircraft travelling much faster than his own, rocking his small craft in the turbulence. As the fighter manoeuvred around behind him he looked aghast at his map willing there to be an excuse but none of the features made any sense to him. He was totally and thoroughly lost and the arrival of the Mig meant that, this time, his mistake was serious.

"Delta, Echo, Bravo, Oscar Victor. You will follow me to Zerbst," he heard as the transmission intruded on his thoughts, his slowly receding mental capacity finally registering the implications. The callsign was his own Cessna so there could now be no doubt.

Johann's day was going downhill rapidly.

CHAPTER 14

THE FLIGHTLINE, RAF WILDENRATH

The dominant building on the Wildenrath flight line was the imposing hangar occupied by No. 60 Squadron, the Communications Flight. Work had begun back in 1963 to modify three Pembrokes for covert photographic missions by installing a removable camera installation in each aircraft. Once modified these Pembrokes became known to those in the know as the 'fit' aircraft. Although it was impossible to disguise the modifications as each aircraft now sported large camera hatches on the belly, only a few key individuals at the base knew the details of what they were really used for. The rest of the personnel at the base spent hours speculating, some getting much closer to the truth than others. Operation Hallmark was a closely guarded secret and only the Station Commander, OC Operations Wing and a few select aircrew on the Squadron who flew actively were briefed-in. Only selected groundcrew were allowed in the cabins of the modified aircraft whilst the rest were allocated simple tasks on the more sedentary communications Pembrokes.

The 'fit' consisted of three F96 cameras sporting 12 inch lenses protected by sliding hatches on the underside of the fuselage. The cameras, designed for the specialist photo reconnaissance Canberras, were fed by bulk film magazines producing hundreds of high definition photographs on each mission. Mounted in a fan arrangement in the rear cabin the cameras covered the whole of the area under the flight path of the aircraft. If operated carefully, almost uninterrupted coverage of an area of interest was guaranteed. Two additional F96 cameras with even bigger 48 inch lenses stared from each side of the aircraft configured to capture events along the route. With the substitution of the normal windows with specially treated and tailored replacements the quality could be quite remarkable. Flying at low altitude and at slow speed the Pembroke was an ideal camera platform. But for the heavy vibration of the ancient Alvis Leonides piston engines the fit would have been perfect. Nevertheless, when fitted with the heavy cameras the Pembroke was operating at almost the maximum allowable takeoff weight.

Missions followed a routine which in intelligence circles might not have been advisable as they could become predictable. Crews nominated for Operation Hallmark flew the "corridor" for a week completing one but, occasionally, two trips during that time. Good weather was critical as the cameras were weather dependent and often missions would be delayed waiting for better conditions. Targets of interest were identified from a number of sources but controlled from the Air Intelligence Cell at the Headquarters at Rheindahlen. Once a target was nominated the appropriate corridor was identified and the primary navigator would begin to plan the route including preparing both the navigation flight plan and the Air Traffic flight plan. One such crew had been nominated for the Operation for this week and the navigator would be Flight Lieutenant Pocklington.

In the 60 Squadron hangar a technician was installing the cameras for the following day's trip. His job complete, he pulled the curtains back over the windows sealing the secret fit from prying eyes or lenses. The Pembroke would stay in the hangar overnight and only be pulled out onto the ramp in the morning. Flight servicing would be the final task before crew-in but it was rare for last minute snags on this old but reliable classic.

What the technician did not know was that their covert activity was about to spark a serious incident which would begin to question the validity of the title "The Cold War".

CHAPTER 15

THE LETZLINGER HEIDE TRAINING AREA, EAST GERMANY

With its impressive title of The British Commanders'-in-Chief Mission to the Soviet Forces in Germany, BRIXMIS was set up in the immediate aftermath of World War 2 to provide liaison teams to assist cooperation between the military occupation authorities in the two zones. Similar missions were set up by the French and American authorities, although the British contingent was by far the largest. In a shrewd initiative, the British Mission also secured the right to fly a Chipmunk light trainer aircraft within a 20 mile radius around the British airbase at RAF Gatow in Berlin. This allowed limited aerial reconnaissance over the Soviet-controlled zone. There was always a robust Soviet military presence around Berlin and, at various times, almost 95% of the order of battle passed through that small circle. To have a light aircraft with a spare cockpit that could be occupied by a passenger with a camera was an intelligence coup.

Throughout the following years, the Mission undertook "tours" to monitor troop movements and to provide reassurance to the Western powers that the Soviet intentions were harmless. Despite this headline role, the reality was that with their relatively free movement authorised by the Soviet Headquarters, the teams gathered intelligence on installations, troop movements, equipment and deployments. During social events, members of the teams enjoyed close relations with their counterparts and often gleaned key impressions of morale and intentions.

Once allocated to a task, three man teams wearing military uniform travelled in olive green Mercedes Geländewagens or Opel Senators marked with prominent Union Flag symbols. From their base in the Mission House at Potsdam in Berlin, they entered East Germany crossing over the Glienicke Bridge by virtue of their Soviet-issued passes towards their nominated "targets". The East German authorities were not recognised and although the Stasi would tail the teams trying to disrupt the surveillance, only Soviet personnel could apprehend the teams if they were deemed to be operating outside the rules. Once in open countryside they were supposed to avoid the published restricted areas, which, normally, contained interesting items of military hardware. For that reason, such places were often a magnet and high on the list of places for the teams to visit.

Today was one such day and the three-man team had departed from Berlin at first light in a futile attempt to catch the Stasi "narks" unawares. As they crossed the bridge in the company of a second decoy vehicle they had separated. For once, they had been lucky that the narks had followed the decoy and the driver would take them on a serene trip around the local countryside before depositing them back at the bridge in an hour. Modified with long range fuel tanks and performance enhanced engines, the Senators allocated for this tour were wolves in sheep's clothing. Not only would they sit happily at 160 Kph all day on the East German autobahns, they were equally happy to go off-road if called for and mud and ditches were no obstacle. On the rare occasions they bogged down, a specially installed winch could extricate them from many unfortunate predicaments.

The NCO driver who was an expert in defensive driving powered the vehicle along the main autobahn to the west. At this early hour they were hoping to make good progress before the traffic increased. Tourist traffic was not a feature of East German life and even the wealthiest citizens were lucky to own a basic Trabant. However, as the day progressed they were more concerned about the increasing amount of military traffic. Any military convoy they fell across was fair game and would be a target for their cameras but routine traffic could be problematic. If they were spotted by the Stasi minders it was vital that they try to make their escape unhindered. The details of their vehicles were widely circulated and it was not unknown for an enthusiastic Soviet driver to use his Ural truck as a battering ram in an attempt to block their progress or even drive them off the road. As they approached the training range they took the exit heading north and eased the car off the main roads onto the minor routes. Normally used by Stendal airbase the range was some way north of their present location and air activity could be quite heavy when the range was in use. If their intelligence was correct, the range was quiet today and they should be able to dig in overnight and secure a safe place from which to watch the flying the following day. As they looked up prompted by the sound of a jet engine, a green Mig-21 flew past, manoeuvring hard. The officer in the rear of the vehicle trained his camera on the receding fighter and the motor drive clicked rapidly.

As they arrived at their target location the warrant officer climbed from the vehicle and eased the red and white striped barrier upwards allowing the British vehicle to pass through. Luckily the barrier was not locked and the chain had been carelessly wrapped around the post. He rearranged the links satisfied that their intrusion should go unnoticed hoping that the barrier would remain unlocked in case they had to beat a hasty retreat. Up ahead the track through the dense forest opened up onto flat ground before falling away down a slight incline towards the open plain below.

A secondary track led off the main route and the driver manoeuvred the car out of sight some distance from the main track. The trees were dense enough that, even if a patrol passed along the road, they should be invisible. A camouflage net pulled over the vehicle finished the job. Checking around the location and satisfied that they would not be spotted they made preparations for the night. The driver secured the best bed in the car and, although the seats would not fully recline, he managed a modicum of comfort. The warrant officer and officer slid into their arctic sleeping bags and shuffled into the lee of the vehicle out of the biting wind. Despite the cold they were quickly asleep.

As dawn was breaking they moved tentatively around the temporary camp site checking for evidence of patrols. There had been a few engine sounds and shouted commands during the night but they had all been in the distance and nothing which had given any cause for concern.

With his breath condensing in the cold brisk air, forming clouds in front of his face, the officer damped down the embers of the fire which they had lit to boil a mess tin of water for the morning brew. Breakfast had been a can of bacon grill sliced into individual portions which had sizzled appetisingly in another mess tin over the fire. The oatmeal block crumbled down with powdered milk and water had made a passable substitute for porridge. Other goodies from the 24 hour ration pack that they had drawn from stores before leaving Berlin were laid out for inspection. In addition to breakfast, each ration pack contained a main meal packed in tins along with snacks and the makings of a warm drink. The contents of the ration pack varied and, in theory, it would be a different menu for each trip out into the field. They had been delighted to find that they had drawn the most sought after menu - Menu A - Chicken Curry. Even so, they had balked at the idea of curry for breakfast. That would be for later if they could retire to the anonymity of the trees in order to warm up the food without attracting attention to their presence. To tide them over, the packets of sweets and chocolate bars were shared out and tucked away safely.

With the overnight gear re-stowed in the boot of the vehicle they moved slowly and carefully towards the tree line searching for a good vantage point. A small hedgerow gave perfect cover from view from the plain below and they went to ground and waited for the day's activity to begin. It was not a long wait.

"I don't really believe what I'm looking at," the warrant officer said under his breath.

"What have you spotted," asked the team leader gripping the camera closer to his chest. "Talk me on."

"Look down by the tank track in the two o'clock; in the gap in the woods. If I'm right this is the coup of the decade."

"Oh my God," the officer replied. "It bloody well is you know. That's an SA-10 Grumble launcher. They've only just been declared operational after testing and I thought the things were only deployed around Moscow for air defence of the city."

"Up to now that's been true but I'd bet next month's drinking money that we're right on the money with the identification. I saw some pretty good pictures last week. Some sort of company publicity that the manufacturer has been touting around at an airshow. If it is a Grumble, the associated radars are somewhere around here. It can't operate without the Flap Lid and the books say that it needs a Clam Shell for height finding and a Tin Shield for battlefield coordination. What the hell is it doing here at Letzlinger-Heide?"

"Have you got a picture yet?"

"Give me a second and I'll have one."

He clicked a few rapid-fire shots before changing the lens for a long range 300 mm telephoto. He retrained the camera on the launcher and clicked off a few more shots but, as he did so, he felt a gentle tap on the shoulder and his team mate pointed at a small clearing some distance from the first position. Tucked in a small clearing was the unmistakable profile of a Tin Shield surveillance radar rotating slowly on its rectangular plinth, the toned down structure barely visible against the foliage. Until now, the only pictures available had been of glossy painted systems paraded on Red Square for the benefit of the world's media. As the camera clicked away quietly that status quo between the superpowers was about to change.

"That's a seriously capable air defence system if the analysis is to be believed. I can't believe we're seeing it in the flesh."

As they watched, the tubes containing the missiles elevated to a vertical position from which the missiles were normally fired. Another tap and a pointed gesture and he slewed his gaze to a small radar dish standing proud above the canopy of the trees. Positioned on a massive tower, the radar antenna of the Clam Shell height finder was nodding up and down clearly tracking an unfortunate target in the distance, its position in three dimensions being carefully correlated by the computers within the camouflaged control cabins. The Flap Lid phased array was stationary, as yet looking out across the training area and they could only assume that a simulated target was being engaged as they watched. They had carefully checked the planned activity for the day and there had been no notifications for live firing so when the crack of a missile eject motor sounded out across the forest they were all taken aback. A huge missile rose from the launcher and headed, initially vertically upwards, before bending over and picking up a wide arcing course away to the north. This was unprecedented and they could only imagine the chaos which would ensue as sensitive receivers in space registered the significance of a missile launch from close to the Inner

German Border. Luckily its trajectory away from the border towards Sweden would cause sane minds to prevail but sanity seemed a long way from the present to the three men huddled in the undergrowth capturing the firing on film. As the missile tubes lowered back onto the launcher bed a few bodies emerged from around the complex and began working their way towards the control complex in the trees. The exercise was over for the day.

"Right, time to extricate ourselves and get this back to base," the officer said hurriedly. "This stuff is important and we need to let the people back in The Old War Office work out what's going on. It's way above my pay grade."

They shuffled backwards trying not to show a profile above the ridgeline on which they were perched. Once safely shielded from the SAM complex below they beat a hasty withdrawal to the Opel, fired up the engine and made their premature departure. It would be a long and nervous drive back to the Mission Headquarters.

Heading back south along a minor road a dark green vehicle approached in the opposite direction. As it passed alongside the occupants eyes were trained on their faces and only yards behind them, it threw a frantic 180 degree turn and set off in pursuit.

"Bugger, and it was all going so bloody well," the driver muttered accelerating hard. The warrant officer alongside had already pulled out his map and, anticipating the risk, had mentally rehearsed an escape route.

"There's a track off to the left about a mile down the road. Come off left and head down there. It's pretty rough and it crosses a ford about two miles east of here. If we're lucky we can strand them in the river crossing."

He glanced over his shoulder and the green car was slowly closing them down despite their own speedometer nudging 130 Kph. It looked like a Lada or some such Russian make. Luckily it wasn't a western design which might have made their task somewhat harder.

"It's about 300 yards, keep a good look out for the turn. There; hang a left now."

The Opel lurched crazily as the driver hit the brakes hard, the ungainly limousine probably slightly better equipped for touring Berlin than for throwing around the country lanes. It made the turn with some protests and settled down onto the rough surface through the countryside its suspension protesting even more. Although it had dropped back some distance the Lada also made the turn and began to follow. In the back seat the team leader had stowed the cameras in a compartment between the seats, hopefully out of sight should they be apprehended. He had taken the precious 35mm film and the small canisters were now secreted in a small hideaway behind the trim panel. It would take a full strip down of the car to find them now. He doubted that their cover story of being out taking photographs of the wildlife on the range would hold much sway if they were stopped. Although their pursuers were undoubtedly Stasi "narks", it would take no time at all to call the local Soviet Military Commander if they were forced to stop. Please let this be one day when they could make good their escape.

In the passenger seat the warrant officer was poring over the map. The ford was only a half a mile ahead and approaching rapidly. He had spotted a farm track which doubled back south towards the autobahn. If they could get across the short stretch of rough ground they would be back on a decent road and may yet shake off the pursuers. It was then that the stakes were raised as a crack heralded the disintegration of the rear window. The occupants ducked involuntarily, although it was far too late to affect the flight of the bullet. The fact that the windscreen had not shattered meant that the bullet had lodged somewhere within the cabin. It was way too close for comfort and it was rare to be fired upon during a pursuit. What the hell had got into them today? Had they been warned of the presence of the SA-10 complex? If so the stakes were indeed high.

The Opel careered through the ford throwing up a bow wave as it crossed the shallow stretch of water leaving damp tyre tracks on the road beyond, evidence of its passage. The road took a sharp turn to the left and just beyond the turn, the wooded track split off at an angle. The driver hauled the Opel into the leaf-covered roadway and accelerated hard, throwing up twigs and gravel in his wake. Behind them the Lada sped past the track entrance, only visible for a fraction of a second as it passed. The team leader breathed a sigh of relief urging the driver to keep up the momentum as a semblance of normality returned. Within a few minutes they picked up the main road and headed back towards Berlin, their prize intact.

*

The technician pulled the sheet of photographic paper from the trough of chemicals and washed it quickly in the sink arresting the developing process. A sharp image of a mean looking military vehicle with a slab-sided radar antenna started back at him. Impressed but not immediately aware of the significance of the image he clipped it to a drying line and moved back to the other tray. More pictures were being developed and a series of shots captured the scene on the military training area. He had a good idea, having looked at many similar images since he had arrived at BRIXMIS in Berlin, that this team had struck gold.

Within minutes the pictures were arranged on a plotting table in front of an analyst who pored over the detail with a stereoscope. Staring at a pair of the images through the binocular-like device the original scene sprang to life transformed into three dimensions by the cunning gadget. That the SAM system was new was beyond doubt. His challenge now was to try to identify it, although the notes from the team gave him a good clue. Normally he pored over minor changes to an SA-2 tracking radar or a Mig-23 weapon comparing it to grainy pictures from earlier tours. To have such a clear set of pictures of a newly deployed weapon system was a coup. Such magical moments were rare.

He would get the pictures off to the experts in Defence Intelligence in Whitehall and allow them to do their magic. Engineers and analysts would pore over the detail and make complex calculations to decide on the electronic characteristics and capabilities of the new system. Time was of the essence but as he stared at the images he could not know how critical any delay would prove.

CHAPTER 16

CHARLIE DISPERSAL, RAF WILDENRATH

The BRIXMIS teams were not the only ones to play the intelligence game. In the woods to the south of Wildenrath airbase, their Soviet counterparts, SOXMIS, were playing a similar role. After leaving the E46 autobahn the team had threaded its way through the local villages and parked up near the village of Gerderath. The car was hidden in a small wood and, although concealed from a casual bystander, would not avoid detection by a determined search team. Against all the rules they had left the vehicle and made the short trek across open ground to the southern perimeter fence of the airfield where they waited for the dawn.

Ringed by dense forest, the hardened shelters at Wildenrath were reasonably well concealed from the air but much of the woodland lay inside the perimeter wire. A single copse close to Charlie Dispersal but outside the perimeter road allowed the Soviets to approach quite close without risking detection. The small team had camped in the woods and, as dawn had broken, they had moved forward to an observation post adjacent to the fence. The tools of their trade were arranged around them and a single-lens reflex *Zenit* camera with a massive telephoto lens sat on a tripod trained at the dispersal opposite. Directional microphones captured the voices of the few personnel who had ventured outside at this early hour. Anyone working on the open revetments had been targeted and already the tape recorder had been capturing the sounds as an armament team moved weapons trolleys around the site. Activity in the shelters built carefully around the taxiways and aligned inwards was shielded from them, the stark rear shelter walls with their massive blast deflectors provided a frustrating shield preventing the Soviet watchers from seeing anything going on inside. Nevertheless, the trip was proving useful because, already, a lone aircraft had taxied out through the dispersal towards the distant runway attracting the attention of their long lenses.

At the sound of an approaching vehicle a camouflage net was thrown over the tripod and the team went to ground, motionless. A green Land Rover sped past only feet away from their position, the driver oblivious to their presence. After a short interval with everything once more quiet, the net was drawn back and they resumed their vigil.

On the dispersal, unbeknown to the watchers and until now hidden from view, the Station armourers were taking the opportunity to catch up on some much needed cross training. A key performance goal was to undertake servicing of other NATO aircraft so that, in the event of wartime diversions, they were able to re-arm the jets and send them airborne prepared for a further operational mission. The presence of the F-4E and the Mirage fighters was a perfect opportunity and not to be missed. A tractor pulled an F-4E onto a revetment in full view of the road joined within minutes by a Mirage III.

Beneath the Phantom, easily distinguishable from its RAF counterparts by its brown and green camouflage, a K-loader had been manoeuvred into place and a missile was being raised into the forward semi-conformal launcher. As the watchers clicked away the white projectile was eased into place and latched tight and the remaining guidance fins were slotted onto the missile body. Although the missile body fitted snugly in the housing, the angular fins broke up the smooth lines of the lower fuselage of the Phantom. Alongside, a second team was manhandling a Sidewinder onto the launcher rail of a Mirage III, the yellow stripes around the forebody marking it as a war shot round. The fact that the Mirage normally did not carry the Sidewinder was lost on the Army members of the SOXMIS team.

Conclusions were quickly drawn and a whispered conversation between two of the watchers resulted in a series of hand signals before the team began to pack up the gear. The speculation between the Soviets may have been premature but the presence of the armed aircraft was enough to form a false assumption. As they withdrew, the report that would soon be making its way to the Lubyanka was already being formulated and would warn of preparations for an armed mission by a combined NATO and French force. What they would not see after their hasty departure was the armament team removing the missiles and returning them to the adjacent trolleys.

A dangerous game play was being set in motion.

*

Teufelsberg, or the Devil's Mountain, was the highest landmark in Berlin and an ideal location for a listening post. Accessed via a steep, winding road from Grünewald in the British sector of West Berlin, the white radomes and antenna farms stood out against the skyline. Built on a man-made mountain of rubble cleared after World War 2, the installation was home to an international military community and one of NATO's electronic intelligence stations. To be allowed to pass through the doors meant that rigorous background checks had been completed and personnel had been cleared for access to the most sensitive Cold War secrets. Inside, operators maintained a round-the-clock watch on almost every aspect of East German and Soviet communications in the surrounding area. What they heard would never be discussed outside the facility not even with their closest friends and family. A small army of technicians kept the antennas, which were hooked up to sensitive radio receivers, serviceable. Communications dishes not only transmitted data back to London and Washington but also scanned the electro-magnetic spectrum for snippets of information which might add to the complex jigsaw.

The RAF contingent, part of No. 26 Signals Unit, operated from both RAF Gatow and from Teufelsberg itself. Across the city on the airfield at RAF Gatow, a pair of seemingly innocent Chipmunk trainer aircraft were the most unlikely candidates for a spying role. Operating within the 20 mile radius of the Berlin Control Zone, they exercised the right to fly across the city and the surrounding countryside, their mission enshrined in post-war treaties and agreements. Carrying a pilot in the back seat and a photographer in the front, the small trainers captured the activities of the Group of Soviet Forces Germany ranged around the city in their forward deployed bases. On the airfield and hidden by an anonymous rubberised radome, a radar antenna scanned the local airspace and RAF technicians monitored the aerial activity of the Soviet Air Armies based in East Germany. It was all legal but the game of tit-for-tat was endless as the opposing forces sought to maximise their own intelligence haul but limit their opponents.

At Gatow, one such sortie was in progress. The pilot in the back cockpit of the Chipmunk peered around the bonedome which obscured his forward view. He canted the nose of the small training aircraft off to the side to give him a clear view of the taxiway ahead. Pointing into wind he brought the throttle up allowing the RPM to stabilise as he checked the magneto drop and the carburettor heater. With the gauges cooperating he nodded imperceptibly and retarded the throttle checking the idle settings. Content that the engine was behaving, and with only a single engine to keep them aloft that was reassuring, he called the air traffic control tower. With takeoff clearance granted he snaked along the taxiway kicking the rudder pedals left and right to clear his path, the nose of the Chipmunk and the observer obscuring his view. Needing only a few hundred metres takeoff run, the expanse of concrete which stretched ahead was a luxury and without stopping he advanced the throttle and the small aircraft surged forward, lifting off into the bright morning sunshine. He had already passed through 500 feet as the white piano keys of the easterly threshold passed below and he set heading over the dense forest which ringed the easterly end of the airfield. To the left of the nose the "Berliner Funkturm", a huge 150 metre high radio transmission mast dominated the skyline and he adjusted his heading to pass to the south of the landmark. In the front cockpit his passenger began to set up the single lens reflex camera ready for the task they had been set. Within the 20 mile radius of Gatow he planned to make the most of the regulations and, perhaps, a little extra, and much of the short sortie would be spent over the eastern sector of the city which stretched out ahead of him. To the northeast lay the fighter base of Werneuchen which was home to two squadrons of supersonic Mig-25 Foxbats. He would give the airfield a healthy margin, keen not to antagonise the residents. The slipstream from a close pass from a Foxbat would give him more problems than the other pilot. If the reports were correct, there was a troop concentration in one of the regular holding areas near Buchholz on the edge of the Strausberger Forest. As he cleared the urban sprawl he let down to 500 feet keeping the Neuer Mehrower Strasse off his right wing. Passing over the village of Altlandsberg the pair looked ahead straining to pick out any military vehicles against the green backdrop the propeller obscuring the view. Their efforts were unnecessary and, within minutes, they had the target in sight. Entire fields had been requisitioned from unfortunate East German farmers and ranks of armoured vehicles were set out in neat rows ahead, the landscape dissected by rutted tracks churned up in their wake. In military parlance it was a target rich environment. Used to seeing Soviet military formations, the masses of T62 tanks, BMP1 armoured personnel carriers and Zil trucks which greeted the crew surprised even them. More importantly, the sight of four ZSU 23-4 self propelled anti aircraft artillery pieces focussed their imagination. With evident relief the pilot realised that the barrels were stowed in the transit position and relaxed slightly knowing that he would be unchallenged. Although the Army formation would include embedded SA-7 Grail missile launchers the tiny infra-red signature of the Chipmunk conferred immunity. The front seater began to snap away capturing images of the assembly area. There was no effort at concealment and, as the pilot dropped the wing to give a better view, the photographer zoomed in on the nearest vehicles capturing rare close-up shots which would keep the analysts busy for months.

As the tiny trainer stood on its wingtip overhead the tanks, the crew could see faces staring up at the noisy intrusion. Often this would send the Soviet troops scurrying to fit covers to shield sensitive equipment from prying eyes. Today there was no such hesitance. Arrogant gestures from below suggested a swagger unusual around the capital city. Set apart from the main assembly area the pilot spotted the familiar layout of the communications battalion, the trucks festooned with antennas, confirming his impression that this was a fully formed Motor Rifle Division. The communications battalion was the eyes and ears of the formation and provided connections with higher command and the neighbouring divisions in combat. Somewhere close by would be the Divisional Headquarters, the heart of the unit. The camera snapped relentlessly, capturing the detail.

With another intelligence coup in the bag the crew, after a hurried discussion, decided to cut short the sortie and return to Gatow. The pilot set heading and the range back to Gatow began to wind down when there was a frantic call from the back.

"Left, nine o'clock, range two miles, closing."

The pilot swung his head around staring down the bearing quickly spotting the gaunt profile of a Hind attack helicopter bearing down on them at the same height, the rotors a blur. He unconsciously eased down, checking the familiar features on the ground, willing the city boundary to appear beneath him. Pushing up the throttle the airspeed indicator hovered at the limiting airspeed where it pegged. The light trainer would go no faster. The Hind, and by now it was obviously a Delta model, swept past ahead of the Chipmunk disturbing the crisp air and leaving the tiny aircraft rocking in its wake. It swung round in a wide arc and closed in from the 5 o'clock the disparity in the speeds clear.

"Gatow Tower Lima Bravo Echo 34, reporting a confliction with rotary traffic, 090 range 12. Request you contact their operators and advise them of our intentions to recover." His tremulous voice gave away his concern.

"Lima Bravo Echo 34 roger copied, willco. Stand by."

The pilot hoped he had the time to stand by. The gaunt concrete of the East Berlin suburbs flitted by and the watch towers of the Berlin Wall emerged from the haze. The brightly coloured Chipmunk with its red and white colour scheme was a regular feature in the Berlin skies and one of the few that could cross the Wall with impunity. The pilot hoped that today would be no different. Even so he tensed as the Hind closed inexorably. Armed with a 23mm chain gun, if the Soviet pilot was about to make a statement, they had no defence against the brutally functional killer. His tiny infra red signature was no defence against a visually aimed gun. The needle wavered at 120 knots yet the second hand of his watch seemed to stand still.

As the Hind pulled alongside and stabilised there could be no doubting the meaning of the gesture from the rear cockpit occupied by the pilot. The two faces stared at them impassively but the universal symbol left little doubt as to the Soviet crew's opinion of their heritage. The helicopter peeled away and disappeared into the distance.

With the Berlin suburbs passing below, the pilot ran through his recovery checks feeling relieved at the narrow escape. The precious film would be scrutinised in detail but already they knew that this troop build-up was extraordinary. Such aggression was extremely unusual and the actions unprecedented.

CHAPTER 17

RUNWAY 09, RAF WILDENRATH

The 60 Squadron Pembroke lined up on Runway 09 at Wildenrath and the pilot ran through his pre takeoff checks. The clock ticked down to 1000. There was no set time for this type of mission and, if an unusual event had been identified in East Germany, the Pembroke crews would respond. The Alvis Leonides piston engines split the early morning calm as the aging piston plane rumbled off down the runway picking up speed slowly.

"RAFAIR 3637 airborne to Clutch Radar."

"RAFAIR 3637 to Clutch on Stud 13, the regional QNH is 1024, good day."

"Good day Sir."

The pilot switched frequency and checked in with the military air traffic control agency in Düsseldorf as he reset his altimeter watching it wind up slowly through 2,000 feet. He eased the nose of the aircraft gently left as he settled down on his outbound heading aiming directly for the entry point to the central corridor many miles to the north east. His course would take him through the congested airspace of the Cologne/Bonn air traffic control zone and his slow rate of climb would mean he would be dodging airliners departing from Cologne for exotic destinations, for the early part of the flight. It was a well rehearsed routine and he settled down for what he assumed would be a typical sortie along the corridor to RAF Gatow in West Berlin.

In the rear, the extra crewmember unstrapped and began to move around the cramped cabin stepping around the bulky camera installation. Strapped down alongside the row of ancient rearward-facing, blue leather seats, the fixed photographic installation looked complex. More heavy containers holding the latest Pentax single lens reflex cameras and their telephoto lenses would be opened once the important tasks of the day were complete and would provide some fill-in shots which the fixed cameras might miss. The high tech of the photographic gear was a stark contrast to the aging technology of the old plane. Despite the clandestine nature of the mission, the first priority of the day was to pour a coffee and break out the in-flight rations.

*

At Zerbst airbase across the border in East Germany a pair of Mig-21 Fishbed Deltas fired up and taxied to the operational readiness platform at the end of the runway. As they closed down a fuel bowser pulled alongside and hooked up the refuelling receptacle to the underside of each jet in turn. Critically short of fuel under the best of circumstances, no risks were being taken today and the tanks would be topped off to full before the jets took off. In one cockpit the pilot had unstrapped and sat casually on the ejection seat, his helmet plugged into the intercom waiting for instructions. They had been given their mission and the only information missing was when they would launch. The other pilot watched closely as the refuelling operation was completed on his jet and he signed the obligatory paperwork for the fuel. With a thumbs-up to his wingman he climbed back into the cockpit and assumed the vigil as his partner stretched gratefully and climbed down the boarding ladder.

*

As the Pembroke passed Braunschweig, by now level at 10,000 feet and cruising at a sedentary 120 knots, the spare navigator broke open the camera case and began to check his equipment. Today's route would begin at the TACAN beacon at Wolfsburg at the western end of the central Berlin corridor. The corridors were a mere 20 miles wide and the maximum height of 10,000 feet was constrained by Soviet mandates. For the Pembroke crew this was no problem and, for their task today, the lower, the better. It also allowed the civilian airliners, which were restricted to the confines of the air corridor to fly into Berlin at the highest possible level.

The primary navigator up front sat next to the pilot whereas his colleague down the back would operate the equipment today. Although they interchanged in their roles they were fulfilling completely different roles. The navigator in the cockpit was responsible for the route navigation and keeping them out of trouble. The rear-seat navigator without a view forwards had to rely entirely on his information to align the cameras and when to switch on the vertical cameras. The drift sight, rescued probably from a Lancaster bomber, was merely a telescope that pointed down under the belly showing how the aircraft was tracking over the ground. Using it was like trying to watch a football match through a straw. If the aircraft was off track course corrections passed by the second navigator might realign the aircraft and, hence the cameras and recapture their target but it was fraught with difficulties and much could go wrong. If the pilot was over-enthusiastic on the controls even a gentle turn would move the subject away from the staring lens. Most important of all, the front seat navigator had to make sure the aircraft remained inside the corridors during these manoeuvres. With such a short distance to the crucial boundary, a drift too far from the centreline would take the Pembroke worryingly close to East German airspace attracting unwanted scrutiny.

The second navigator's collection plan was attached to a clipboard with carefully marked boxes annotated along the route identifying each of his targets for the morning. The central corridor passed directly overhead the airfield at Mahlwinkel and close to the training area at Letzlinger Heide. He would be ready to capture anything that might be of interest on the ground. An exercise had been running for a few days and Mig-23BNs from Jagdbombenfliegergeschwader 37 of the East German Air Force had been deployed forward from Drewitz on the Polish border and had been flying ground attack missions on the training range. There was a rumour that the new Hind Delta attack helicopters were also flying from Mahlwinkel in support of the exercise and if he could get some shots of those he would be an overnight sensation. A shot of a Flogger during an attack run would still gain him some serious kudos with his fellow aviators and the intelligence analysts. He checked the batteries for the exposure meter carefully and lined up the spares. Removing the lens cap he fiddled with the filter and wiped down the lens making sure the last vestiges of dust were removed. The last thing he needed was to spoil the intelligence coup of the year with a dust spot in centre frame. Happy with his efforts he stowed the camera and its huge 300 mm lens in the carrying case and checked that his spare reels of 35mm film were to hand. As he passed the Hawk site on the western side of the border he would run a few test shots to make sure the camera was working correctly.

Up front, the navigator watched as the TACAN range to the beacon at Wolfsburg wound down slowly. In 15 minutes they would descend to 3,500 feet, the height at which they had flight planned to penetrate East German airspace to begin the run along the corridor to Berlin. A secondary radio set was tuned in to the air-to-ground radio frequency of Letzlinger Heide Range and he would listen carefully for the codeword "Dvorets" which was used by the Warsaw Pact pilots to identify the training range. The chatter would be recorded for later analysis. Although the navigation would be simple and they merely had to follow the TACAN radial into Gatow, the navigator had drawn a line on a low flying chart and he would walk his finger along the track to make sure they stayed in the corridor. It was a well known tactic of the Soviet electronic warfare battalions to use "meaconing" of the radio beacons to give false readings in the cockpit. Any deviation from the flight path would result in interception by Soviet fighters and it was an opportunity the Pembroke crew did not want to offer.

*

At the eastern end of the airfield at Gatow in the western sector of the city of Berlin, a seemingly innocent radome covered a rather more sinister purpose. The radar housed in the bubble, ostensibly for ground controlled approaches into the airfield, was used for other more covert tasks. On the average day its beam spread out over the surrounding airspace monitoring and recording any air traffic within its coverage allowing analysts to monitor and evaluate the tactics of the Soviet 16th Air Army and the East German Air Force. Without its input the alarm systems which warned of an attack on the West would, effectively, be blind.

Alongside in a small hut, sensitive radio receivers sat in racks alongside other intelligence gathering equipment. Two operators were huddled over the sets their headsets clamped to their ears. For the last 30 minutes the level of chatter on the primary air defence frequency had gone through the roof and an incessant chat was continuing between the controller at Zerbst airfield and the central sector controller. The operator was alert waiting for any of the key Russian phrases he had been trained to identify. At the sound of the word "Pembroke", completely out of context in normal discussions, he became even more focussed. Something was amiss. He listened with alarm as the scramble message was passed to the fighter controller at Zerbst. MiG-21 Fishbeds of the 833rd Soviet Fighter Regiment were being scrambled to intercept something and it seemed likely to be the hapless Pembroke. Or was it a scramble? The pilots seemed quite relaxed under the circumstances; almost as if it was planned. His instructions were quite clear for this situation. He opened his noddy guide and thumbed down to the emergency alert procedures. Picking up the phone he dialled the number in the intelligence cell at HQ RAF Germany. The phone rang masking the noise of his fingers tapping a beat on the counter, nervously waiting for a response.

*

"Crossing the IGB," now said the navigator, Carl Pocklington. "The wind is right behind us so there's not much drift to worry about and it's pushing up our groundspeed. With an extra 30 knots on the tail we should be there 10 minutes ahead of schedule."

"Thanks Carl. Did you get that down the back? We'll hit the fix points a few minutes ahead of schedule so better have your kit ready now. It's about 120 miles from here to Gatow so it'll take us about an hour. Estimating Mahlwinkel in 25 minutes from now."

"Roger that, all ready back here and the gear is all checked and ready."

The engines droned on.

*

Colonel General Portnov stood on the bridge of the Combined Operations Centre watching the backlit operations tote closely. Activity was intense over the Letzlinger Heide Training Range but further east the airspace was quiet. It would be some hours before the rest of the planned air activity began.

"The track entering the corridor at Wolfsburg. It's not a civilian aircraft, confirm?"

"No Sir", said the harried operations officer, a Major of Aviation, suddenly distracted by the intervention from the senior officer. "It's a British Pembroke inbound to Berlin."

"A communications flight?"

"Yes Sir. They are regular visitors but we know they carry a reconnaissance suite onboard. It's a standing joke with the soldiers on the training range."

"They carry cameras?"

"Indeed Sir and we suspect they monitor our frequencies too but there are no obvious additional antennas on the airframe."

"So what is our normal reaction?"

"Nothing Sir. We have equivalent flights operating over West Germany, and beyond, so it's treated as a tit-for-tat arrangement. The post-war agreements allow free passage into the Berlin Control Zone."

Portnov went quiet for a moment. Having asked to see a practice scramble by the Migs deployed forward to Zerbst, he was moving inexorably towards a decision point. Quite soon there would be no turning back. He watched the symbol denoting the Migs as a clerk updated the position with a grease pencil. A target, an An-24 Coke, had been arranged which was tracking parallel to the Berlin corridor but some miles north. The Migs closed slowly on their quarry.

"What is the aircraft's position in the corridor?" he asked gruffly.

"On the centreline Sir. It's a perfectly normal flight. Entirely routine."

"Intervene. I want to inspect that aircraft and find out what they are carrying."

"But Sir, there is no reason to do so. The pilot is complying with all the regulations and his squawk is correct."

"Are you questioning my decision Major?" the General challenged.

"Of course not Sir but the implications. . . . ."

The staff officer hesitated but quickly deferred, wary of incurring the wrath of the Communist Party Commissar. His hesitation was irrelevant. Portnov had mulled over the implications countless times over the preceding days and the Major could have no inkling of the political ramifications of the actions which would follow in the coming hours. The interception would be discussed at the highest levels in the Politburo; and quite soon.

"I'm waiting Major."

He watched as the operations officer picked up the handset and relayed the crucial instruction. What the operations officer could not know was that more sinister undertones were driving the intervention and onboard the Pembroke, all was not as routine as it might seem.

*

Without a radar warning receiver the first the crew knew that they had company was as the polished, silver Mig-21 pulled alongside on the right, its delta wing planform glinting in the sun as it jockeyed to stay in position. At 120 knots it barely accomplished the feat and the white bonedome in the cockpit moved urgently on gimbals as the pilot struggled with the reluctant controls. Despite the reflected image of the Pembroke in the burnished fuselage, the presence of the five-pointed red star on the fin and the large red numbers that adorned the forward fuselage left no doubt as to the fighter's origins or its intentions. The bullet fairing in the nose housing the air-to-air radar and the four pylons under the wings carrying AA-2 Atoll missiles spoke more than words. Unable to hold close formation the pilot eased the small fighter away from the flight path and took up station a few hundred yards away on the right. Almost immediately his wingman appeared on the left and the small wings began to rock violently as it positioned itself ahead and slightly above the Pembroke's flight path. In concert, its navigation lights began to flash rhythmically.

"Oh Jeez," breathed the pilot, you know what that means don't you?"

"I wish I didn't but it means you've been intercepted, follow me."

"Are you sure we're still in the corridor, Carl?"

"Spot on mate; bang down the centreline and the TACAN backs that up."

"In that case we don't need to comply. We're flight planned and we have diplomatic clearance for the flight. I say we tough it out."

"Sounds good to me."

As he spoke, the jet on the left dropped back and took up station on the left side in the 8 o clock position about 200 yards behind. The navigator in the rear cabin began a commentary of its position. The jet on the right also dropped back but within seconds cranked on 60 degrees of bank towards the lumbering transport and began to track.

"Jeez, it looks like he's about to shoot."

The Mig closed inexorably before breaking out at the last moment and passing feet above the cockpit in a hard right turn back out onto the perch. At the same time the second Mig drifted in towards their flight path and began to rock the wings violently once again.

"This is getting serious. This guy doesn't look like he's going to give in."

The original manoeuvres were repeated but as the Mig bore down on them from the right, the nose came off and tracked ahead of their flight path. The relieved commentary in the cockpit was short lived as the sound of gunfire could be heard above the noise of the clattering pistons and the unmistakeable sight of tracer rounds passed across the nose only narrowly missing the Pembroke.

"OK that's enough; I'm not going to die for a matter of principle. Let's do as they say."

The pilot began to rock the wings in acknowledgement and, as the Mig turned to the right, he began to follow. They quickly left the corridor entering East German airspace, their escorts following closely. At this stage not a word had been said on the Guard frequency so their control agency could have little idea of their fate. With the thought of the warning fire fresh in their minds, neither crew member in the cockpit made any attempt to transmit over the radio. With hindsight it was a serious mistake. The Migs began a slow descent.

They had flown southerly for some time and were now well south of the safe confines of the corridor. As they approached the airfield at Zerbst the Mig immediately alongside lowered his undercarriage pointing, purposefully, at the Pembroke pilot urging him to respond similarly. Looking ahead, the runway was clearly visible and the pilot dropped the landing gear and settled onto short finals.

"OK seats for landing. Please tell me that you ditched the maps and films over the side?"

"I did. The cameras are still here but the evidence is gone. I fogged the films so that they can't be developed and I dumped the hand-held film canisters out of the window with the maps."

"Maybe the cameras should have followed but it's too late now. The guy on the wing would see them being ditched."

"And I suspect a worried East German citizen would hand them in to the nearest Soviet barracks. Not sure how we're going to explain them away though. They're not exactly useful for taking tourist snaps on the Kurfürstendamm!"

The Mig drifted ahead giving the pilot a wide berth to choose his touchdown point on the runway. Behind and unsighted to the pilot the second Mig held silent sentinel, its weapons system live and infra red missiles locked to the rumbling pistons. Even if they could run away, which at a speed of 120 knots was laughable, the Mig would quickly run them down. Discretion seemed to be the order of the day. He lowered the flaps and eased the throttles up to compensate for the additional drag and the Pembroke lumbered across the runway threshold and settled onto the concrete surface. As the speed washed off the trailing Mig passed low over the cockpit rattling the airframe before pulling up in a gentle wingover ahead and turning downwind. Suddenly alone for the first time in some minutes the pilot felt a strange sense of isolation and the cockpit was quiet. The unsaid question between him and his navigator was what would happen next. The answer would become obvious very quickly.

A drab green utility vehicle with a yellow flashing light appeared on the runway ahead of them and positioned itself on the centreline blocking further progress. When its intentions became obvious to the crew it arced around and returned back along the taxiway from where it had emerged. The pilot eased the Pembroke onto the taxiway and followed. After a short taxy he approached the parallel taxiway to the north of the main runway where a large hard standing opened up in front of him. The reception committee left little doubt as to where he should stop. The "Follow Me" truck pulled to a halt and the driver made frantic gestures placing his crossed hands above his head. With one engine already stationary and after receiving the universal signal to stop, the pilot resignedly braked to a standstill. As the noise died he cautioned his crew to follow his lead and pulled off his headset.

As Carl Pocklington walked down the hastily positioned steps, no one seemed to notice that he was carrying his Navbag yet all the other gear had been left aboard the Pembroke. Perhaps it was the Soviet guards brandishing AK47 rifles which caused the temporary lapse in attention or, perhaps, it was the sinister looking man dressed in the archetypal raincoat who waited at the base of the steps. The fact the civilian did not appear to be armed added to the air of menace.

The crew were hustled into the waiting crew bus at gunpoint. The thought of resisting was far from their minds. For once politicians and diplomats seemed vitally important as the events of the coming days would be determined in the corridors of power not in the cockpit of an aeroplane. The diesel engine in the bus fired up sounding remarkably like a sack of hammers and belching fumes.

The convoy moved off across the dispersal to an unknown fate.

CHAPTER 18

DIVISIONAL HEADQUARTERS, 16TH TACTICAL AIR ARMY, EAST GERMANY

Portnov waved his aide into the seat in the dingy office and sat down in the faded armchair, his features beginning to show the strain.

"We need to start a few things in motion Petr."

The aide scribbled furiously in a small notebook, alert and attentive.

"Send a signal to Moscow and update them on this latest move. The news will arrive fast enough through other sources and I don't want them pre-empting my plans."

"Already being drafted Comrade General. I'll make sure the signal is released as soon as possible."

"Good. What do we know about this navigator at Wildenrath who Meier has been running?"

"Very little General. He's played him close so far and we've had little need to know the details. The information we've been receiving has been checking out and there has been little need to dig deeper."

"Are we happy it's all genuine? I wouldn't be surprised if we were being fed a few false trails."

"It's been checked out Comrade General and all seems well. I can have them go over it all again to make certain."

"Do that. Some of the decisions will rely on reading their responses correctly. I need to be sure."

"Immediately Sir."

"Have Meier contact his agent over there; Kolbe isn't it?" he asked distractedly not waiting for an answer. "If our friend is not already in possession, have him pressure her to deliver the operational plans we talked about. Without the detail of the Western responses I'll be working in the dark. This is important so I think we can afford a few risks. Make sure he knows that the stakes have just risen.

"Of course Sir."

"Then that just leaves me to initiate the next phase of the operation. Thank you Petr."

Portnov could have no idea that not only the navigator but the operational plans had just come into his possession somewhat sooner than anticipated.

*

As the military trucks pulled up outside the Kaserne, the gaunt Germanic headquarters building, the squad of guards tumbled out, their AK47 rifles clattering against the tailgate. With barely a pause, the aircrew were bundled out and ushered into the building at gunpoint jostled by their unsympathetic captors. Locks rattled and doors banged amid shouted commands as they were hustled along the anonymous corridor and into a soulless room. A small barred window allowed a trickle of light into the temporary cell and, as the noise from the guards receded, the pilot took stock only then realising that Pocklington was not with them.

"Did you see what happened to Carl?" he muttered still disorientated.

"No, the AK47 had me mesmerised and the way the guard was waving it around, I wasn't sure if I was going to survive the journey."

"Carl!" the pilot shouted, his call echoing in the small space. There was no reply. He paused taking stock before returning to the door. He banged aggressively, the noise reverberating along the now empty corridor.

"I am a British Officer and I insist on seeing a Soviet officer; now!"

His demand was met with silence as were his further, futile attempts to persuade his unresponsive audience. He slammed his hand hard against the door in frustration. Silence descended as the men sat down to wait, plotting their next moves yet seemingly bereft of the ability to control the rapidly escalating events.

CHAPTER 19

THE INNER GERMAN BORDER

"Major, have the pilots been briefed for Phase Two?"

"Yes Comrade General."

"Implement."

"At once Sir."

The operations officer moved back across to the console and thumbed the microphone relaying the message to the operations controller at Zerbst. His eyes flicked nervously back towards Portnov as he spoke giving away the fact that the conversation was taking an unexpected turn. He remonstrated with the man on the other end of the line, seemingly reaching a compromise before returning the handset to the cradle. His demeanour spoke volumes, his reply less than confident.

"The aircraft are being serviced as we speak General. They will be airborne as soon as possible."

The hostile stare he received in return chilled his blood and he busied himself with another trivial task to temper his growing apprehension. His nervous glances at the tote did little to expedite events at the distant airfield and it seemed like an age before the symbols changed denoting a launch.

Portnov scanned the airspace along the IGB. Already the message that the Pembroke had been forced down would be working its way up the command chain prompting questions in Moscow as faceless bureaucrats tried to fathom out who had initiated the provocative act. He would ensure that the decision makers were not given the chance to evaluate the tactical situation too deeply before he set the next phase in motion. Always ask for forgiveness rather than permission was his motto. He tapped his fingers impatiently as the clock ticked away.

*

The Battle Flight Phantom headed towards the border approaching the Buffer Zone, it's airspeed indicator tickling Mach 1. Launching from Gutersloh for the second time today it had entered the Zone almost immediately, the radar in the nose scanning left and right registering nothing but empty airspace on the other side of the border. All flights in the Air Defence Interception Zone had been grounded temporarily as soon as the Battle Flight hooter had sounded but the crew were oblivious to the fact.

The controller rambled, his monologue failing to calm the racing pulses of the crew still on an adrenaline high after the scramble. His platitudes were little justification for the hectic manner in which they had launched. Although the second scramble in a few hours, as was so common, the buzz of a scramble seemed certain to be replaced by the monotony of a wasted alert.

*

The Migs lifted off the runway in close formation, the pilots barely having had the chance to celebrate after they had forced down the Pembroke. At the morning briefing, the range of possible missions that had been briefed seemed unlikely but already events were running into a single, increasingly blurred episode. Normally confined to the rear area of the operational theatre the pilots were specially selected and their instructions were unambiguous yet disturbing. They were to run at high speed towards the border at medium level where the western radar systems would easily be able to detect and track their progress. At a mere five miles from the boundary, the Leader would turn at maximum G towards the north and descend to low level. What he did not know was that the number 2, a rising star in the political hierarchy, had subsequently received even more aggressive instructions. He was to penetrate western airspace before turning in the opposite direction and making his escape to the south where a prominent protrusion of the border into West German airspace would allow him to cross back to the east and provide sanctuary. The gesture was designed to ramp up the pressure on the western controllers already nervous after the earlier events. One mistake might prove to be the elusive trigger. As a "150 percenter", that he would comply was assumed. Whether he complied implicitly might come as a surprise during the final stages of the manoeuvre.

*

"Contact 090 range 45, single contact, low, fast."

"Mike Lima 26, I hold the contact. Investigate."

"Are we cleared hot pursuit?"

"Negative Mike Lima 26, hold clear of hostile airspace unless authorised."

"Mike Lima 26, hold clear, acknowledged."

The Phantom crew took an immediate cut-off closing down the range to the target and vectoring towards the extended centreline, the ideal position to launch a missile. Weapons switches armed, missile status checked, chaff and flare systems primed and ejection seat straps tightened, the crew watched the blip track inexorably down the radar scope. Mental calculations in the rear cockpit confirmed that the target was well inside East German airspace but moving rapidly towards the border. The navigator broke the radar lock and checked the scope for other contacts. His caution was rewarded.

"Contact bearing 090 in 20 mile trail."

"Affirmative, I hold the trailer. He shows 15,000 feet," came the reply from the controller. Like pulling teeth the navigator thought frustratedly. A clue would have been good.

With the prospect of an engagement occurring close to the border increasing, the nervous Phantom crew felt isolated.

"Instructions!"

96

"Checking, stand by."

Expressions of exasperation cut through with expletives filled the cockpit in response to the indecision. Evaluation time was short and if they were to enter the fight on equal terms they needed clearance now. If the intelligence was to be believed, the contacts on the scope were Soviet Mig-21s pushed forward as reinforcements for the East German regulars and significantly more agile than the Phantom. The navigator checked his position yet again concluding that, on the present track, they would merge exactly overhead the border towers. He needed the engagement to be over western airspace and now was the time to engineer the geometry of the engagement or be sucked into a disadvantageous position. The last thing he needed was to merge over hostile airspace. Reluctantly, he prompted the pilot to reverse the heading and the edgy front-seater hauled the heavy Phantom around onto a reciprocal heading breaking the lock as the contact disappeared off the side of the radar scope. The navigator, equally frustrated as the radar reverted to search mode, played with the controls anticipating the turn back. With the contacts now invisible, firmly trapped in the six o'clock, he endured an anxious 60 seconds as they dragged the geographical point at which the merge would occur back towards the west onto safer ground. He was oblivious to the fact that the coming events would make his caution redundant. Facing back up to the threat and listening to the renewed position calls from the fighter controller the blips reappeared on the radar display and he re-locked to the lead Mig.

"Mike Lima 26 contact, 090 range 20, request instructions," he prompted yet again.

"Roger 26, if the hostiles penetrate friendly airspace you are clear to engage, acknowledge," came the heavily accented German voice over the ether. Adrenaline kicked in.

"Clear engage over friendly airspace, Mike Lima 26."

In the control bunker, the tracks on the huge display screen of the air defence surveillance radar slowly merged and the controller tapped his foot on the floor in rhythm with the rotation of the time base. He had done all he could and it was now down to the aircrew. As he watched, the hostile track closest to the border suddenly turned away and began to parallel the border heading north. He transmitted the evasion turn watching impassively as the Phantom dragged northwards in sympathy but the control frequency remained quiet. Aloft, the crew were busy. Without clearance to penetrate East German airspace the friendly response from the Phantom remained to the west of the Inner German Border. A standoff ensued as both aircraft headed north on parallel tracks split by only a tiny margin. Mesmerised by the aerial ballet the controller was momentarily distracted from the activity behind which should have been his main concern. Unseen by either him or the Phantom aircrew the second Mig pressed onwards towards the border. A minor dogleg in a southerly direction increased the separation from the rapidly opening Phantom but, even on the revised heading, its track would take it perilously close to the border. The indolent controller finally spotted the danger.

"Mike Lima 26, heads up, vector 180. Second contact 150 range 25, heading west. Expect border crossing in zero two minutes. Buster."

He watched as the friendly squawk on his radar tube responded and he could visualise the stresses in the cockpit as the Phantom crew responded with a maximum rate turn. Immediately, he breathed a sigh of relief realising that the crew had turned westerly. He should have been clearer with his instruction. A turn easterly would have taken them across the border. He cursed quietly at his mistake.

Within seconds it was clear that the Phantom had been dragged too far north in mirroring the response of the northerly Mig and that the feint had achieved its aim. The trailing Mig continued relentlessly west. This was not a typical penetration run he finally accepted as the Mig crossed into his area of responsibility.

*

In the cockpit of the Phantom a new danger registered with the crew as they turned south in response to the urgent warning from the controller. A gentle ping in the headsets turned into a metallic rattle as the radar warning receiver sprang alive. The navigator glanced down at the small circular display buried in the corner of his cockpit and analysed the vector. A strong India Band signal pulsed in the 9 o'clock position flashing its warning, the noise in the earphones emphasising the threat. It was unmistakeable. An

SA-6 Gainful low level air defence surface-to-air missile had locked them up and was tracking their manoeuvre from its hitherto hidden position close to the border. The threat from the ingressing Mig-21 to the south was instantly forgotten as he called a defensive counter manoeuvre to his pilot dragging the Phantom, once again, away from the border onto a westerly heading. The pilot pushed the stick forward as he executed the turn and the reluctant jet dived towards the forest below. As the height wound down, the tone in the headset remained strident for a few seconds longer before ceasing, the crew breathing a collective sigh of relief. Distancing themselves from the unexpected threat the pilot tried, without success, to raise the controller but the rapid descent and the hills which now sheltered them from the lethal radar beam were affecting the radio. With the capable surface-to-air missile so close to their position there would be no returning to medium level until they were sure they were outside the lethal range of the Gainful missile. Returning south and scanning the horizon to the left for signs of the watchtowers they headed for the last known position of the southerly Mig. Suddenly, being down in the weeds, with or without radio contact, seemed more inviting.

*

In the control centre Portnov watched aghast as the second track continued west and crossed into West German airspace. His plan was unravelling.

"What is that idiot doing?" he shouted.

"Sir, he was supposed to cross the border briefly and return back south but he has pressed on westwards. I'll try to find out what is going on," replied the harried Ops Officer.

Portnov lowered his head into his hands. As he looked up again, the stress in his eyes was palpable but the tactical picture was no less depressing.

*

Once more in contact, the crew of Mike Lima 26 listened intently to the calls from the fighter controller as the range to the contact closed down yet the radar remained stubbornly blank. Somewhere just ahead was a Mig-21 but frustration built as the navigator thumbed the scanner increasingly urgently meaning the chances of detecting the target lessened as his impatience grew. Relax he urged himself when, suddenly as if by a sixth sense, he glanced upwards over the centre arch of the canopy and spotted the rapidly diverging profile of a fighter well above and already crossed ahead. His strident command to the pilot elicited an immediate climbing turn away from the border towards the receding Mig. The afterburners bit and the Phantom surged upwards to medium level. He hoped they were outside the lethal zone around the SAM. A border infringement was turning into a serious episode as the tiny fighter headed deeper into western airspace.

*

The controller was already inundated by questions from the Master Controller. Was he in contact with the intruder? What height was it flying? Was it armed? All the questions were relayed to the harassed Phantom crew in rapid succession eliciting a curt response to each query. The Phantom slowly closed on the tiny radar contact.

"Mike Lima 26 confirm the weapon fit," he prompted yet again.

"Stand by, closing in," he heard, the response irritable. "Mike Lima 26 he seems to have only air-to-air weapons."

The Guard frequency burst into life.

"Aircraft in the ADIZ this is Mike Lima 26, come up 364.2 and identify yourself."

The request was ignored.

"26, confirm he is not carrying air-to-ground ordnance," the controller hectored.

The reason for the question was clear. The Mig had taken a direct track towards the airfield at Gutersloh.

"Confirmed, 26, air-to-air weapons only."

At least they could be hopeful that this was not a prelude to an air attack.

"26, request further instructions. Am I clear to engage," the pilot prompted, conscious that the stakes had changed. A simple air-to-air interrogation had morphed into a potentially more serious scenario.

"26, negative, weapons tight," the controller directed, immediately hitting the line to the Master Controller to confirm his caution. His request for guidance was pre-empted.

"Loneship Mike Lima 26, the bogey has lowered his landing gear."

"Roger 26 acknowledged. "Shadow and report."

With the threat diminished, a seemingly compliant Mig pilot showing signs of capitulation and armed with only air-to-air missiles, the tension eased. Things could still go wrong but sanity was returning.

*

The squawk box on the control console in the Tower at Gutersloh had been hot for the last 10 minutes as the emerging crisis escalated. The controller's eyes scanned to the south and east as he strained for the first elusive sight of the approaching aircraft. Suddenly, he detected a flash as his binoculars tracked through the horizon. It was difficult to recognise the indistinct shape at such long range but, as reported, the undercarriage was undoubtedly lowered. As he adjusted the focus, the image of a Phantom weaving around behind the shape flashed through the field of view, its bulk and heavy smoke trail immediately recognisable. Double checking his radio box he satisfied himself that the International Distress Frequency was selected yet the radio remained stubbornly silent. Whoever was flying the approaching aircraft had no intention of asking for clearance to land. As the image refined he felt a chill as the unmistakable profile of a Mig-21 emerged. With the range closing, the detail began to break out and he could see missile rails slung beneath the delta wing.

"Gutersloh Tower, Mike Lima 26 on frequency."

"Mike Lima 26, loud and clear, request intentions."

"26 is holding hands with our visitor. No joy on Guard but it looks like he intends to land. We'll shadow until he's down."

"Roger 26 understood. He is clear to land runway 27, surface wind is 240 at 12 knots."

"Roger understood. Once he's down I'll hold off until the runway is clear."

The Local Controller picked up a handset and, as he pressed the transmit button, his voice echoed around the Station.

"Noduff, noduff, noduff, Operation Renegade is now in force. I say again Operation Renegade is now in force."

He hit the crash alarm sending the fire and emergency crews scurrying towards their vehicles. All around the Station, personnel nominated to respond to the arrival of a defector aeroplane exchanged incredulous looks, reacting instantly. A well rehearsed plan sprang into action.

The Phantom crew in the Battle Flight Phantom orbited the airfield at 3,000 feet watching the unfolding scene below. The cluster of toned-down green fire engines, interspersed with tactical green Land Rovers converged on the scene, blue lights flashing atop a few. Ant-like figures swarmed around the Soviet jet, its burnished silver fuselage and wings reflecting the bright sun, standing out against the toned down concrete of the main runway. As they watched, the canopy opened, the tiny figure of the pilot barely visible from their lofty perch. It soon became obvious that the prospects of clearing the runway to allow the Phantom to land were diminishing.

"Tower Mike Lima 26 is joker and diverting to Wildenrath. Can you advise our operators of the situation and ask for a replacement Battle Flight jet to be brought on state. We'll return when the runway is clear. We'll transit VFR at low level. Talk to you on the ground. Best of luck!"

"Roger 26, looks like this may take some time. See you later, Sir."

Out on the airfield the chill of the Cold War gripped RAF Gutersloh. From the Fire Chief in the fire tender to the RAF Police corporal in his Land Rover to the young SAC in the arrestor vehicle there was a common thought. Each of them had leafed through the latest copy of Air Clues, the RAF Magazine, at some time over the last few days, fascinated by the striking photographs of Mig fighters captured by the BRIXMIS team over East Germany. It was rare to see anything other than grainy shots of the

"Red Hordes". Little had they thought that the burnished silver airframe which now sat only yards away blocking the main runway would feature so prominently in their lives so soon. As the tug dragging a towing arm joined the fray the driver glanced with disbelief at the prominent red star on the fin and the bold red number 45 emblazoned on the nose.

The cacophony of sound reduced by a fraction as the Tumanski turbojet of the Mig closed down leaving just the throaty roar of the Alvis crash tender dominating. With the canopy of the Mig open the pilot stood up on the seat and raised his hands in submission. Luckily his intentions seemed peaceful or the single 9mm Browning pistol hefted by the RAF policeman might have proved a poor match as an armed response. Some minutes later, another Land Rover pulled to a halt and the small armed response team from the Station Rapid Reaction Force tumbled out from the tailgate brandishing self-loading rifles aimed at the bemused pilot who, by now was seated on the canopy rail waiting for a set of steps to allow him to climb down. With a 10 foot drop to the ground the reluctant pilot stayed firmly apart from his captors.

The Storno radio clipped to the fire chief's belt crackled into life as his section commander in a remote office somewhere on the airfield pressed for information. It would be some time before a clear picture emerged.

CHAPTER 20

STATION HEADQUARTERS, RAF WILDENRATH

The door to the Station Commander's outer office opened and he beckoned to the visitors. Following him into the comfortable enclave, each gave a smart salute before removing their hats.

"Gentlemen, my apologies but the phone hasn't stopped ringing for the last hour. Come in, sit down, coffee anyone?"

He waved towards the seats which ringed the office, the green-clad aviators eying the photographs around the wall as they sat. The pictures told the story of a flying career in microcosm, some of the aircraft which were depicted in grainy monochrome pictures looking decidedly ancient. There was no preamble.

"Thanks for coming over and I know how busy you are with Bold Challenge but the reality is that this is no longer a training exercise. I've just come off the phone to CinC RAF Germany who, as you know, also holds a NATO appointment as COMTWOATAF. He's a very worried man at the moment and suffice to say this is now very much NATO business."

"I've been getting the same vibes from the Command Post at Ramstein," interjected the American detachment commander. "The buzz is that the tension along the border is the worst we've seen for ten years, Sir."

"Without a doubt. The bad news is that the Soviets just took it to a new level. This is still close hold but during the last few hours they intercepted one of our Pembrokes on its way into Berlin and forced it down. The good news is there were no shots fired and the crew appear to be safe and well but they were forced to land at Zerbst."

"That's a Flogger base isn't it Sir?" asked Roy South struggling with the geography to the east of the "Iron Curtain".

"It is. Flogger Bravos in the air defence role. Worryingly, the aircraft involved in the incident weren't Zerbst-based which is causing some confusion amongst the intelligence experts. A pair of Fishbeds has been operating from the base over the last few days for no obvious reason. Normally when the Soviets deploy forward, and these are Russian airframes, they arrive en masse in squadron strength. This is only two aircraft. There's a suggestion that there might be some power politics in play. We've had reports that a senior general, General Artur Portnov, has been seen in the forward area. Portnov is a very politically savvy military officer and well connected in the Kremlin. He has aspirations of taking the Soviet Union back to its post-war glory days and he doesn't seem to mind who he steps on en route. We think the Fishbeds might be PVO Strany assets deployed forward into East Germany from Russia. That would give him direct control over the pilots rather than having to go through the command structure of the 16th Tactical Air Army in the forward area. If these reports prove to be true that might suggest that he's playing a dangerous game."

The senior officer paused as his PA entered carrying a tray of coffees. She probably knew as much about what went on around the Station as the Station Commander but the habit of "need to know" lingered. As the door clicked closed he resumed, noticing the American flyer wince at the cheap instant coffee which had been served.

"Turning to the specific aspects that affect you, how do you all feel about the training scenarios that you have been practising? Have they been realistic? Are the crews getting to grips with the challenges?"

He listened as each of the detachment commanders summarised their progress, their replies reflecting national stereotypes. The French flyer was non-plussed, seemingly relaxed at the challenges. The American was typically ebullient offering guarantees potentially beyond his ability to deliver. The British commander delivered a familiar litany of inexperienced crews, unfamiliar scenarios, insufficient flying time on the squadrons and temperamental aircraft. Despite the frank exchange, there was a unanimous agreement that they would make it work when called upon.

"I think SACEUR will probably want you to lead any operational mission Lieutenant Colonel Fairchild. He seems to want the USA to control events," he added, failing to hide a hint of irritation at the apparent slight from the Senior NATO Commander. With the exercise-turned-operation centred on his own Station, secretly he had hoped that the British contingent would lead the mission.

"I think we have time for one final training mission today so make the most of the opportunity. Hold off on the announcement to the crews that we are going live. It's not worth putting extra pressure on them until necessary. Even so, anticipate that we might be flying this for real tomorrow if efforts to release the Pembroke and its crew fail. Make no mistake; the politicians will not accept this aggression without response. Make sure your people are ready and if you need any extra support from the Station let me know immediately. It will happen."

Fairchild had been making rapid notes.

"What about the rules of engagement, Sir?"

"Good question. There's a meeting between "Their Airships" at the Headquarters, underway as we speak," he said glancing at his watch. "I'll make sure you receive the signal with the RoE as soon as it arrives."

The rules of engagement would be critical as the operation unfolded and restrictive conditions might mean the loss of an aircraft against an aggressive opponent. He sensed the unspoken tension.

"Don't worry, I'll intercede on your behalf if necessary. I won't let you go into this with one arm tied behind your back. You'll have robust RoE, be assured. Any other issues so far?"

The question hung in the air, the silence disconcerting, the sudden reticence tangible.

"There is one more thing," he added. "We've known for some time that an East German agent has been active in the local area but we've had no luck up to now tracking down the source. It looks like we just made some progress and the Provost Marshall has sent out a team to pick up a suspect. Again this is close hold but, if she is the one - and the "she" is significant - there may be a chance that one of our officers has been compromised." There was a dramatic pause. "It gets worse. That officer was aboard the Pembroke which was forced down today."

The momentary silence hung in the air as the significance became apparent but the lull was quickly broken.

"That needn't affect your planning and you can leave that aspect to me but make sure that your people are briefed on the need for absolute operational security. There's to be no loose chat about operational matters and I don't just mean in the Officers' Mess bar. No calls home to Mum, OK?"

The squawk box on his desk buzzed and he eased behind the large mahogany desk to take the call, irritated at the unexpected interruption. His curt response and his raised eyebrows left little doubt that he was unimpressed. His PA sounded breathless.

"Sir, sorry to interrupt but I thought you should know. I've just had a call from Battle Flight. A Soviet aircraft has just landed at RAF Gutersloh. Battle Flight intercepted as it crossed the border but has been forced to divert back here to Wildenrath as the runway at Gutersloh is blocked. OC 92 Squadron is trying to get hold of you."

The looks around the table in the small office needed little interpretation.

"Thanks Gentlemen. Needless to say, this is another thing to keep under your hats until I find out what's going on. We'll speak later."

By the time the door clicked closed he was already dialling a number.

*

At the Joint Headquarters at RAF Rheindahlen the Commander in Chief was closeted in his office with a small number of key advisers. The decision from his NATO Commander, SACEUR, to delegate control of the operation to him at HQ TWOATAF had come as a surprise given the political ramifications. With opening shots being fired by the Soviets, the potential for escalation was enormous and the implications were not lost on him. One careless shot from an over enthusiastic fighter pilot and his carefully nurtured career could be reduced to ashes. The discussion had been wide ranging and they slowly homed in on the operational imperatives. With the multi-National force already co-located at Wildenrath the complexities of mounting the operation were eased. That the French were already part of the exercise helped and even his French counterpart in Paris had been easily persuaded that the Soviet aggression should be challenged, despite detente being so fashionable in the Elysee Palace.

His aides were fractious and he was slowly losing patience. The air defence expert, an RAF Wing Commander, was bullish and was lobbying hard for unrestricted latitude His political adviser, a civil servant, was typically reticent and it seemed that his caution might put lives at risk. Somewhere in between was a compromise.

"Rules of Engagement. Views?" the senior officer snapped. The military officer responded first.

"Sir, the key issue is identification and we're well placed on that. The American Phantoms are fitted with TISEO which is an electro-optic sensor tied to the radar. Once the weapon system locks-on the crew see a magnified picture of the radar track at well beyond visual range. They can visually identify the target and, in the case of Soviet fighters, well before the opponent can launch a weapon. Our own Phantoms are also fitted with TESS which is an optical telescopic sight. Once the radar locks-on, the crew can see that target magnified. It's good out to about 10 miles at medium level."

"A telescope you say?"

"Yes Sir and, bizarrely, it's fitted in the back cockpit."

The CinC shook his head.

"Are they going to be in radar contact with the ground units when they push down the corridors?"

"Yes Sir. We've moved the German mobile air defence radar units forward to the border so they will have good coverage almost as far as Berlin. If the Soviets push fighters into the air we'll see them. The LLADS is a pulse Doppler radar system so it's not quite as effective against helicopters but works well against fighters."

"So if I understand what you're telling me, we'll be able to see any fighters that launch against the package and we can identify an aggressor as a last resort using onboard systems. If it's a Soviet aggressor we'll know in advance. What about IFF?"

"Yes Sir, all the players have IFF but it's never a guarantee. It will tell you that the target is friendly but will never guarantee that it's hostile if you follow the nuance. We often experience systems failures and we don't want to risk shooting at a friendly track in error."

"As a precaution, we can sanitise the corridors during the mission. We don't want airliners getting tangled up in the melee."

"Indeed Sir, we'll divert all civilian traffic down one of the other corridors."

"OK, I approve the use of all weapons out to the limits of radar coverage but only if fired upon. The force will be "weapons free" once they enter the corridor. Anything that enters a five mile bubble on the transport aircraft can be engaged. Anything else which enters the confines of the corridor can be engaged in self defence. That way they should be able to employ beyond visual range weapons. Get back to me if the commanders have any issues with that."

"Will do Sir. That should be workable. If the Sovs penetrate the corridor they deserve to be reminded that we are serious."

"What have we said to the Soviets so far other than the usual political hand wringing?"

"Very little Sir. I recommend we draft a strong signal to the airspace coordinator in the Soviet Command HQ in Berlin. We need to reassert our rights of navigation before we put fighters into the neck."

"Agreed. Draft something for me will you? It needs to go to London, Paris and Washington at the appropriate level. Reiterate our disquiet at the violations and make it clear we reserve the right to use combat air to enforce access."

"Will do Sir. That only leaves us to talk about weapons loads. The French are delivering missiles to Wildenrath as we speak. Although the Americans use the same weapons as we do, it appears they want to send their own weapons. Maybe all Sparrows are not equal after all."

The CinC raised an eyebrow but let the point go.

"This aspect is not negotiable. My direction is that each aircraft will carry a full war load unless the Mission Commander elects to reduce the load for tactical reasons."

He looked around the faces challenging a response but the staff officers were silent.

"Good. Cut along Gentlemen. Let's get those orders on the wires. The first mission runs tomorrow. I aim to make a statement of intent."

As the group dispersed the phone rang and as he digested the new information his expression darkened.

"A Mig?"

CHAPTER 21

DIVISIONAL HEADQUARTERS, 16TH TACTICAL AIR ARMY, EAST GERMANY

Back in the control room, Portnov pondered his next move knowing that he would need to react quickly to counter the unexpected defection by the Mig pilot. His intervention in forcing down the Pembroke would not go unchallenged in the Kremlin and he had prepared his response carefully. Maybe he could turn the defection to his advantage. It would certainly divert the attention of his opposite number at Rheindahlen for some time and ramp up the pressure. Some of his peers back home had grown too lax and it was time to shake up the old order a little. He had pre-warned a few key allies and the coming hours would be critical. An aide scurried across the ops room floor towards his dais clutching a signal message.

"General, this has just arrived marked "Flash" for your immediate attention. It's an intercept message from the surveillance post in Berlin. There's an additional report from the Soviet Liaison Mission following a trip to the base at Wildenrath. That's the air defence base on the Dutch border."

"I know," he snapped aggressively silencing the aide, snatching the proffered paper from his hands whilst scanning the message. A smile creased his features. This was exactly what he needed. The SOXMIS report went into some detail describing the joint exercise which was underway at the base. He focussed on the critical section describing the arming process. Weapons had been seen on the detachment dispersal and had been fitted to each of the participating fighters emphasising his concerns. Why would live weapons be fitted if the exercise was merely for training purposes? He could use this as a key indicator of something more sinister and it would take more effort from the "naysayers" to challenge his stance. He switched his attention to the intercept report. The Ramona listening post on the Inner German Border had caught a short conversation between a deployed control and reporting post and a LLADS commander deployed in the vicinity of Helmstedt. A commuter airliner had been diverted from the airway taking a wide detour around a temporary restricted zone. It was most unusual but the conversation had been tense and the reaction of the controller was unusually tetchy. The mention of a major exercise coincided with the arrival of one of the formations from Wildenrath in the local area. It was highly unusual for the German air traffic controllers to be so compliant. Civilian traffic so often received priority over the military.

He summoned the aide rattling off a raft of instructions barely pausing for breath. The urgent gestures towards the ops tote made his intent clear. The remainder of the operational staff maintained a respectful distance but anyone who had strayed too close to the animated senior officer would have heard a perfunctory summons for his intelligence officer. As the instructions were relayed rapidly back to Moscow it would provoke a swift response.

His plans would quickly filter back down to Meir, presently in West Germany and blissfully unaware of the rapid escalation of events.

*

At Zerbst the sound of a pair of Mig-23 Floggers died away into the distance, and the sound of boots on vinyl echoed down the corridor as the locks rattled before the door was flung open. The German NCO shouted from the sanctuary of the corridor, the guttural command familiar and requiring little interpretation.

"Heraus. Mitkommen," he bellowed.

The Pembroke crew roused themselves and moved towards the belligerent interloper, stirring the fetid air in the makeshift cell. Emerging from the gloomy room, the presence of the six armed guards spread out along the corridor was sufficient incentive to behave. Two guards clutched each of them tightly and marched them along the corridor.

Entering another non-descript room it was obvious that a staged event was underway. A pair of Soviet flags had been hastily positioned behind the chair and provided a dramatic backdrop, the hammer and sickle dominant. A photographer snapped away. The Soviet officer, his rank indecipherable, struck a pose, his neat uniform a contrast to their dishevelled working dress uniforms. The high fronted, peaked dress hat seemed somehow threatening with its prominent red band. When he finally spoke his English was perfect.

"You have been detained and stand accused of spying. The pilots who intercepted you report that you were flying outside the published air corridors and observed camera ports on your aircraft. When we inspected your aircraft on landing we found camera equipment but surprisingly no film. I find it difficult to believe that you might be carrying them for no purpose. Your colleague," he looked down at his notes, "Flight Lieutenant Pocklington has even more to explain as he has been found to be carrying compromising documents. We found an operational plan which clearly contains a strategy to attack the Soviet Union and its Warsaw Pact allies. Supplan Mike I believe it is called. Do you have anything to say?"

The implications were dawning and the British pilot was silent for a moment shattered by the prospect that he had been party to a momentous compromise of the NATO operational plans. Challenging the accusation of carrying cameras seemed futile at this stage but it was the only course of action open to him.

"We were flying legally within the confines of the published airspace and did nothing wrong. You had no right to divert us from our course and I wish to make a formal complaint. I demand to speak with a representative of the British Government."

"I acknowledge your request and you will, of course, be offered consular access in due course. Arrangements are being made as we speak. In the meantime I would like an explanation for the presence of the photographic equipment. Once I understand your role I can ensure we contact the correct agencies to progress this delicate matter."

"I have nothing to say and demand legal representation if we are to be charged."

"I will make arrangements. Dismissed."

The pair were bundled unceremoniously from the room. As they were hustled through the door the pilot glimpsed Carl Pocklington being frog-marched down the corridor slumped between two guards. His head lolled alarmingly and he seemed unresponsive, perhaps even drugged. For the other aircrew a further stretch in the cramped cell beckoned.

CHAPTER 22

THE COLOGNE/BONN AIR TRAFFIC ZONE

The Captain of the Illyushin IL-18 transport aeroplane, a Soviet copy of the Bristol Britannia declared a minor in-flight emergency as he descended towards the holding stack for Cologne/Bonn International Airport. The Cyrillic script extending along the length of the fuselage spelled out Aeroflot and the red flag pennant on the fin left no doubt about its country of origin. Inside the cabin the distinction was less obvious and the few passengers dotted around the cabin could not have known of the real function of today's flight. The aircraft was, in reality, a military airframe and the main cabin was split into two sections. If anyone had been allowed to measure the distance from the doors to the rear bulkhead it would have been readily apparent that it was able to take more than the 80 seats arranged down its length. A false wall concealed a hidden cabin which contained signals intelligence equipment and camera gear operated by a concealed crewman who would never be made known to the airport authorities. On closer inspection of the exterior of the airframe, camera ports under the fuselage hidden behind carefully disguised retractable doors only opened in flight. The servicing personnel on contract to Aeroflot barely gave the access doors a second glance.

Persuaded by the ruse and, in the universal spirit of lending assistance to an aircraft in difficulty, the civil air traffic controllers allowed the airliner to take a leisurely extended flight path as its wide turn back towards the easterly facing runway extended its flight path almost to the Dutch border. Conveniently flying overhead the military airfields at Brüggen and

Wildenrath, the operatives in the concealed cabin tuned their receivers to their pre-briefed frequencies. The motor drives in the cameras clicked rapidly at the appropriate moment as the airliner passed overhead its target, tape recorders capturing the chat on air-to-air and air-to-ground frequencies, transcribing them indelibly onto the reels of magnetic tape. Conveniently, the temporary emergency miraculously cleared in sufficient time to allow the crew to make a normal long straight-in approach to the runway at Cologne/Bonn International. As it flew low over the housing complex on the final approach to Runway 06, the Soviet airliner looked like any another civilian flight in the traffic pattern.

The IL-18 pulled up to the terminal building, its turboprop engines reverberating against the glass structure. The Jetway eased outwards towards the forward door, the heavy pads making gentle contact, shutting out a little of the incessant whine. As the pilot closed the throttles, the noise died and the door popped outwards, slotting in along the side of the fuselage. The smile on the face of the Aeroflot cabin crew greeting the West German operator gave little cause for concern as the document bag for the West German Bundesgrenzschutz was offered up. As the passengers began to disembark, the fact that there were only 20 of them seemed of little interest to the airport workers who began to service the airliner for its return trip to Moscow. Equally, the fact that the cabin seemed unnaturally short compared to the other airliners stacked along the terminal frontage would not even be noticed. None of the small army of cleaners who trooped into the cabin would be invited beyond the false bulkhead at the rear of the cabin nor would the occupants disembark during the short turnround.

No one paid much attention to Dieter Meier as he followed the line of smartly dressed businessmen which snaked its way up the enclosed Jetway towards the customs hall. He tucked his hat forward on his head keen not to offer too much sight of his face to the banks of security cameras which monitored the arrivals hall. His documents and credentials were, of course, scrupulously correct and there was no risk that he would be taken for anything other than a normal East German businessman. He had no intention of spending any more time than was absolutely necessary in the airport terminal. He had business to take care of. He joined the line of passengers as the short line at passport control shuffled closer to the bored-looking border official.

CHAPTER 23

ACROSS EAST GERMANY

A carefully crafted plan was slowly being instigated and, with each successive measure ratcheting up the pressure, tension was rising.

The supervisor at the signalling control centre in East Berlin studied the official document for the third time looking for any signs that it might be a forgery. Try as he might everything seemed authentic and the distinctive stamp at the base of the authorisation originated from the Stasi Headquarters in Berlin. The order was detailed and quite specific. For the next 72 hours every train leaving West Berlin was to be held up for at least an hour before departure. Ostensibly, the reason for the disruption would be given as technical problems caused by routine maintenance of the signalling equipment. The reality was somewhat simpler and only his authorisation for the train to depart would delay the schedule. The 0720 express to Hannover was due to depart shortly and he would not release it for departure until 0820. Such things, however, needed top-cover and he dialled his manager. The man would be grumpy at this time in the morning but some things, despite the official orders on the desk, were best cross-checked.

*

In the operations centre of the airbase at Juterbog, the communications clerk ripped the signal from the teleprinter and walked it over to the harassed operations officer. The officer scanned the flimsy sheet rapidly taking in the significance. The orders brought two Mig-21 Fishbeds to cockpit alert. They would stand by to scramble to intercept and interdict

118

airliners routing down the corridor to Tempelhof airport in West Berlin. No shots were to be fired but the Mig pilots were cleared to enter the corridor, normally reserved exclusively for the civilian traffic, and show an overt presence. After the recent interceptions and so soon after the defection of the Mig it was provocative. He picked up the line to the alert shed. The first launch would be in 45 minutes so he had little choice but to use the East German alert fighters at first. Once he had them primed he would call out the squadron and generate more fighters. He hoped that the pilots had not downed too much vodka last night. This was an early start for them and nothing had been planned to fly today. Their problem, not his.

*

In the barracks of the local Nationale Volksarmee Regiment, the NVA or East German Army, the officer called his NCO into the office. Today they would be reinforcing the border guards at each of the three major checkpoints around West Berlin. Established in 1961 shortly after the Berlin Wall was built, the three border crossing points known as Checkpoint Alpha, Bravo and Charlie, were the main arteries for anyone wishing to pass between the two opposing blocs. His orders allocated him to Checkpoint Charlie the most famous of the three crossings. Located at the junction of Friedrichstraße with Zimmerstraße and Mauerstraße in the Friedrichstadt neighbourhood, it was the only crossing point through which foreigners and members of the Allied forces were allowed to pass. Looking at the orders for his troop he could guarantee that passage through the checkpoint today would be a nightmare. The delays would be horrendous and he could see why there might be some friction. He was glad that a Soviet officer had been allocated to work with them. The allied personnel steadfastly refused to acknowledge his men and would insist on speaking only with the Soviet officers, resurrecting the post-war protocols during every trip. Today that was fine. His brief was to slow down the flow through the checkpoint and any prevarication would only help his cause.

*

The Superintendent at the Police Station in Wustermark listened with resignation as the regional controller explained today's grand plan. He was to set up a checkpoint on the main E5 highway between Helmstedt and Berlin and stop any black or green cars, particularly Opels. He was to be particularly vigilant for any BRIXMIS plates. After 10 minutes he was to allow them to proceed but not without stiff warnings about exceeding the speed limit. That would mean stopping virtually every vehicle using the road as most of the traffic was made up of official cars driving into West Berlin. There was very little tourist traffic as the burdensome paperwork deterred all but the hardiest traveller. He would commandeer a rest area outside town that he would set up as a checkpoint. He really did not need the inevitable hassle but questioning the directive, or worse still ignoring it, would invite inevitable scrutiny. The Allied officials knew the rules to the letter and were well briefed before they travelled the route. They would anticipate a level of bureaucracy but he would leave the difficult ones to the Soviet officer who had been allocated to join them. Let him sort it out.

*

The hubbub in the cabin aboard the Pan American Boeing 727 had increased, the passengers down the left hand side staring, intently, from the windows. Alongside, the Mig fighter eased forward and the pilot gestured repeatedly at the Captain in the left hand seat in the cockpit. Undeterred, the jet pressed on along the corridor holding its height rigidly at 9,000 feet, the crew hurriedly checking and cross-checking their position verifying that they had tracked precisely along the centreline of the airway. There could be no suggestion that they had strayed out of the corridor and the needles of the VOR held a steady bearing pointing precisely at Berlin. The Mig's wings waggled frenetically showing off the air-to-air missiles slung beneath. Unless the situation escalated the airliner crew were determined to press on towards Tempelhof and their pre-appointed landing slot. A further camouflaged Mig pulled up from beneath the belly of the 727 and eased out alongside the first Mig but set slightly back. The afterburner cut in and it made a violent slash across the front of the airliner passing metres ahead of the cockpit, an impressive but frightening planform cutting the light out from the cockpit momentarily. The wake turbulence assaulted the airliner which bucked violently and the rapt attention of the passengers turned to screams. Already held in their seats by the "Fasten Seatbelts" sign which had been illuminated from the moment the jet had been intercepted, mercifully there were no injuries other than a bruised flight attendant who had been making her way back to the galley. Dazed and visibly shaking she strapped into her seat grasping at the intercom handset and began an urgent exchange with the pilot. Up front the two pilots conversed. So far the visual interception signals had been following the norm. If it followed the script, the next step would be a warning burst of cannon fire across the nose but to do that the Migs would need to drop back into a firing position. After its lunge, the second Mig banked around and took up station on the right hand wing. The crew waited nervously as the formation pressed on towards Berlin, talking calmly to their controller at the air traffic control centre. Cleared to descend to 5,000 feet to begin their initial approach into Tempelhof, the crew waited. Suddenly, with a violent flash of the wings the Migs broke hard away from the airliner and disappeared rapidly into the distance. Rattled, the crew began to run through the pre-landing check list, the co-pilot making detailed notes of the incident. An inevitable debrief would follow.

*

The Opel saloon car rolled up outside the unassuming house in Wegberg. The shutters were rolled down with no sign of activity at such an early hour. An inquisitive shopkeeper watched as the RAF policemen climbed out of the car donning their white-topped service caps, joined by a German Polizei officer who had pulled his VW Passat in behind the black staff car. They had done their research carefully and there was no exit from behind the property with its hemmed-in plot. There was only one way out of the first floor flat and the three bulky officers were providing an impenetrable barrier. As the knocking became louder and more persistent, curtains were drawn back and inquisitive residents peered at the interlopers. Such drama was unheard of in the quiet suburb and thoroughly unwelcome. The door creaked quietly on its hinges and a nervous face peered from behind the door staring at the three visitors, her eyes darting between the officials.

"Anneliese Kolber?" asked the German policeman in her native language.

"Ja," she replied hesitantly.

"We have a warrant to search these premises. Could you please open the door."

Her demeanour implied that she was assessing her options. The look in her eyes hinted at flight but the overwhelming sense of futility appeared to win over any thoughts of bravado. The door slid open allowing the men to enter, closing behind them swiftly to shut out prying eyes. The green and white police car advertised the fact that this was not a normal day in the sleepy suburb. In the adjacent houses tongues began to wag.

Inside there was little fanfare. After establishing her identity and offering some official looking paperwork she was persuaded to accompany them for questioning. The exchange was brief and efficient and her thoughts of flight quickly extinguished.

Across the street Dieter Meier watched from the safety of a bus shelter, although he felt vulnerable being the only solitary person awaiting a bus at this early hour. Had he arrived a few minutes earlier he would have been inside facing awkward questions from the police, his meeting with the young agent difficult to explain away. He made a show of checking his watch, shaking his head as if frustrated at the delay in boarding his bus. Taking off down the road he searched surreptitiously for a better vantage point as he walked. Cutting into a small park he eased back towards the hedge peering back at the stationary vehicles outside Anneliese's flat. He would not wait long before she was led out by the RAF policemen a coat hurriedly thrown around her shoulders and a scarf covering her face. They bundled her into the back of the Opel where she was joined by the second policeman and the convoy set off along the road back towards Rheindahlen.

CHAPTER 24

JOINT HEADQUARTERS, TWOATAF, RAF RHEINDAHLEN

The hastily arranged meeting was called to order as the Commander in Chief Royal Air Force Germany entered the room, prompting the assembled officers to their feet. The attendees reflected the breadth of his command and, around the table uniforms from a diverse range of NATO nations signified that NATO was taking an increasing interest in events. Nevertheless, the predominance of American and British uniforms and the presence of a French officer, despite the fact that France was not a full NATO member, hinted at the forthcoming agenda.

"Gentlemen, thank you for coming," the CinC boomed from the head of the conference table. "I'm sure you've been briefed about events over the last 48 hours but they have taken a rather sinister turn for the worse. We've been watching a series of incidents in the Berlin corridors for some time and you will know that we've had a number of occurrences over the last few weeks which have escalated significantly today. I had hoped it was simply sabre rattling but I'm afraid, as you'll hear, the stakes have risen considerably. I am now seriously concerned that we risk seeing the corridors closed down unless I act now. As a precaution I've already deployed Battle Flight forward to RAF Gutersloh to be closer to the border. There have been a number of scrambles since the Phantoms arrived. Unfortunately, yesterday, a light aircraft strayed over into East German airspace and we think it was escorted to Zerbst, although there has been no contact yet with the pilot; a German National. It was totally unconnected to current events but I'm sure the Soviets don't see it that way. It's still very close hold but earlier, a Soviet Mig-21 crossed into our airspace. We thought it was the usual probe but he carried on westwards and landed at Gutersloh. The debriefing has begun but there is no clear reason for the timing with everything else going on. It may be a coincidence."

He fussed with his briefing pack in front of him turning to a brightly tabbed annex.

"Sir," prompted an American Lieutenant Colonel. "Squadron Leader Silversmith can give a summary of events to bring everyone up to speed if you're happy."

"Yes, good idea," he replied distractedly, frowning at the content of the document. "John, please go ahead."

Heads swivelled as the intelligence officer stepped up to a small podium at the far end of the room and began his briefing.

"Gentlemen, as you know, Exercise Bold Challenge, a Berlin Corridor reinforcement exercise has been underway for the last few days. So far, three missions have been flown. The exercise involves US F-4E Phantoms from Ramstein, French Mirage IIIs from Dijon and resident Phantoms from 92 Squadron at Wildenrath reinforced by two aircraft from 56 Squadron at Wattisham. The timing of the exercise is entirely fortuitous and had been planned for months. The aircrew have been practising escort tactics using NATO transport aircraft simulating civilian airliners and have been opposed by fighters simulating Soviet aggressors. The scenarios have been carefully scripted by the TACEVAL Team and have worked up through increasingly aggressive action with escalating rules of engagement. So far, our assessors report that success has been mixed but the learning curve is steep. The exercise was planned to run for the rest of the week and then the participants would have returned to their own bases but the CinC will update us on his thoughts. In parallel, in a disturbing trend, we have seen real world events mirroring the exercise play. We know the Soviets have been monitoring the exercise closely but we don't think that their actions are a direct response to the exercise scenarios but the similarities are remarkable."

"Can you give us a summary of the broader intelligence John. Not everyone will have seen the reports."

"Yes Sir, of course. I mentioned the monitoring. A Ramona passive listening post located very close to the IGB has been on 24 hour manning since the start of the exercise. We've intercepted reports to their Divisional Headquarters and they are gleaning quite a lot from the missions. It's clear that they have been analysing our tactics from the recent corridor incidents. Some of their approaches have been scripted to avoid detection by the pulse-equipped Phantoms. A civilian airliner inbound to Tempelhof was intercepted by Mig-21s and, although no shots were fired, the crew felt threatened. The East German jets manoeuvred aggressively and tried to divert him from his flight path. The CinC has already mentioned the Battle Flight deployment and the border penetration. The light aircraft was a Cessna from a flying club based in the ADIZ. By the time Battle Flight reached the border, even operating from Gutersloh, the light aircraft had strayed over into East German airspace. The German authorities are on that one and are attempting to repatriate the pilot and his aircraft but it could be a slow process."

He paused as he turned his notes on the podium.

"Earlier today we had another border incursion by a Soviet Mig-21. It was operating from Mahlwinkel and made a run directly at the border. Whether the penetration was intentional or not we don't know but it spent six minutes in our airspace before it headed back east. Looking at the track it might be that he was supposed to run parallel to the border on their side but he was about 5 miles inside our airspace. We know their navigation kit is useless but he was under GCI control so it suggests a deliberate action. Again, Battle Flight was launched and both Phantoms got airborne but they only got within five miles of the Fishbed before he turned back east. I don't have anything yet from the defector."

"Are there any more indicators from the Soviets?" asked an RAF officer.

"Yes Sir. As you know an exercise in the Letzlinger Heide Training Area has been underway for a week and we've seen unprecedented levels of activity from local units. There has been a steady stream of tactical air from the local bases, mostly Hind Delta attack helicopters from Stendal, but we've also seen Fitter Alphas and Fitter Charlies from units based in the eastern sector operating at low level and dropping live weapons. It's unusual to see them this far west as they normally work their local ranges east of Berlin. The rates of effort are unprecedented. Add to that, the Chipmunk on a local recce flight from Gatow spotted a large troop concentration in the Berlin suburbs. They often have large movements at this time of the year but it's unusual for Berlin to be the destination. They normally try to prevent their troops seeing the bright lights of West Berlin. It's bad for morale, Sir."

There were a few smiles around the table, mostly from officers who had experienced the bright lights of West Berlin at first hand. Given the military privilege of being able to cross into the Soviet sector of East Berlin, the contrast was not lost on them.

"We've also seen Mig-21s deploy forward to Stendal airfield although we're not sure if that's routine or is significant. The most significant escalation was earlier today. A Pembroke bound for Gatow down the central corridor was intercepted by a Mig-21 Fishbed Delta. After a brief intervention the Pembroke was forced to fly back to Zerbst and has landed. The fate of the crew is not yet known but we think they are safe at present. Diplomatic exchanges are already underway. That's about it. Any questions Sir, Gentlemen?"

"Yes John, a good summary but I have a few. The crew of the Pembroke; was it the usual crew complement? They were not carrying passengers?"

"No Sir, only the pilot and two navigators."

"And were they carrying any classified documents?"

"That's an issue Sir. As you know, apart from the intelligence material that they needed for the sortie we normally avoid carriage of any classified material. Their procedures are to destroy any of their equipment and documentation if they think they are about to be detained. This time however, there was a copy of Supplan Mike being delivered to BRIXMIS in Berlin. It's highly unusual but it seems we may have been unlucky. We don't know its fate yet but can I talk afterwards about that Sir?"

"So we must assume it's compromised?"

"At this stage, I'm afraid so Sir."

The CinC rubbed his temple making a scribbled note in his briefing pack.

"And I assume it was a converted Pembroke equipped for the reconnaissance mission?"

"Yes Sir."

A few more scribbled annotations were made around the room as the CinC realised his lapse. Operation Hallmark was less covert by the minute.

"So persuade me why we shouldn't put a covert team from Hereford onto the airfield at Zerbst and bring the crew out. Or even more, why I shouldn't target Zerbst with an air attack and take out a few Migs on the ground."

"We're keen to try to resolve this diplomatically, Sir," said the JAG, an American military lawyer who handled the more complex legal matters such as rules of engagement. "Any overt action which results in destruction of assets would be seen as a significant escalation by the Soviets. We would risk them responding with greater force."

The CinC nodded, not yet decided.

"We might also need to negotiate to exchange the aircrew for Eastern Bloc personnel we have in custody, Sir," said Silversmith. "I haven't been able to brief you yet but we have a significant input from the counter-intelligence team. I would also agree that a diplomatic solution might be more appropriate for as long as we have personnel held in detention over there. I think we should anticipate the need to exchange prisoners."

"OK, so no gung ho response. Relax gentlemen it was not high on my priority list."

There were relieved looks exchanged around the table, although one American officer looked positively distressed at a missed opportunity.

"Gentlemen, any more questions before I allocate tasks?"

There was quiet around the room although each attendee probably had a number of burning questions. They would each investigate further once they got back to their offices but, for now, no one was keen to show any signs of weakness.

"OK thank you for all the inputs. Here is what I want," began the Senior Officer.

"We will exercise an equivalent show of force to demonstrate to the Soviets that we mean business. If they intend to play hard then we must show them that we won't be cowed by their actions. I want Exercise Bold Challenge terminated immediately but their job is by no means over. The next mission will be live. I plan to put an aircraft down the corridor and it will be escorted. I'd like the senior representatives from the UK and the US to remain behind. You too John," he said beckoning Silversmith.

As the rest of the attendees filed out of the room he turned to the RAF Group Captain. The orders were very specific.

CHAPTER 25

CHARLIE DISPERSAL, RAF WILDENRATH

As the meeting wound up at the Joint Headquarters, a short distance away at Wildenrath the Commander In Chief's orders had yet to filter down to the aircrew in the briefing room on Charlie Dispersal. The buzz of conversation was stilled by a Texan drawl.

"OK Gentlemen, listen up. The weather."

The meteorological forecaster, better known as the "Met Man", stood next to the podium at the front of the packed briefing room and flicked on the overhead projector. Only the British aircrew in the audience recognised him as a former weather presenter on the BBC returned to his true role.

"Good morning Gents. This is the synoptic chart for 0600 Zulu. A cold front passed through Wildenrath overnight and is now sitting to the east, overhead Hannover. Conditions behind the front are good and you should have good flying conditions for your sortie later in the day."

There was a contented buzz amongst the aircrew as he switched slides.

"This is the "actual" for Wildenrath and as you see the colour state is blue, forecast blue throughout the flying window. Visibility is 10 kilometres plus and there are no significant clouds. Over the next two hours the front will move further east so your operating area will be clear and you will have similar conditions over the whole of Northern Germany. There may be some wispy cirrus above 25,000 feet but it shouldn't be thick enough to affect you. Your nominated crash diversion is Brüggen and it is also blue, forecasting blue. Any questions?"

Lieutenant Colonel Rick Fairchild, the mission leader for the day, allowed a few seconds for queries but with the continued silence returned to the podium as the Met Man bustled around collecting his briefing slides and made to leave.

"Thank you, Sir. OK gentlemen, today is the next mission of Exercise Bold Challenge. With tensions rising I suggest we make good use of this opportunity. We may be called on to run this for real quite soon. Our overall callsign is "Storm" with element callsigns Chevy for the F-4Es, Bentley for the FGR2s and Renault for the Mirages. Our nominated transport today is an HFB-320 Hansa Jet of the Luftwaffe, callsign Boxcar."

His crucifixion of the pronunciation of the title of the German Air Force, was stereotypical.

"Red Air will be provided by an Alpha Jet also of the Luftwaffe, callsign Ivan. Our job is to see that Ivan doesn't spoil our day and that Boxcar comes home safely."

Scribbled notes were added to kneeboards around the room.

"For this mission we are simulating rising tension along the Inner German Border. An airliner was buzzed yesterday by Mig-23 Floggers from Zerbst as it made its way up the southern corridor."

The fact that the scripted events were disturbingly close to the real events of just a few hours ago was moot.

"No shots were fired but the Mig penetrated the corridor and flew alongside the airliner for 10 minutes before breaking off without intervening. It was armed with AA-8 Aphid missiles and made that fact obvious with some impressive manoeuvring according to the crew debrief. The flying display alongside is unusual and, normally, the Sovs are more cautious. This guy was aggressive and the crew felt threatened and reported the incident immediately on landing, although Berlin Centre was way ahead of the pilot and filed a complaint. On the strength of this provocation, COM2ATAF deployed Battle Flight forward to RAF Gutersloh and brought up two additional QRA birds to Alert 5 here at Wildenrath."

With the departure of the additional Battle Flight jets an open secret, the distinction between the fact and the fiction blurred.

"We have been ordered to mount a response and to escort a transport through the corridor to assert our rights of navigation. The Hansa Jet is simulating a civilian airliner on a routine passenger flight. We'll talk tactics shortly but the use of combat air down the corridor is a significant escalation and we can expect a response from Red Air."

"Do we get the RoE to respond aggressively today Colonel?" called a French voice from the floor.

"We do not have authority to engage without clearance from the controllers on the ground, although our normal rights to act in self defence apply. If you are fired on you can respond. If not, hold fire until cleared. That's important gentlemen."

"So normal authentication procedures apply, Sir?" asked a British navigator from the back of the room.

"Affirmative. Clearance to engage must be approved and authenticated with our control agency. Let's cover that now. Our operating area is over the north eastern area of Germany and will be controlled today by "Backwash" control centre. The coordinates you have for the operating area are an exact representation of the dimensions and orientation of the southern Berlin Corridor. This mission will be as authentic as we can make it with the exception of loading live weapons."

At the mention of live ordnance a few exchanged nervous glances.

"OK that's the overview, let's get into the detail. We'll taxy as elements for runway 09 with Chevy leading. Bentley hold in the neck of Delta dispersal until my formation is done with last chance checks on the ORP. When I call for takeoff, follow me onto the runway. We'll line up as 4-ships for individual pairs takeoffs within elements. After takeoff I'll turn downwind and extend as far as I can to allow the elements to join, although Dutch airspace is only five miles to the west and we will not be crossing the border. Once we're all aboard I'll climb at 90% and we'll chop across to Clutch Radar on button 13 for clearance to climb."

The briefing continued in excruciating detail mapping out every moment of the departure and recovery before the Colonel finally took his seat and his WSO, pronounced "whizzo", stood up to brief the tactics and rules of engagement. The leaders used every last second of the allocated 30 minutes pushing out rapid-fire facts interspersed with questions to check understanding. With the clock slowly ticking down to "Step Time", the Colonel rose to his feet for a final time.

"OK element leaders only at the out briefing in air operations at minute 30. The rest of the crews go direct to your jets after signing out. You step at minute 25. Check in on Button 1 at minute 55 and stand by for a time hack on the hour. Any questions?"

He glanced around but it was clear that no one wanted to be the one who proved that he had been inattentive. The briefing had been thoroughly comprehensive and they all felt ready.

*

Five hours later the briefing room was once again packed. A dejected mission leader entered the room prompting the assembled aircrew to jump to their feet. He waved them to sit down.

"OK Gentlemen, let's start. I'm not going to be diplomatic. That mission was the pits and we have a lot of work to do. I'm not going to get into the domestics. Start up, taxy, takeoff, departure and the recovery were all fine from my perspective. Debrief as elements afterwards and element leads give me any feedback. Let's use our time to dissect the mission."

The leaders of Bentley and Renault nodded acknowledgment, silently sensing bad things to come.

"OK the brief was for Bentley to sweep ahead and clear the corridor. Chevy was providing the outer screen and Renault was in close formation as the inner screen and last ditch defence. My assessment is the plan was sound and we failed on execution. Any challengers?"

Dissent seemed inadvisable.

"Good. Run One was fine and, even though the bogey penetrated the outer screen, Chevy 2 was well positioned and stayed with him all the way between him and the transport. There was never any chance for an opportunity shot. So far, so good but that gentlemen, was the only high point of the mission."

Heads around the room had lowered anticipating the tirade not wishing to be the subject of the inevitable scrutiny.

"Run Two was a rolling goat fuck!"

He paused for effect, the silence ominous.

"At least we agree. Bentley, did you have contact on the bogey?"

"Negative, we were 10 miles ahead, as briefed, and he approached on the flank, well behind us. We continued to sweep ahead to clear the corridor."

"Roger that; as briefed. Who picked him up?"

"Chevy 3, Sir", called the hapless victim. Backwash gave us a heads-up on an inbound and we stayed in the screen until he broke the ten mile bubble."

"What then?" snapped the leader turning to the whiteboard, drawing the opening positions of the jets using coloured markers. Blue white and green marked the friendly elements and an ominous red symbol marked the position of the aggressor at the edge of a perfectly drawn circle. It was apparent that, despite the collective firepower of the formation, none of the elements were covering the approach and the transport was already vulnerable to attack.

"We turned towards after the call and the controller give us clearance to face up to the bogey. He was already inside the corridor but too close for a head-on shot. After a head-to-head pass, he blew through, still headed for the transport. As soon as he passed we called "Heads-Up" and turned back to rejoin."

The leader sketched a new position for Chevy 3 and 4 on the whiteboard, each aircraft symbol trailing a curved vector behind it. The manoeuvre had left the northerly flank of the formation unprotected. Well ahead of the main formation, the British Phantoms were unable to influence events.

"And that would be when Chevy 4 joined the fight," he said looking, pointedly, at the US crew sitting nervously in the second row, staring down his new victims. "What we're you guys thinking?"

"Well, Sir, it looked like . . . . ."

"It looked like a horlicks from where I was sitting, son," shot back the formation leader, vehemently.

"Well we thought that he was about to get a shot so . . . . ."

"So you took a Sidewinder shot."

"Yes Sir."

"What were the RoE?"

"To shield the transport and only take a shot if we came under direct attack, Sir."

"Were you threatened?"

"No Sir."

"Was the Mig in parameters?"

"No Sir but . . . . ."

"No buts. Did you ask for clearance to engage?"

"No Sir but . . . . ."

"What part of no buts are you not getting son?"

"No Sir, I took the shot because I felt the transport was in imminent danger."

"Where were the Mirages at this point?"

"In tight box around the transport . . . . . Sir."

The Phantom pilot rapidly adjusted his attitude realising that a defensive and subordinate response might be advisable given his blatant error.

"Correct and I put them there for exactly that reason. They're fitted with self protection chaff and flare dispensers. You . . . . ." he said jabbing a finger at another hapless "wizzo" from the F-4E detachment. "What dispensers are the Mirages carrying?"

"Err, I'm not sure Sir."

"Find out from Renault lead and brief the team later. You," he said jabbing the same finger at the No 4 pilot. "What infra-red counter-countermeasures does the basic Aphid carry?"

"Err, If I'm right Sir it does not have IRCCM."

"Correct. So a properly executed chill manoeuvre and a rapid break will defeat the missile tracking. With the Mirages tight on the transport, the aggressor pilot won't get a look at the IR source. It'll be shielded by the screen. See now why I put the Mirages in tight?"

"Chevy 3", he said turning back to the hapless F-4E pilot, "Congratulations, you might have started World War 3 if this had been for real. You engaged a Soviet Mig without clearance to engage when the RoE said self defence reactions only. We may not like it but until the guy takes a shot we are weapons tight. Our job is to make it impossible for him to get a shot by staying between him and the transport. If he shoots, we shoot, is that clear?"

Watching the exchanges within the US formation, startlingly frank given the international audience, the Mirage pilots seemed mildly bemused. Perhaps the fact that they had been positioned as Mig fodder was dawning. Maybe the language difficulties took away some of the vitriol. Only the British crews at the back of the briefing room felt safe from the onslaught, glad that they had been pushed out front and had held off on the desire to enter the melee.

"OK moving to the next phase of the engagement. . . . ."

The debrief rumbled on, dissecting each and every engagement candidly, drawing out every learning point, dissecting each move. The mission had been a baptism of fire.

"OK let's knock it on the head there. If we had problems with the Hansa Jet today, tomorrows transport is a Transall C160 of the French Air Force and Red Air is a Mirage F1 simulating a Mig 23 Flogger. The transport will be way slower tomorrow so that will add to the problems of formation keeping. When we move on to the British Pembroke on the following Mission, he'll be flying at 120 knots and we won't be sitting in close formation on him at that speed. Think hard about those debrief points overnight and let's move forward tomorrow. The next mission is a Brit lead and Squadron Leader South will be the mission leader. Roy."

"Thanks for the honest views today, Gents. That was a heavy debrief but I think we all learned something. We'll brief tomorrow morning at 0700 local. Be in place five minutes in advance so we can start on the dot. I'll see you all in the bar at 1900 tonight and we have a table reserved for us all to eat at 1930 in the Dining Room. No jokers tomorrow so make sure you keep the alcohol intake down tonight. Thank you Gentlemen."

The debrief broke up amongst a buzz of disquiet. The pilot of Chevy 4 looked decidedly mauled.

CHAPTER 26

THE PROVOST MARSHALL'S OFFICE, JOINT HEADQUARTERS, RAF RHEINDAHLEN

The interview had been slow and Anneliese was withdrawn and sullen. Her mouth was dry and she craved a glass of water or, even better, a cold glass of wine. She realised that she had become soft during her time in the West. Hardly the hard-bitten James Bond style villain was she?

Look, you've told me that Meier is in the country," the interrogator pressed for the third time, " . . . and that he was to have met with you in Wegberg but I know that already."

His needling persistence was beginning to break down her resistance. She pushed her thoughts into the comfortable corner of her mind as she had been taught to do under resistance to interrogation training. It was unlikely that they would revert to violence but the psychological pressure was ramping up progressively. It could only be a question of time but if she could hold off for a while longer it would give time for Meier to reach the airport. Her knowledge was limited but if Meier was compromised it would open Pandora's Box. Another question dragged her back to the present.

"Let's try another tack Miss Kolber. What if I told you that we know all about your family and your family history? Your Mother struggled to give you a decent start in life, did she not?"

The unexpected reference to her Mother caught her unawares.

"What if I also told you that we have Herr Meier in custody and he's already giving us the details about his network over here. He can be quite eloquent."

The reality was that the interrogator had no idea of the whereabouts of the East German spymaster other than that he was somewhere in Nordrhein Westphalia but he was not about to offer that snippet just yet.

"We've researched your family circumstances quite carefully Anneliese. I can call you Anneliese? Is that OK?"

His efforts to ingratiate himself were transparent but she let him carry on talking. Perhaps there was a way through this nightmare.

"It would not be difficult to arrange for your parents to leave Magdeburg you know. We have resources and contacts and under the right circumstances we could arrange a passage. The only question is whether the gain is sufficient to justify the effort and you, my dear, have total control of events. Just say the words and we can start the ball rolling."

She resented the patronising tone but for a moment, she was tempted by the thought. It did, after all, solve one part of her dilemma. Logic won over. It was too soon.

"Perhaps with some accommodation on both sides we can find an arrangement that is mutually beneficial?"

She had made many compromises over the past months and began to wonder whether one more would be so bad. Her present situation offered little prospect of a happy ending and it was not as if she was ideologically tied to the East. She would need reassurances that the offer was deliverable. Her own masters in the Stasi, had made similar promises to captured agents before now and not all had been honoured. What if it was an empty promise?

"What I need you to do is to fly back to Berlin and visit your organisation. I'd like you to spread some rumours of the premature and unfortunate demise of Dieter Meier."

Did they really have him in custody?

*

Annaliese lay on the hard bed, sleep elusive, her thoughts in turmoil. She ran through the options, endlessly, trying to convince herself of the wisdom of her choice. There could be no other alternative given the stark choices she had been given. She hoped her new master would honour the promises. Was her life destined to be a mess or would her decision offer any hope of a better chapter unfolding?

*

Back in Wegberg Dieter Meier knocked on the door of an innocent looking house in a quiet suburb.

"Guten Tag. Darf ich bitte Fräulein Kolber mitsprechen?"

The conversation continued in his native tongue.

"I'm afraid she's not been seen all day," replied the German hausfrau pleased at the prospect of digging deeper into the apparent scandal. "She left in a car with what looked like military policemen and she hasn't returned."

"Thank you," he replied cutting the conversation short. The longer he engaged in idle chat, the more likely it would be that he would be recognised later. The woman had no idea of what had taken place and persistence would be futile. He would not fuel her curiosity. The presence of the German police officer was indisputable and might have been the lesser of two evils. It may have been a simple case of paperwork or credentials. The military police had no jurisdiction in the local community so, for them to be involved, had sinister overtones. That they were working in concert generated a sense of foreboding that would not disappear yet he was no closer to understanding why she had been compromised.

Walking quickly back to his rental car he tried to blend in, anxious to remain anonymous. The sense of relief as the engine fired up was tangible. Why was he so edgy? All might yet be resolved. He threaded his way through the quiet streets of the residential district picking up the ring road before driving out into the rural countryside once again. Spotting a secluded lay-by he pulled in dragging out a local street map. He needed a public telephone box and preferably one not in a public place or close to a military installation. He doubted whether the public networks would be monitored or even if it was technically possible but he was not prepared to take the risk. Unless Allied intelligence was tapping the lines at Stasi Headquarters a rural public call box offered the safest option. The call he was about to make was important and being overheard was not a risk he was willing to take. He thought back to earlier visits trying to recall the location of a suitable call box. The box on the forecourt of the local petrol station in Wildenrath village was too close to the base and was often used by the airmen for calls home, or perhaps for calls closer to home. There was one on the outskirts of Wassenberg which would be ideal for his needs. Although it was on the main road, if he took a few simple precautions he could disguise his features to avoid scrutiny from casual passers-by and it was sufficiently exposed to make sure he would spot another potential user if he should be approached. Surely that was unlikely at this time of the day? He fired up the car and headed south towards the small German town. If anything better materialised en route he would take it.

"Niedermeier, thank God where are you," replied the familiar voice on the end of the phone, purposely using his cover name. "I've been trying to track you down all day."

"It's been moving quickly here. You go first. What have you got for me?"

Meier pulled the scarf around his face pressing the phone to his mouth keeping his features covered. He glanced around the immediate vicinity checking for signs of undue interest but all was quiet. A few neatly painted houses edged the road alongside the Deutsche Bundespost phone box, the shutters down. The clear glass walls of the booth gave him a good view along the street and traffic on the road was light. He felt secure with only a short distance back to the rental car in the lay-by.

Switching to Russian in a vain attempt to confuse a potential eavesdropper he immediately realised his error. If he was being overheard, German would have been far less likely to attract attention but it was too late to worry. The damage had been done. The recipient switched effortlessly into the unfamiliar language.

"I don't know how much had occurred before you left but things have been moving fast. There was another incident yesterday in the air corridor and our friends in Moscow intercepted a transport aircraft on its way to Tegel. Earlier a Pembroke en route to Berlin was forced to land at one of the Soviet bases by fighter aircraft. The crew have been apprehended. I think you know one of the officers onboard."

The revelation unsettled him.

"Damn. I expected the incident but my contacts told me it wasn't supposed to occur for a few days. Where are they now?"

"I'll update you on your return but let's say you have a package that you need to accept. You need to work with our mutual friends if you want to take delivery."

Meier cursed quietly. The idiots had pulled the schedule forward despite all the planning. It had to be when he was in the field.

"We have other reports that something is going on at your present location. One of our teams spotted weapons being loaded and we think an operation is about to be mounted. With the loss of their aircraft I doubt they'll roll over without a fight. We need to anticipate the next move. This could well turn into something of a showpiece event unless we pre-empt matters."

"Have you heard that they picked up Anneliese?"

"No I hadn't. That's not good. When?"

"Within the last few hours. I don't know where she's been taken but I'm making enquiries as we speak."

"OK, get back here and we'll work it through other contacts. I need to know what you had planned. I'm being dragged in to see the Director in a few minutes and he wants to know how we plan to proceed. I'd better break the bad news. Our Soviet friends will not be happy."

"How did that it go so bad so quickly? We need to find out what the Soviets plan to do with the aircrew if we're to have any negotiating power. Are they contemplating one of their futile show trials? If so we need to stop them. There's more to gain by keeping this quiet."

The response did not fill him with confidence.

"Look I haven't got long. This call is not secure. We've probably already said too much. The situation here is difficult. My other contact at the Headquarters at Rheindahlen is not answering. If he's been taken in for questioning we've had a major compromise. I'm coming back right away. I'll head for the airport and we'll regroup. The situation is too volatile at the minute and I'm getting nervous. I'll book a commercial flight at the airport and I'll see you as soon as I return."

He hit the cradle not waiting for acknowledgement and glanced at his watch. The call had been too long but if it was being monitored, by now they knew his location. No matter. He didn't intend to stay here any longer than a few more minutes before heading back to Düsseldorf airport.

*

At Teufelsberg, an analyst ripped off a note headed "Intercept Transcript" and set off across the operations room towards the supervisor. The key words contained in the telephone conversation had triggered the tape machine to begin recording and the use of Russian had done little to divert the trained analyst. He had no doubt that the content of the transcript would be of interest to the hard pressed counter-intelligence team.

*

As Meier made his way back to the rental car he scrutinised the driver of the nondescript, silver VW Golf as it passed down the road towards Wassenberg. Seemingly indifferent, the driver stared blankly at the empty road as he flicked the ash from his cigarette through the window. Despite his best efforts Meir would not spot the car again even though it would tail him for the next hour, nor would he see the blue Peugeot 205 GTi which would tag-team him along the A46 autobahn as he made his way to the airport.

*

That night in the Officers Mess at Wildenrath the drinking was restrained, the ferocity of the debrief still fresh and the prospect of a full flying programme planned for the following day weighing on the minds of the crews. The serious drinking would be reserved for after the final debrief once the exercise had finished. In a quiet corner the American Lieutenant Colonel pulled the detachment leaders aside, the group locked in a serious discussion.

"Today's sortie was a mess and, I hate to admit but it was mostly my guys. Trust me, the post-exercise debrief will be ugly."

"I don't think any of us were that sharp today Colonel. Don't be too hard on them," said Roy South, the British element leader. "A lot of the guys are youngsters and this is probably their first real NATO exercise. We've all been there."

"Look I probably shouldn't say any of this because my briefing back in the Command Post was NOFORN. They are all pretty tense down at Ramstein and our intel guys are telling me that tensions are at breaking point with the Soviets. This exercise and our presence here, although planned a long time ago, might be timely."

"We've had a similar briefing from our own people. It's probably about time they fessed up and, if the risks are increasing, we need to know. I'm sure after our discussion with the Station Commander today that he'll be pressing hard."

"If your guys are anything like ours they get a weird pleasure from sitting on stuff that would make our lives on the squadrons a hell of a lot easier. Sources, sources, sources is all I ever hear."

"So what was the briefing?"

"I heard this morning that there has been another incident in the southern corridor. One of our C-141 Starlifters inbound from Rhein-Main was intercepted by a pair of Mig-21s. There were no shots fired but the Migs got close enough to divert the transport from its course and it came close to the edge of the corridor. Despite what the Sovs will say those Migs were well inside the lane. I've lost count of how many interventions we've had this week."

"Has your Embassy taken it up?"

"Oh it's way higher than that. The Soviet Ambassador in Washington was called in and the Secretary for Defense gave him a horoscope. It was ugly from what I heard. So with the Pembroke missing and a go at our airplane today it could be you guys next. Anything from Paris, Phillipe?" he asked turning to the French Detachment Commander who had been quiet.

"Mais, Non," he replied switching to English. "We don't put military aircraft into Berlin any more. Our Government sees it as provocative and they are trying hard to build relations with Moscow. Money talks and there are lucrative contracts to be won. Too much antagonism and the contracts will be placed elsewhere. We have invited them to the Paris Airshow again this year and I'm surprised we have been authorised to take part in this exercise. If things go live I would not even guarantee we will participate. Politics and detente can be powerful antidotes."

"Well whatever gives, we need to have this team ready to go for real. Time may already be short."

With the consequence of a potential split in unity resonant, the impromptu meeting broke up and they returned to the knot of flyers clustered around the bar. Such decisions were beyond their control and politicians not flyers would decide on such matters. For now, their job was to make sure they were prepared.

CHAPTER 27

THE POLITBURO, MOSCOW

The two grey haired men appeared relaxed but subtle mannerisms reflected the tense tone of the conversation.

"I assume we can agree that Portnov is driving this?"

"We can. He is well connected and, I have to say, his ebullience is going down well with many of the hard-liners. We need to be wary of challenging a course of action that is seen to be traditional Soviet."

"I accept the sentiment but we have come a long way since 1948 and the Americans and British rode out that campaign during arguably more difficult times. The politics of Perestroika are far more subtle. If this escalates further we can forget thoughts of normal relations."

"Let me have a few discussions. The Chairman is still keen to see progress. But for his ailing health we would be secure and could rein Portnov in. The fact that the Chairman may not be around for too long is a risk we must anticipate. His condition is worsening and he may yet prove to be the shortest incumbent of the post in recent years. Already potential suitors are appearing and Gorbachev is manoeuvring for primacy."

"Let me gauge the mood. If I can secure enough backing we can issue direct orders to stop the interventions. Even Portnov is not brave enough to ignore Politburo direction, particularly as he has moved forward to the 16th Tactical Air Army Headquarters. Without the ability to influence the policy makers face-to-face he would have to desist."

"Are we sure that detente is the way?"

"At least the two of us agree and with a few more behind us we can carry the day. I still carry a decent number of supporters with me."

"I will talk with the Commander of the 16th. I know him from my days at the Officers' Academy. He is an astute leader and should see reason. If he can't challenge Portnov, at least he can make it harder for to orders to be passed down the line. We need to move quickly."

"I will contact you immediately after my discussions."

The impromptu meeting lasted only three minutes but the outcome would shape events immeasurably.

CHAPTER 28

ZERBST AIRFIELD, EAST GERMANY

The strain of captivity was beginning to show as the pilot paced around the perimeter of the small room adjacent to the flight line. Conditions were cramped, the temperature rising in the confined space and tempers rising. Peering through the grimy, barred window it was obvious that the activity on the flight line had slowly dwindled. The sound of the Mig-23 Floggers based in the hardened shelters on the far side of the runway had rattled the windows for some hours as wave after wave had launched and recovered. For the last hour it had been quiet. A large propeller-driven transport had landed and parked somewhere close by on the ramp but even that had now gone. The vain hope that they might soon be released had faded as they watched in dismay as the Pembroke was pulled into an adjacent hangar and the doors hauled closed. An imminent release did not seem likely despite their protestations to the Soviet officer.

"I wonder where they've taken Carl?"

"Who knows. Why would they split us up?" the navigator replied. "Maybe he knows the base commander and he's been asked around for tea?"

The weak attempt at humour didn't lift the heavy atmosphere. It had been some time since lunch had been unceremoniously deposited on the table inside the door. The armed guards had left no room for manoeuvre during the brief moment the door was open and the sound of the heavy boots retreating down the corridor only emphasised their plight. So far, their protestations had fallen on deaf ears and requests to speak with the British Consular staff had been ignored repeatedly. They could do little but wait and ponder, charges of espionage featuring prominently in their thoughts.

"Did you see that Cessna sitting on the apron outside?"

"I did. It had a civilian registration didn't it?"

"Yes but it was West German. What the hell is a West German-registered Cessna 172 doing sitting on the pan at Zerbst?"

"Beats me. This is not the sort of place I'd want to visit on a land away. The afternoon tea sucks."

"I used to fly those things as a kid. I did my licences at Oxford Air School before I joined the Service. It was loads of fun in those days. No pressure. All I had to do was bimble around the countryside and watch the world go by."

"Could you still fly it?"

"Yeah, of course I could. It's like riding a bike. I bet I could still remember the checks if I thought about it."

"That would solve a transport problem wouldn't it?"

"It would if we weren't locked in this bloody room. Not much point in thinking about a lift home when we can't even get out of the building."

"I must admit I'm still worried about Carl but if that's all that's stopping us why didn't you say so? I didn't get my pilot's licence as a kid but my Old Man was a locksmith. He taught me a few things over the years and he said they might come in useful at some time. I doubt there's a set of lock picks in here but I'd bet there would be something in this office that I could improvise with. Here, help me look in these drawers."

They began to rummage through the desk discarding pens and other items of stationary. Eventually, armed with an old plastic identity card and a pair of prongs prised from a discarded metal filing tray he began to attack the lock. The lock clicked alarmingly and he paused regularly, conscious of the risk of discovery if a guard passed along the corridor. If his efforts were detected, any chance of escape would disappear along with his improvised lock picks. Without the correct equipment he struggled, prodding at the lock mechanism in frustration. Occasionally, he moved over to the window where he rubbed the metal tips on the exposed brickwork around the window frame filing the ends of the prongs into a point. He held them up to the light, filing and bending, forging the ends into a hook. Satisfied, he returned to attack the lock once more. With a contented grunt he pushed the card into the gap adjacent to the lock wedging the reluctant mechanism. It gave way; the door ajar. A tentative glance down the corridor confirmed that all was quiet as they worked their way slowly past empty offices towards the rear entrance. The stuttering ring of a telephone stopped them in their tracks and they retreated into the closest office but it went unanswered. With pulses returning to normal, easing open the outer door they emerged from the gloom of the building into the bright sunlight on the flight line which was, by now, deserted. From the far side of the building came the unmistakeable sound of the military truck accompanied by the crash of doors and footsteps in the corridor behind. There was an exchange of glances and a rapid reassessment. Their RAF-issue green flying suits blended in like an advertisement hoarding and the challenge of crossing the expanse of concrete, which stretched out across the apron between them and the small red Cessna parked in front of the hangar, seemed insurmountable. Skirting along the front of the flight line buildings they stayed mostly out of sight but, at some stage, they would be forced out into the open to cross the concrete to where the small aircraft was parked. The lofty control tower gave a perfect view over the movements area and, if it was still manned, their presence would be impossible to miss. They could only hope that the Tower was empty. If night flying was planned their bid for freedom would be cut short.

"There's no good time to do this," the pilot whispered. "If we meet anyone we're going to stand out like a dog's balls so, once we hit the end of the building, I suggest we brass it out and go straight for the Cessna. If the door's locked or the keys have been removed we've had it anyway. There's no way I can hot-wire a Cessna."

He received a nod in acknowledgement and they began to walk, casually, along the narrow path alongside the office building. Keeping a low profile but trying to act naturally, their hope was that they may fool a casual observer. Reaching the end of the building and ducking down behind a servicing trolley they dropped out of sight, temporarily, pulses racing.

"OK, there's no other way to do this other than to look as though we're supposed to be here. Once we move, look confident as we walk out to the aircraft. Let's hope both doors are open. I need to be on the left so you take the far door. I think I'll forgo a walk round for this trip. Once we're inside I need to remind myself of the location of a few switches and hope to God that the keys are on the coaming. If not, we're toast. Ready?"

"As I'll ever be."

Standing up, they began the long walk towards the waiting Cessna chatting amicably as if they had every right to be there. Expecting to be discovered at any moment during the 50 yard walk, the relief was palpable as they ducked under the high wing of the light aircraft. The strident challenge never came and with a swift tug on the door handles they climbed into the small cabin dropping onto the bucket seats registering with relief the presence of the keys hanging in the ignition.

"Once I start up there's going to be no way of disguising our intentions. I only need about 1000 feet to get airborne so I'm not taxying all the way to the runway. The parking apron is not big enough for the takeoff roll so I need to get to the taxiway but it's not that far. Can you see the entrance there? It looks like the wind's across the runway so I'm going straight ahead from here and as soon as I'm lined up we roll, OK?"

"Sounds good to me, let's do it."

His hands moved automatically despite the intervening years as he refamiliarised himself with the controls and the layout of the instruments. He flicked on the battery master switch and was rewarded with the quiet hum of the gyros as they wound up. The instruments flickered briefly as the gauges sprang into life, the artificial horizon bobbling in its gimbals. With a glance at the fuel gauges he saw with relief that the fuel tanks were showing about half full. If his memory was correct it meant that they had about an hour's flying time which should be plenty to get across the border. That is if the QRA pilots across the airfield did not have other ideas.

"OK, everything looks fine. Ready to start?"

The question was superfluous and a force of habit. They had no choices left. He primed the engine with a few strokes of the primer and set the throttle slightly open. Turning the key to the start position the engine turned over slowly; once twice, three times before it reluctantly kicked into life and the prop began turn under its own power. Without fanfare he flicked off the parking brake and gunned the throttle and the light aircraft leapt forward. As it emerged from the lee of the hangar into full view he could imagine the panic which would ensue in the tower if it was still manned. Dabbing the brakes and satisfied that they were working he flicked his hands across to the radios and avionics firing each one up in turn. Rushing through a few vital checks which would normally have been run at the holding point, he aimed directly at the entrance to the parallel taxiway only a few hundred yards away. As yet their movement had not attracted attention but that was about to change.

"So, what heading after takeoff nav?"

"I think west might be a good plan Biggles!"

Without maps there had been little preparation but precision was far from their thoughts. As the small aircraft homed in on the neck of the taxiway a red flare arced into the sky from the balcony of the control tower. A figure leaned over the rail and for a moment, the pilot thought the green-clad figure was about to turn the flare gun on them. It turned running back inside the tower disappearing rapidly from view. As they reached the end of the small concrete apron he lined up with the taxiway and gunned the throttle. There was no time for the luxury of an engine check nor would they be turning back if it showed any signs of petulance. Used to the wide runway at Wildenrath the taxiway looked narrow but it was plenty wide enough for the tiny Cessna. The engine note picked up and the still cold engine made its displeasure known before picking up strongly and accelerating the small craft along the concrete strip. The airspeed indicator increased rapidly and, as the nosewheel lifted, with the speed passing 65 knots, they rose into the evening air and picked up a westerly heading. More used to transferring to a radar unit after takeoff, he held the nose down, staying low and heading out across the green fields, the radio mercifully silent. At that moment, a feeling of remorse struck him, disturbed by the fact that they had abandoned Pocklington to his fate yet there had been no alternative.

With the lack of headsets there was little desire to challenge the noise of the engine with superfluous chat. With a flourish the navigator pulled a tattered map from the small pocket next to his knee and began to pore over the unfamiliar chart. It had been folded carefully but was centred on a small light airstrip to the west of the border. Clearly the last pilot had not anticipated navigating in the vicinity of Zerbst. He unfolded the map which stopped just to the east of the Inner German Border and pored over the detail. The central corridor was clearly marked and running his thumb to the south he checked out the topography. Trying to visualise the position of Zerbst in relation to the corridor he slowly orientated himself and adjusted the small heading bug on the compass. Pointing to the gauge, he persuaded the pilot to ease the nose to the right by a few degrees. It was a guess but a route towards Gutersloh seemed like the best plan for the time being. The fuel gauges remained, reassuringly, steady.

Back inside the control tower, the controller who had unsuccessfully tried to persuade the crew to abort the takeoff, snatched up a phone and was in hurried discussion with the operations room attempting to convey the urgency of the situation provoked by the unexpected departure. Even to his own ears it sounded unlikely. The exchange became increasingly animated before a reluctant supervisor eventually hit the scramble button that would alert the Mig pilots in the hardened shelter on the far end of the runway. A few personnel across the base reacted instantly to the claxons which rang out in unison. Others stared morosely into their drinks and ignored the warning. In the small annex next to the alert shed pilots and groundcrew raced towards the waiting Migs.

*

A few miles away the small red Cessna headed west towards freedom, its Lycoming engine pulling it along as fast as possible. With the throttle parked fully open the airspeed indicator peaked at a nervous 130 knots and would go no farther. With the drama of their escape subsiding, neither of them was under the illusion that the journey would be anything but tense. If they were to arrive back safely they would have to penetrate some of the most heavily defended airspace in the western hemisphere. Their only advantage was that to the radar systems which would already be searching for them, the tiny aircraft was all but invisible. The IFF transponder that would normally exchange electronic signals with air traffic agencies, providing instant indications of their location, was dormant. If a tracking radar was to detect them it would have to work hard to break out their primary radar response from amongst the electronic noise at low level. The simplicity of the Cessna and its slow pace across the terrain might be its salvation. The town of Zerbst had passed on the port beam some time before and the river Elbe which split the flat landscape loomed ahead. It was tempting to turn and follow its meandering path which would eventually lead them to the North Sea near Cuxhaven in West Germany but that would take them through miles of East German airspace and, throughout that time, they would be vulnerable to attack. Against them was the slowly diminishing fuel reserve that dictated a shorter track. Safety lay to the west and it was a short, albeit predictable track to the Inner German Border. With depleted fuel tanks it was doubtful they could make it far beyond the border and there were few options other than a direct track. To have made good their escape only to land short of sanctuary would be a cruel fate. Little did they know that the first challenge to their progress was, at that very moment, taxying out from the hardened alert shelter at Zerbst and powering towards the active runway. The wingman followed and very soon the pair of Mig-23 Floggers would be lifting off and in pursuit.

The ground ahead was depressingly flat and a wind from the northwest was slowing their progress reducing their already pedestrian groundspeed. The pilot had laid off a few degrees to offset for the drift but, until they could pinpoint their position on the rudimentary chart, they were working from memory. A roughly westerly course should take them almost directly to the Army garrison town of Goslar nestled in the Harz Mountains. To the northwest the border crossing at Helmstedt was heavily defended as it was the major entry and exit point via the corridor. Drift too far north and they would tempt fate. Following the main E30 highway that linked Helmstedt to Berlin was easy but would be folly as it was an obvious magnet for a pursuer and would be predictable given their unfamiliarity with the territory. A further complication was that the course of the border veered considerably further west just to the south of the border town penetrating well into what might logically have been West German airspace. Drift too far south and they would spend longer in East German airspace than was necessary, something they were keen to avoid. Their route was slowly becoming predictable. The ideal would be to aim for the small town of Hotensleben if their imprecise navigation could achieve it. From memory, having entered the Berlin Corridor many times in the Pembroke, a huge quarry close to the village was visible from miles around and would be a good feature to pinpoint their position. By turning northwest once they were clear of Magdeburg they should cross the huge forest of "Waldfrieden und Vogelherd" and reach the border shortly afterwards. There was a gulf between their hasty plan and reality and the nervous conversations in the cabin were not helped by the steady downwards progress of the fuel gauges already showing just above quarter tanks.

*

"Wildenrath, alert two Phantoms."

"Mike Lima 25, Mike Lima 64."

"Mike Lima 25, Mike Lima 64, vector 070, climb flight level 150, Gate, contact Loneship on TAD 072, scramble, scramble, scramble, acknowledge."

With the frantic activity at Gutersloh the two additional Battle Flight Phantoms at Wildenrath were needed. The pilot hit the button on the telebrief box to acknowledge the call with the alert claxon loud in his ears, his navigator already sprinting towards the hardened aircraft shelter which housed the QRA alert aircraft. Across in the adjacent Battle Flight HAS their actions were being mirrored by the second crew. Coincident with the hooter, the clamshell doors had begun to move automatically and he squeezed through the narrow gap between the opening doors. At the base of the steps he hoisted his lifejacket onto his shoulders and clipped the chest plate together before sprinting up the rear ladder into the cockpit. His pilot was only feet behind him struggling into his own lifejacket and already the whine of the Houchin external power set dominated as it wound up, the flight line mechanic coaxing it into life. Leaping onto the canvas cover of the ejection set he dropped into the cockpit his pilot now only seconds behind. With external power applied the cockpit sprang to life, the lights on the instruments bright in the gloom. Reaching down he fumbled with the controls of the inertial navigation system and began the short alignment sequence that would dictate how soon the Phantom would roll off the chocks. He plugged in the intercom lead from his helmet into the pigtail and slotted the personal equipment connector into his ejection seat simultaneously hitting the floor-mounted transmit switch.

"Mike Lima 64, scrambling."

The right hand Spey was already screaming and he was vaguely conscious of the flight line mechanic poised on the ladder waiting to help him strap in the top straps which were impossible to connect encumbered by the bulky flying gear. He dragged the lower seat straps around him and fed the fasteners through the bulky canvas parachute harness clipping them into the harness box. In response to his thumbs-up the flight line mechanic offered the shoulder straps which clicked into place, closely followed by the top ejection seat pin, slotted without question into the storage housing on the canopy arch. The body disappeared over the side before, seconds later, the rear ladder was pulled clear. With the final obstruction removed, the left engine wound up adding to the pandemonium.

"Seagull, 64, say again the scramble instructions."

As he jotted the brief message onto his kneeboard the significance of the instructions became clear. "Gate" authorised them to fly at supersonic speeds using afterburner and the course took them across the city of Cologne at only 15,000 feet. This was serious.

*

As the Cessna passed the small town of Bottmersdorf the navigator in the right hand seat gestured upwards through the windscreen. The view above was obscured by the high mounted wing but, invisible to the pilot, a pair of Mig-23 Flogger Bravos, the air defence version of the Mig, sped past only 5,000 feet above. Holding a swept tactical formation their course was diverging which suggested that the pilots had not yet spotted the bright red, light aircraft. Despite an urgent desire to make for Hotersleben the pilot jinked a few degrees to the west increasing the divergence between their courses. He had no idea of the location of the air defence radars on the ground around here and he began to wish that he had paid more attention to the intelligence officer at the Friday afternoon briefing when the intricacies of the air defence structure had been explained. What he remembered clearly was that the coverage in this region was dense and overlapping. If they were close to an air defence unit it was only a question of time before they were detected despite their tiny radar signature. With detection would come retribution and their safe passage would no longer be guaranteed. To the north the pair of fighters began an ominous turn back towards them moving relentlessly closer.

*

The Phantoms appeared from the Battle Flight shelters simultaneously, canopies closing, as they emerged from the lee of the concrete roofs. Inside the cockpits the crews were frantically running through the pre-flight checks readying for takeoff. Holding "Readiness 05", the scant five minute time limit in which they were required to be airborne gave no leeway for tardiness or mistakes. The 92 Squadron jet reached the taxiway first and covered the short distance to the runway in seconds.

"Mike Lima 64 taking the active."

It was a statement not a request. There was no seeking permission to takeoff and the only way the momentum would be stopped was with an authenticated codeword from the controller. Even then, the time taken to verify its authenticity would take longer than the time taken to engage the reheat which was what the pilot now did. The burners bit almost before he was lined up with the runway and the first Phantom sped down the tarmac strip, the shock diamonds reflecting from the surface, a visible sign of the immense power of the Spey engines. The second aircraft followed only seconds behind.

"25 airborne."

"Mike Lima 64, 25, TAD 072, Go!"

*

The Migs passed directly overhead the Cessna still oblivious to its presence. Suddenly conscious that he had almost stopped breathing the navigator sucked in a lungful of air, watching the pilot tweak the heading bug once more, pointing the nose towards the massive forest which had emerged from the haze. With the sun now low on the horizon visibility into the glare was becoming difficult making it harder to pick out reliable navigation features but also making it more difficult for their pursuers to detect the small Cessna visually when looking into sun. Remarkably, their ad hoc plan seemed to be working and they estimated about another 20 miles to run to the border. At this speed the 10 minutes flight time would seem like an age. To the east the Migs made another turn seemingly homing in on their position. Whether the search was random or deliberate would become obvious quite soon.

*

" Loneship, Mike Lima 25 and 64."

"Mike Lima 25 and 64 this is Loneship, I read you loud and clear. Vector 085. Your targets bear 090 range 60 miles at low level. You have cut off. Targets show 350 knots."

There was none of the usual tactical preamble and the navigators in the rear cockpit of each jet settled into the familiar routine rolling the scanners down towards the ground beginning a methodical search of the airspace. The target, over 60 miles away, was on the other side of the border.

"Request instructions," the question from the lead aircraft curt and functional.

"Mike Lima 25, 64 interrogate and report. You are not cleared hot pursuit. I repeat, you are not cleared hot pursuit."

The manacles applied by the controller were becoming commonplace for the hard pressed Battle Flight crews. The blips on the radar scope appeared almost simultaneously and rapid calculations put the merge ten miles beyond the border. Without clearance to penetrate and, if nothing changed, they would be forced to haul off before the merge.

"25 contact."

"64 contact."

"Your targets bear 090 range 48 miles, check switches safe."

The safety check was acknowledged in turn but whether the intercept would conclude without weapons being traded was not yet clear.

In the cockpits of the Phantoms a stalemate ensued. Stumbling into the merge without clearance to engage, particularly if the geometry of the intercept dragged them close to, or worse still, across the border, put them at a tactical disadvantage. So far their instructions were to determine the intentions of their opponents. The launch of an Apex missile might be their first indicator. Further calls to confirm their restrictive rules of engagement elicited the same cautionary response. It was time to force the issue. The navigators locked up their respective targets and with a simple switch selection, the continuous wave guidance radars illuminated the distant targets.

"25 is on the southerly."

"Roger 64 has the northerly."

The picture flickered into full track. With the steering dot centred in the display and the Phantoms now on a collision course for the targets only 20 miles away the outcome of the engagement would be determined by the response from the Soviet pilots.

"Loneship, Mike Lima 25, range to the border?" the lead navigator queried.

"25 you have 10 miles to run," came back the terse response.

The opposing formations would merge directly over the disputed territorial boundary. It was too close. As the navigators fretted over the tactical dilemma the decision was made for them as the closing velocity rolled off, the targets turning away and returning onto an easterly vector.

"Targets turning away, 25 and 64 hauling off," called the leader, relieved not to be turning his tail to a high speed contact. Whether the Soviet fighter controller would have been so cautious as his own controller would remain unanswered. Was the turn away coincidence or planned?

*

In the Mig cockpits 20 miles to the east, now heading away, the pilots were oblivious to the imminent threat from the Phantoms. Concentrating on tracking the elusive light aircraft their own controller had failed to warn of the fighter's approach on the western side of the border. That their radar warning receivers stayed silent was testament to the critical lack of spares on the East German based squadron. With no likelihood of a radar detection, the pilot's eyes scanned the surrounding countryside striving for the elusive visual contract.

*

Skirting the edge of the woods at Waldfrieden the vivid red colour scheme of the light aircraft was marginally less prominent against the greens and browns of the countryside and the tall trees provided an element of cover. Clearing the woods their goal was tantalisingly close. Ahead, a watch tower stood tall on the horizon, positioned to dominate its surroundings. As a consequence, it could be seen from every vantage point in the surrounding terrain. The navigator recognised the BT-11 observation tower with its octagonal observation deck and slender concrete column. Positioned at regular intervals along the border it was too common to be a useful navigation feature and he scanned the track for something distinctive which they might recognise. Something which might be stored in his memory from the numerous trips down the Berlin corridors. All around, the landscape seemed nondescript, worryingly flat and featureless.

"I thought it was going too well," he sighed, unheard by the pilot over the noise of the engine, gesturing at a point in the windscreen. In the distance between them and the Inner German Border, a Mil-24 Hind Delta gunship tracked slowly northwards. Flying at a similar height to the tiny Cessna, avoiding detection would be impossible, sky-lined against the horizon and easily visible at the slower speeds. With its ability to hover and armed with a 23mm cannon mounted in the nose, it was a formidable threat and altogether more dangerous to a slow flying light aircraft than the Migs which had disappeared from view.

The pilot aimed for a point behind the helicopter attempting to increase the separation from the new threat. If it held its northerly heading they would diverge rapidly but if it turned, detection was guaranteed. Ominously, the helicopter followed the line of the border, its search methodical and precise. So far there was no indication that they had been seen despite the dense radar coverage in the area. Salvation was still tantalisingly close. Up ahead, the hinterland fence rose from amongst the trees, emphasising the proximity of their goal. They were a mere five kilometres from the border and safety. The pilot eased the Cessna lower ignoring every low flying rule, skirting the treetops. His only hope was to remain invisible.

"I've got a truck in the one o'clock, stationary on the patrol road," the navigator called. "Looks like a team of border guards."

"Bringing it further left," he heard in response.

On the road below the members of the "Grenzregiment" had deployed around the front of the vehicle, their attention fixed on the light aircraft passing overhead. The jink was insufficient to avoid the green-clad guards and, as they passed directly overhead, there was a loud crack and the right hand wing juddered briefly drawing their attention to the gaping entrance hole made by the 7.62 millimetre small arms round that had pierced the skin of the Cessna. A thin line of fuel emerged from the hole smearing the underside of the wing, rapidly dispersing in the airflow. The pilot glanced down at the fuel gauge and the indication from the gauge for the right tank began to run down rapidly from its already parlous level. He reached down, feeling for the tank isolation switch reassured that with individual tanks, the damage was not terminal but their hitherto marginal fuel load was reduced even further.

"We've taken a round in the fuel tank," he said, stating the obvious. "It's a serious leak but I'll run on that tank until it empties," he announced, little able to influence events. The confidence in his voice belied his concern. It would be a tense few moments as he could not allow the engine to stop starved of fuel yet he needed to eke out every last litre of the precious commodity. Anticipating the thud of further rounds striking the airframe they were rewarded with a lull and the sound of the Lycoming engine pulling strongly. They were past the first barrier but hardly unscathed and more was yet to come. To the north the rotor disk of the Hind helicopter flashed briefly in the fading sunlight as it reefed hard around and its nose came to bear on their position. Words were unnecessary and their heads tracked the inbound gunship in unison.

With a collision seemingly inevitable, at the last minute the Hind deviated and passed in front of the Cessna at co-altitude dipping its stub wings, the range of weapons clearly visible. The light aircraft shuddered as it passed through the turbulent wake, rocking alarmingly. The helicopter extended to the south before slowing, rotating in place and holding its position in the hover. There was a short standoff, the ugly profile demanding attention before it closed in, once again aiming directly at them. Seemingly intent on collision the nose tracked unerringly, causing the pilot involuntarily to push hard forward on the controls bunting the Cessna towards the ground. Overhead, the helicopter passed within feet, filling the windscreen, the noise of its turbines reverberating through the cabin before wheeling round in a wide arc and positioning in the 5 o'clock. As it closed more slowly now, it filled the rear window. With the attempts to intimidate having failed, attack seemed imminent. Recovering from the crazy manoeuvre and only feet above the ground, the pilot pulled back sharply, avoiding the stall by a tiny margin as, yet again, he hit the turbulent air in the wake of the attack helicopter. It was at that moment that the engine faltered and the pilot cursed realising he had forgotten in the heat of the moment to switch the fuel selector from the damaged tank. With the contents depleted he switched to automatic urging the engine to respond. The rough note continued for some seconds eliciting a nervous glance from the right seat. Fuel flow restored, the engine gave a threatening cough before the note returned to normal. The calls from the navigator that the border was approaching seemed both reassuring yet ominous. So close.

After the last ditch evasive manoeuvre the heading was taking them close to a smaller watch tower, a situation they had hoped to avoid. The observation deck of the squat, square "Kommandoturm" was only 20 feet above ground level but their manoeuvre had taken them down almost level with the windows. Behind, the Hind tracked relentlessly. Why was the pilot not opening fire? The gun in the nose followed their progress and they could only hope that the ultimate sanction had not been approved.

In fact the real reason was less dramatic. Urgent requests from the pilot had been passed up the command chain as he, repeatedly, asked for clearance to open fire. Ordinarily the approval would have been granted but in such unusual circumstances, caution prevailed. That the Cessna held two fleeing airman was common knowledge and self-preservation had prevailed, the political implications of a mistake prominent in their thoughts. The request had been shuffled upwards, each official deferring to higher command and even the cajoling from the helicopter pilot that his quarry was approaching the border had no effect. No one was prepared to approve the intervention.

Unheard in the Cessna further shots rang out from below as the border guards in the watch tower trained their guns on the small craft, its slow forward motion making it an easy target. Their instructions were less complex and anything which attempted to cross the cleared strip in a westerly direction was to be targeted. No exceptions. The sound of bullets winging past could be heard inside the cabin heralding a piercing crack as the rear window crazed and the noise of the air rushing past the canopy was magnified tenfold, turbulent air sucked in through hitherto airtight seals. It was to be a last gasp defence as, within seconds, the scar of the Inner German Border slipped by only feet below them, the momentous event seemingly lost in the mayhem. Behind them, the Hind hauled off.

Once clear of the border, they hugged the contours of the rising ground their course dictated by the shallow valleys before the pilot eased up to 1,000 feet to give a better view of their surroundings. The fuel gauge now dictated their priorities and with the right needle pegged on E and the left dropping towards empty, a landing site was an immediate priority. The inaccuracy of the gauges was legendary and running close to the mark was ill advised. With the danger from the Hind and the border defences past and, once again safe in West German airspace, any landing strip would suffice. Pressing on towards Gutersloh was a futile gesture. The pilot flicked on the IFF transponder and selected 7700 on the display, the code for emergency. He flicked the radio to 121.5, the international distress frequency and transmitted.

"All stations, Delta, Echo, Bravo, Oscar Victor on Guard," he called, the rush of wind noise clearly evident to anyone monitoring the Guard frequency. There was a momentary pause before the radio sprang into life.

"Delta, Echo, Bravo, Oscar Victor this is Loneship on Guard, confirm you are squawking Emergency?"

"Loneship, Delta, Oscar Victor, that's affirmative, I estimate my position to be five miles east of Schöningen, presently climbing to 1,000 feet."

"Roger Delta, Oscar Victor, state the nature of your emergency."

Suppressing the urge to respond with a sarcastic comment and realising that he would only just have popped up into radar coverage, the pilot bit his tongue.

"I am inbound from Zerbst, I say again Zerbst and request immediate diversion to the nearest landing strip. I am on fuel minimums and require immediate recovery."

"Roger Sir, are you familiar with the local area?"

"Negative Sir."

The engine coughed and faltered before picking up but sounding rough. He checked yet again seeing the same depressing indications. With the selection he had made, the fuel should have been transferring automatically between tanks but not wishing to test his hazy knowledge of the Cessna fuel system he reached down and flipped the tank selector across to "left". The engine immediately returned to a smooth note and he breathed a sigh of relief. Not wishing to tempt fate again, and convinced there must be a myriad of potential landing sites around them on which to set down, they began to scan the local area.

"We need to get this thing down right now," he urged. I have no idea how much is left in the left tank but I don't want to find out. A dead stick pattern I can do without."

"I'm with you my son, no arguments here," came the instant response.

"Loneship, Delta, Oscar Victor, experiencing engine problems. I need urgent vectors for recovery, do you read?"

"Affirmative Sir, Helmstedt bears 360 degrees and the tower has been alerted to your emergency."

"Negative, negative, insufficient fuel to make Helmstedt I need a local strip to put down."

"Roger Sir I'm checking for light airfields, standby."

He knew the controller was doing his best and fought the urge to pressure further. With the town to his right and with the ground rising into the foothills ahead, his best options were more likely to lie to the south. He began to turn the control wheel to the left when the engine made the decision for him as it coughed twice and the propeller stuttered to a halt the noise of the engine replaced by the rush of the wind across the surfaces.

"Oh crap."

At such a low height the luxury of an academic forced landing pattern was soon discarded. He had few options but to look ahead for a safe strip of ground on which to land the Cessna. Steadying his heading into the north westerly wind he scoured the area ahead through the windscreen for a potential landing site.

"Mayday, Mayday, Mayday, Delta, Echo, Bravo, Oscar Victor, Mayday. Engine failure, carrying out an immediate forced landing in my present position."

"Delta Oscar Victor, Mayday acknowledged," came the concerned response from the ground controller.

The fields ahead had been ploughed and the surfaces looked rough and uneven. To the west of a small town the welcome outline of a golf course emerged from the darkening haze and, with its manicured grass fairways, he hoped that a par five landing strip would emerge. There had to be a 500 yard fairway somewhere ahead and, if he could stretch the glide, he might yet stop safely. Looking ahead he could see a series of six long, straight fairways lying parallel in a north-south direction and almost into wind. With the propeller stationary his time was limited and he eased the pressure on the yoke to stabilise the speed at 75 knots. "Seventy Five for Life" he chanted, sub consciously, as he dredged up the words of his old flying instructor from his subconscious. He trimmed the aircraft into a shallow descent trying desperately to eke out his remaining height. It was a long glide to the golf course but, with luck, he could do it but it crossed his mind that he had traded in a good deal of his luck already today. As he passed over the western suburbs of the small town clearing the houses only feet above the roofs the altimeter read 400 feet and he began to feel a little more confident. Dropping a notch of flap to improve the handling, he pointed the nose at the southern end of the middle fairway which seemed wide and free of bunkers. The speed was pegged and he dropped full flap, confident that he could make the landing. An enticing but undulating field passed below the aircraft and he wondered whether he should have been more cautious but his approach was looking good. The tee box appeared below as he went into the flare and the ground rushed up towards him. Easing the nose up gently to wash off the remaining speed he dumped the small aircraft onto the smooth grass and immediately dabbed the brakes gently. The long straight fairway was as smooth as many grass runways he had used in the past and, without drama, the Cessna slowed to a walking pace and came to rest, perfectly framed by the 14th green. That he had demolished the pin or destroyed the green with tyre tracks were the least of his worries.

Overhead, the Phantoms held station at medium level the voice of the controller occasionally breaking the quiet of the frequency. Twenty miles to the east, the Mig pilots had yet to be informed that their erstwhile prey had escaped and patrolled, ineffectually, on the eastern side of the border still searching. An easy stalemate developed.

The 14th fairway was looking more like a heliport by the minute. A camouflaged RAF Puma clattered inbound from a westerly direction and set down next to a German search and rescue helicopter which had been first on the scene. As the Puma closed down, a Bundesgrenzschutz Iroquois and a Police Bölkow 105 which sported the familiar green and white colour scheme, so common around the towns and villages, joined the throng. A medic aboard the SAR helicopter had already assessed the medical condition of the crew and declared them fit, the pronouncement coming as no surprise to the bemused aircrew. The arrival back on terra firma had been as smooth as any landing in a Pembroke despite the lack of help from the engine. Offers of a ride to the local hospital had been rejected in favour of a swift return to Wildenrath and, with the arrival of the Puma from Gutersloh, an easy compromise had been reached. It would whisk them back to a debrief with an eager intelligence staff. As the crew climbed aboard the Puma and it lifted off, a bewildered German police helicopter crew began discussing options over the radio, asking for ideas on how to remove a stranded Cessna 172 from the 14th green.

In the military headquarters on both sides of the border lights would burn well into the night. Although the crew had escaped, with Pocklington still in custody and access to Berlin via the air corridors still challenged, tensions between East and West were spiralling out of control.

CHAPTER 29

DÜSSELDORF AIRPORT, WEST GERMANY

Dieter Meier stood patiently in line at the Interflug airline check-in desk at Düsseldorf airport. Unlike the packed Lufthansa desk alongside, the queue was mercifully short and, at any moment, he expected to be called forward by the agent. Unbeknown to him, his progress had been tracked by invisible security cameras overhead from the minute he had walked through the large glass entrance doors. Alerted by a mysterious phone call, an anonymous security officer was checking each face that entered the terminal against a short database of known Stasi agents. As Meier presented his false passport at the desk a flag had already been set and the moment the agent entered his details into the reservation system, a warning message appeared on the screen and she discretely pressed a button beneath the counter in acknowledgement. A local West German girl, the Bundesgrenzschutz logo prominently displayed on the message was enough to ensure her meek compliance. As she fussed with the boarding pass in a vain effort to delay the check-in process, a uniformed airport official moved alongside, speaking quietly to Meier.

"Herr Niedermeier?" the man asked using the false name on Meier's passport.

"Ja, etwas los?" said Meier beginning to feel a little edgy. The conversation continued in his native tongue.

"I wonder if you could step this way Sir. I have a few questions for you and then we'll get you safely onboard your flight."

Meier's immediate reaction was to bluff his way out of the situation but as the check-in agent passed his boarding card to the official his options diminished, deprived of his means of escape. A glance revealed two uniformed customs officers homing in on the desk and, if he delayed any longer, the trap would close and detention would be inevitable. His thoughts turned to flight but by more traditional means than the IL-62 airliner which had been his preferred method. Turning, readying himself for a dash to the exit, an armed Police officer barred his way.

"Come with me Sir," the man urged, looming over Meier. "Hopefully, this will not take long."

With all routes barred and out of options he meekly allowed the man to steer him along the frontage past the mob of passengers at the Lufthansa desk towards an ominously marked door. The sign: "Airport Security" warned of trouble ahead.

CHAPTER 30

THE POLITBURO, MOSCOW

"I'm afraid it's not good news," the politician offered, the signs of his advancing years heightened by the ravages of recent events. "Gorbachev has agreed to support us but at a cost. It was a difficult negotiation."

"But is there any good news?"

"That was it I'm afraid. Events have spiralled. It seems that a Pembroke transport plane was forced down and the crew taken into custody. In what I can only describe as a farce, two of the officers have escaped but a third is still being held. I hate to say but the escapees stole a light aircraft to make their bid for freedom. It seems that the remaining detainee may be complicit in events. He may even be working for Portnov in some way. What is certain is that Portnov has dragged his "friends" in Berlin into the affair. You already know about the recent actions of our fighter aircraft in the corridor. Sadly, it seems the intervention you had been made aware of was not a one-off and there have been quite a few similar events. There can be no doubt that we have stretched the NATO commanders to the limits of their patience."

"We need swift action. What a shambles."

"I'm afraid that's not all. It seems that a number of East German agents have been detained in the West. It is not clear whether they were being controlled directly by the KGB or whether we have a rogue operation underway. I sense Portnov's influence. I'm checking as we speak."

The older man rubbed his brow distractedly.

"It seems that a NATO mission to reinforce the air corridors is underway as we speak and the aircraft are preparing to takeoff. I cannot find out whether our forces have been ordered to act against it but we shouldn't under-estimate the consequences if shots are exchanged. With the recent provocation this may be seen as a final trigger point by their political leaders. I'm attempting to have orders issued to place a hold against offensive action but the normal lines of command seem to have been disrupted. A number of the commanders seem to be responding to directions issued by Portnov. It may take some time to restore order."

"How can that happen? The procedures should be above reproach. We have checks and balances to ensure a rogue officer cannot act alone."

"True but when someone of Portnov's stature intervenes, particularly with his connections in the command chain, subordinates assume a legitimacy which may not be real."

"I'll leave that aspect to you. With the appropriate direction from the upper echelons we should be able to re-establish the protocols quickly. Make sure we consult each of the Frontal commanders individually. They must be under no illusions about strategic policy. If our friend Portnov has his way we'll be rolling through the Brandenburger Tor before the week is out. It is for us to re-establish order. We have no choice but to let immediate events take their course but once we see the impact of what he has set in motion we can respond. It will be a difficult few hours but after that we will take control. Let us issue the order to place all our forces in Germany on stand down. That should send a clear enough message to our counterparts that we have backed away from direct confrontation. This provocation must end now. Make sure the alert state is lowered and pass the order in the clear. That way the listening stations will hear the orders and disseminate the intent. I will have the Chairman approve the strategy. Pull the reinforcements around Berlin back to the rear areas as soon as it is clear that the message has been received. In parallel I will speak to an old friend in Bonn and make some diplomatic concessions. I will ensure he knows that a rogue officer is being disciplined for his ill-considered actions. I will also reassure them that the rights of navigation will be restored and that aircraft will be allowed to pass unhindered. That after all, seems to be the crux of the matter."

"Would you like me to start arranging an exchange of prisoners?"

"Yes, immediately. I want the man we are holding on an aircraft within the hour; whomever he is working for. It is too late to do anything about the NATO operational plans but once we have chance to evaluate them it may salvage something from this mess."

"I will begin right away. The RAF navigator was moved from Zerbst to Berlin shortly after he was detained. He is in Stasi custody but I'll make sure instructions are issued to have him released immediately. We can offer to hand him over at Checkpoint Charlie or, if they prefer we can fly him back to his base on the Dutch border."

"Make sure you secure a reciprocal agreement or it may look suspicious. We need those Stasi people back here for a debriefing. I want to know how this was allowed to degenerate so quickly. If Portnov was acting alone we may be able to isolate the ringleaders."

"I mentioned Gorbachev. His price is that you support his bid for power. He has designs on the top job you know and his ambitions for accelerating detente are garnering favour amongst the new elite. I suspect that our efforts to neuter the hard liners may well go in his favour. He is demanding total support for his plans. He wants payback. No ambiguities."

"He's a canny politician that man but, for once, maybe he might be right. This has come close to triggering conflict with NATO and we all know that our plans would quickly escalate to a limited nuclear exchange. Nuclear and chemical weapons are integral to our plans and where would that leave Western Europe? Much of the Low Countries would be uninhabitable. No; for once his price is worth paying to prevent this madness."

*

In a secure vault at the rear of the Combined Operations Centre at Wildenrath two 92 Squadron crews were receiving a hastily arranged briefing that would change, drastically, their role in the operation. It was emerging that their contribution would not, after all, follow the scripted scenarios they had practised during the exercise but would be altogether more overt. It was true that their task would involve a transport aeroplane but not the western types that they had escorted for the last few days. This particular airliner had been built in a factory deep in Soviet Russia and its fate was in their hands.

*

In the CinC's office at the Headquarters at Rheindahlen there was a polite knock and his Personal Staff Officer popped his head around the door.

"Sir, we've just had word that the Soviets have begun making diplomatic noises in Bonn. There may be a chance that they are backing down. The suggestion is that this may all be down to a rogue officer and they are willing to offer concessions. Do you want to abandon the mission? We have procedures to issue a cancellation order before corridor penetration."

He pondered momentarily.

"No, let it run as planned. If they are serious then there should be no intervention and the mission will run without incident. If not, we may have to call their bluff. Either way we'll have a clearer view of their intent within a very short time. Send John Silversmith. I need to have a word."

CHAPTER 31

ON THE OPERATIONAL READINESS PLATFORM, RAF WILDENRATH

Some hours later, at the western perimeter of Wildenrath airfield, Razor had pulled the Phantom onto the operational readiness platform and allowed himself a moment to reflect. With the cockpit canopy open, the cool breeze provided a welcome relief from the heat from the instruments already building up in the cockpit. Alongside, his wingman had lined up in echelon, the heads of the pilot and navigator moving slowly as they made a few final adjustments inside their own cockpits. The load-out for the Phantom had been specific for the mission and the jet was in fighting trim. Although the Suu-23 gun pod hung on the centreline station and a full weapon load of four Sparrow and four AIM-9L missiles hung from the missile stations, the *Sargent Fletcher* external fuel tanks had been removed making the airframe more manoeuvrable and, at the same time, increasing the G limit. A transmission on the operations frequency that he had been monitoring since he had pulled onto the ORP brought him back to the present, the message brief but unexpected.

"Shell 55 on station."

"Shotgun 1 acknowledged."

The American KC-135 tanker was already approaching the tactical tanker towline where it would provide the fuel which he would otherwise have dragged around in the external fuel tanks. Once topped off they would leave the towline and set up the combat air patrol his fuel tanks full.

To the right, along the southern taxyway, the first F-4E emerged from Charlie dispersal, its brown and green camouflage blending into the wooded background. As it turned down the taxyway towards him he tapped the canopy rail impatiently, his fingers shrouded in the white flying gloves. He was anxious to be on his way but could not pre-empt the takeoff time that had been carefully coordinated to tie in with the mission plan. As he bided his time, the KC-135 tanker would assume its orbit in the upper air well to the east and await his arrival. Until he had refuelled, the other training tasks allocated to the tanker for that day would be delayed. His was the number one priority.

The F-4E passed in front of his Phantom and pulled onto the ORP closer to the runway followed by the remainder of the US formation, lining up in a perfect echelon, their canopies already closed and locked. The US crews carried out "last chance checks" before takeoff and, as the wingman pulled into the slot, an American armourer scurried underneath checking panels for security and giving the airframe a final once-over for leaks. The wingman received the same treatment. Eventually, after what seemed like an age, the armourer emerged showing the pilot the armament flags which had been withdrawn from the weapons pylons slung under the Phantom. He received the briefest acknowledgement despite the fact that the lethal load of air-to-air weaponry was now armed. The pair pulled off moving towards the marshalling point ready for takeoff as the second pair received their own final check.

The Mirage formation was also holding short of the neck of Delta Dispersal where the nose of a 56 Squadron Phantom peeked from the trees and in the back cockpit, Flash felt the familiar buzz of excitement as the large formation assembled. Finally cleared to line up, the pair of British Phantoms emerged from the neck moving rapidly to catch up the American element. Inside the cockpits the crews heads were down as they ran through their pre takeoff checks determined not to delay the mission. The crescendo of noise from the runway announced the departure of Storm formation, the first pair rolling in close formation, the afterburners of the J79 engines shimmering as they accelerated down the strip. Twenty seconds later the second pair of Phantoms rolled, also in close formation, a mirror image of the lead element. The choreographed departure was perfect and as the first pair, by now cleaned up and travelling at 300 knots, turned downwind, the second pair arced the turn easing out into a fighting wing formation and pulling inside the lead pair ready for the join up. The British Phantoms wasted no time, easing onto the runway, stationary only briefly, before the first jet rolled, followed a few seconds later by its wingman. With gear and flaps retracted and afterburners still cooking the leader reefed into a hard turn downwind turning even tighter than the trailing American element. Before the first section had reached the end of the downwind leg the six Phantoms were in loose formation. They turned back through initials still within easy sight of the airfield. The Mirage pilots repeated the familiar routine lining up on the piano keys as a 4-ship and, as the gaggle of Phantoms passed overhead the threshold, the first pair rolled followed seconds later by the second pair. With the formation receding into the distance, ten aircraft had joined up and turned north easterly for the transit to Hannover where they would rendezvous with the Pembroke transport aircraft.

Back on the ground, Razor and Flash waited. They would not be joining the formation as originally envisaged as today they had a new mission. It involved an airliner but not the one originally envisaged. Flash looked at his watch as the hands ticked down to the nominated takeoff time.

"Two minutes," he announced.

"Shotgun 1 and 2, Stud 1, Stud 1, Go!"

"Shotgun check."

"Two."

Tower, Shotgun 1 and 2 line-up," Razor called. "Looking for departure at minute 22 and hand off to Clutch Radar."

"Shotgun line-up," came the disembodied response from the Local Controller. "Coordinating your departure with Clutch Radar now."

Anticipating the clearance, the two pilots wound the Speys up checking the temperatures and pressures, one final chance to check that all was well. With the runway checks complete the engines wound down, idling, waiting for the nominated departure time. Unbidden, with exactly 10 seconds to go, the controller announced the takeoff clearance, his words coinciding with the engines spooling back up to full power. Razor glanced over at his wingman who returned his gaze his thumb raised in confirmation. Turning back to the front he tapped his bonedome and two seconds later the exaggerated nodding gesture coincided with his opening the throttles. The Phantoms began to move, slowly at first as the thrust of the jet engines overcame the inertia of forty tons of airframe. Unencumbered with the heavy external fuel tanks, the jets surged forward, picking up speed rapidly, more a sports car than the usual hot hatchback. As the afterburners cut in, the thump could be felt in the cockpit and the jets surged ahead. As they lifted off he hit the transmit button.

"Tower, Shotgun airborne, to Clutch Radar. Shotgun, Stud 13, Stud 13, Go!"

With the Phantoms heading out over the urban sprawl of Düsseldorf below, the military controller offered occasional course corrections to keep them clear of airliners arriving and departing from the airfield. Their departure had not coincided with the peak traffic and their passage through the dense airspace was swift. Anxious to save fuel the sooner they could climb into the quieter upper air, the better. He prompted the controller for clearance to climb. The more fuel remaining in the tanks, the less time he would wrestle with the bucking refuelling hose behind the KC-135. Down below, the urban sprawl gave way to green fields.

"Shotgun Flight, climb to Flight Level 240 and call me level. Your playmate bears 065 range 70 miles."

"Climb to Flight Level 240, Shotgun."

Frustrated by the delays and knowing there was an endless supply of aviation fuel waiting for him, his desire for frugality gave way to the urge to make progress.

"Gate, Gate, Go!"

The afterburners surged once more as the jet suddenly took on a new persona. Gone was the sluggish performance and it accelerated willingly. As the airspeed indicator registered Mach 0.9 he pulled back on the stick and the Phantom climbed rapidly, the wingman matching the manoeuvre alongside. With the needle toying with Mach 1 the altimeter soon reached

23,000 feet and he rolled inverted, pulled back down towards the horizon before rolling upright, once more level at exactly 24,000 feet.

"Shotgun 1 and 2, level Flight Level 240," he called to the controller as his wingman slotted in alongside, holding his position in tight battle formation, joined by an invisible cord. The rendezvous datum was now only a few miles away at the south western end of the tanker towline.

The KC-135 used a radically different refuelling technique to the RAF tankers. Rather than the probe and drogue system an operator controlled a large boom mounted under the rear fuselage. USAF combat aircraft were fitted with receptacles on the upper, rear fuselage which opened in flight. Once in close formation on the tanker, the "boomy", facing rearwards and staring through a small window, would fly the refuelling arm using a hand controller, slotting the coupling on the boom into a receptacle on the receiver. Once in contact fuel transferred from the tanker to the receiver. Unable to use this system, when RAF aircraft refuelled from a KC-135, a short section of hose fitted with a refuelling basket trailed from the boom in the turbulent airflow. Without the winch mechanism of the RAF tankers, the hose was stubbornly rigid and, once in contact, pilots faced a demanding joust with the short hose. Setting up an "S" shaped kink persuaded refuelling valves in the pipe to open and fuel began to flow but the pilot's task did not end with making contact. Once coupled, the pilot flew a precise formation position, maintaining the kink, ensuring that the transfer valves remained open. With little lateral tolerance, mistakes would be punished severely either by straining the hose, which made its displeasure instantly known, or with the ultimate insult of a broken contact. Refuelling from a KC-135 using the probe and drogue method was not for the faint-hearted and the risk of failure was foremost in his mind as Razor lined up behind the boom.

*

It had been only hours since the tasking had been received at the air transport tasking cell at Divisional Headquarters in East Berlin. The Antonov An-24 "Coke" transport aeroplane had been reallocated immediately and without question, the urgent priority guaranteeing that its original passengers would have a frustrating delay. It rolled down the runway at Berlin Schönfeld airport, the wheels retracting into the undercarriage bay beneath the turboprop engines and turned in a wide arc westwards, immediately appearing on the scope of the surveillance radar on the airfield at Gatow. Produced in huge numbers and by far the most common Soviet regional transport aircraft, it attracted little attention on the ground and, but for the red stars on the fin it was just another routine flight. Climbing out over the dismal East Berlin suburbs it set course for the neck of the corridor even though, with its Aeroflot markings, it could have taken any route across East Germany that the pilot chose.

The radar operator at Gatow hit the button on his mini-comms box making a connection with the Master Controller at Loneship GCI site confirming the departure. The message was immediately relayed to the intercept controller for Shotgun formation and, before the Coke had even entered the corridor, a codeword had been issued and a pair of Phantoms holding over the ADIZ were alerted, primed for their task.

Unbeknown to the Soviet aircrew, some miles away at RAF Gatow in West Berlin, a Pembroke idled at the marshalling point, its crew patiently staring at the runway caravan waiting for the agreed signal. In the blacked-out rear cabin the lone passenger would not be taking any photographs on this trip and tried to relax despite the sound of the piston engines that rattled the airframe. Suddenly, an Alvis lamp flashed green from across the runway as the Local Controller's instructions were relayed to the waiting pilot. There would be no words spoken over the radio as the frequency was monitored by the listening station across the boundary in the Soviet Sector. Their flight would not be totally covert as the flight plan for their route through the corridor had been coordinated and cleared by the Soviet controllers but the crew would not be offering additional clues of their movement or, at least no more than was absolutely necessary. The identities of the passengers aboard each of the flights were a closely guarded secret and the passage of the two transports had been closely coordinated by officials in London, Moscow and Berlin. The Pembroke would remain at the holding point until the An-24 had entered the corridor but would then follow behind.

Switching frequency the harsh Russian accent of the An-24 pilot filled the air traffic control frequency. His position report placed him safely on track on the centreline of the air lane and with everything progressing to schedule, the carefully, if rapidly orchestrated plan seemed to be working.

*

Razor listened to the commentary from his back-seater and felt a smug satisfaction as the probe slotted into the coupling in the basket on the first attempt. With such little practice at air-to-air refuelling and with the added complexity of the American refuelling system he was satisfied with his performance. He hoped it augured well for the coming mission. Above them, behind the window in the rear fuselage, a grinning "boomy" offered a congratulatory greeting. Distracted, Razor glanced quickly at the fuel gauge as the numbers increased, his attention rapidly transferring back to the unwieldy basket.

"8-2 over 10-6, fuel's transferring," he intoned as the precious liquid sluiced into the tanks in the wings. Without the external tanks the gauges quickly moved towards full. His watch showed 12 minutes to the "Vul. Time" at which point the formation to the north would press into the corridor. Their task was confirmed. He would stay plugged in for another few minutes to ensure that his fuel tanks were topped off before vectoring for the entry point which Flash had plugged in to the inertial navigation system. His own target was the central corridor to the east.

*

"Backwash, Storm Lead has a contact bearing 060 range 50, confirm I hold "Singers?"

"Singers" was the affectionate nickname for the Pembroke earned during its service with the Royal Navy because its engines had sounded like a sewing machine. The nuance was lost on the international audience.

"Storm, affirmative your playmate is at Flight Level 100."

"Storm is Judy," replied the "whizzo" in the lead F-4E as the formation approached the slow-moving transport from above. With the Mirages and the single pair of British Phantoms in trail, the ungainly formation manoeuvred towards the tiny Pembroke already holding position close to the northern corridor entrance. It would not begin its run towards Berlin until its defensive screen was in place.

"Storm renumber," called the leader. "Storm 1 to 4 adopt the callsign

Chevy."

"Chevy 2."

"3."

"4."

"Storm 4 to 8 adopt the callsign Renault."

"Renault 1."

"2."

"3."

"4."

Storm 9 and 10 adopt the callsign Bentley."

"Bentley 1."

"2."

From now on the individual elements had been assigned specific missions. They would fight as an element and recover individually if split from the main formation. Storm formation was ready to fight if the tactical situation demanded. The F-4Es of Chevy formation would run the offensive sweep ahead of the Pembroke and clear the airspace in advance of the package. The Mirages, with their superior slow speed performance would hold close to the lumbering transport with the British Phantom FGR2s remaining free to fend off attacks from the flanks. The aircrew had practiced the profile repeatedly during the exercise. They would now run it for real.

"Range 10 miles. Execute," called the WSO prompting the Pembroke pilot to turn onto a south easterly heading and aim for the entry point for the Hamburg air corridor.

The American F-4Es, flying a loose fighting wing, bracketed the tiny Pembroke passing 1,000 feet above as they entered the corridor, already challenging the Soviet controllers. Dropping the wing, the leader gazed down at his vulnerable charge silently asking for help from a greater power knowing that the events of the next 20 minutes might be as tense as any of the historic stand-offs between the superpowers during the Cold War. It was his task to deliver the transport safely to Berlin and allow the crew to land at Gatow. Once that had been achieved, he would extract his formation, hopefully without incident. At this moment he had little belief that he would be allowed to achieve it unscathed and, despite the assembled show of force, the thought of penetrating East German airspace in a combat jet made him nervous. Ahead of his formation the radars scanned the airspace looking for a hint of hostile activity. So far the scopes were clear.

The leader of Renault formation had, by far, the most difficult task. With the Pembroke flying at its maximum speed of only 150 knots the Mirages were unable to stabilise in close formation alongside. In order to offer the best protection, two Mirages would fly a rolling orbit turning away from the tiny aircraft but keeping within a mile of its location at any moment. Progressing along track, at least two Mirages would be in close proximity at every stage. Even so, as the pilots juggled with their grumbling jets at the minimum manoeuvring speed of 200 knots, they felt vulnerable and ungainly and were grateful for the Phantom screen providing protection around them.

As the American and French fighters began the run down the corridor, the British Phantoms held back, orbiting in a combat air patrol overhead Fuhlsbüttel south of Hannover. Their radars were also searching the airspace adjacent to the corridor alert for potential aggressors but the blank radar scopes gave a false feeling of security at what was to come.

*

In the battery control cabin on Letzlinger Heide Training Range, the Battery Commander of the Almaz S-300 air defence surface-to-air missile system, known to NATO as the SA-10 "Grumble", stared at the radar scope of the 36D6 Tin Shield surveillance radar. Outside his command vehicle, the 30N6 Flap Lid fire control radar focussed on a specific area and electronic commands were already passing to the 5P85 launch vehicles which housed the massive 48N6E missiles in their sealed containers. Optimised to detect low level targets, the 76N6 Clam Shell low altitude detection radar towered above the complex ready to break out any targets which descended to low level. Today it was the medium level targets easily visible to the surveillance radar that interested the Battery Commander.

With its 175 Km range, most of the airspace out over the Air Defence Interception Zone and the adjacent Buffer Zone was clearly displayed on his screens. Equipped with the ubiquitous IFF Mode 3 identification system, used not only by airliners plying the airways but by NATO tactical aircraft, he had watched Storm formation as they headed northeast towards their rendezvous. Their Mode 3 squawks were translated by the combat identification system and, not only did he have a strong primary radar contact on each of the formation members, he held secondary radar contacts on each of them. Electronic tags, provided thoughtfully by the NAOT jets, identified the individual aircraft and showed their heights. Only if they turned off their squawks would he need to employ the full combat capability of his battery. He was confident he would cope under either condition.

In the ensuing minutes there would be drama. His orders were clear and had been reinforced by a visit from a KGB officer to ensure he was under no illusions. His original orders to conduct a further test firing had been superseded and he would be given free rein. Airliners would be allowed free passage but if a tactical formation was to press its luck and fly down the corridor he had authorisation to engage. He had waited and trained for this moment for years.

With a range of 75 Km, the missiles could cover most of the northern corridor from his present location. He wished for the later standard missiles already under development which would extend the range out to 90 Km but, for now, he would accept the minor limitation. Able to track and launch against multiple targets, he had been warned of the likely presence of friendly East German Mig-21 fighters from Trollenhagen which might also be tasked against potential aggressors. Deployed forward to Parchim to be closer to the operational area they were within easy range of the northern corridor. Soviet Mig-21s had also been repositioned and the normal order of battle was becoming confused. His role was to make a statement and he was to select a suitable candidate and make sure it did not return to the airbase at Wildenrath in the enemy rear area. He was utterly confident of his ability to do so. The fact that his system was new went in his favour. It was doubtful whether NATO were even aware of his capabilities yet and his carefully orchestrated test programme would have ensured that stray electronic emissions would have been protected from inquisitive listening posts. He was confident that the NATO countermeasures designers could not yet have produced programs for their jamming pods as all the earlier testing had been on secure test ranges in Mother Russia. Even if they had, he had innovative new circuits that he could employ which would negate even the most capable jamming system fielded operationally in the West. If, or should he say when, he decided to fire he would commit two missiles to increase the probability of kill making the outcome a formality.

He designated the lead element of Storm formation entering the four F-4Es into the tracking computer and symbols appeared on his tactical displays as the Flap Lid radar took a closer interest in their progress tagging them as hostile. He was quietly confident that the radar warning receivers in the NATO combat aircraft would probably not even discern his interest, hidden as it was in the background electronic clutter.

*

The two Soviet Mig-21 Fishbed Deltas sat on the operational readiness platform at Stendal airfield, the burnished aluminium airframes shining in the bright sunlight, the red stars prominent on the fins. Underneath each wing the single weapons pylon carried an AA-2 Atoll infra-red guided missile. The operational readiness platform, set back a short distance from the main runway, edged onto the northern taxiway north of the threshold of Runway 08 and lay within a short taxi distance. Next to the concrete hard standing a small camouflaged caravan had been towed into place and the two pilots lounged on easy chairs which had been pulled outside to take advantage of the warm sunshine.

The briefing had been sparse when they arrived from their home base at Cochstedt but they were used to "mushroom syndrome" - kept in the dark and fed on fertiliser. Given their current circumstances there were few complaints. A small samovar steamed away in the corner of the readiness caravan and hot drinks appeared whenever they desired. Meals appeared regularly unlike normal day-to-day life at Cochstedt. Two more Mig pilots had flown in and they had watched with interest as the An-2 Colt biplane touched down and taxied over to the operations complex. The ungainly piston-engined biplane was a marked contrast to their own sleek fighter jets. The reinforcements would cover the night shift and they had been secretly happy that they had drawn the day shift as the briefing suggested that little or no activity was expected once darkness fell. The pilots hoped to spend the night shift in a local bar drinking German ale. They had been given Ostmarks to pay their way; a rare treat.

Communications were rudimentary and the solitary squawk box positioned prominently on the table in the caravan had remained, blissfully, silent. In true Soviet Air Force style it was adequate rather than glitzy. If a scramble message came they would be brought to cockpit readiness and their radios and data links in the Migs would give them all the information they needed. Once airborne their every move would be choreographed by the controller on the ground leaving little latitude for original thought. The tactics would be dictated by doctrine with responses determined by battle managers on the ground. Their job was as "Driver Airframes Mark 1" and they would follow the controllers bidding implicitly. In the meantime, they relaxed in the sun and watched a pair of Hind Delta attack helicopters clatter off the airfield and head south.

*

The operations room at Teufelsberg in Berlin was a hive of activity and, since the air defence communications circuits had sparked into life a short time ago, the analysts had been busy. With the operation underway in the Berlin corridors, one small omission or one missed keyword might be catastrophic, the implications profound. None of the junior airmen wished to be the one to make the grave mistake. An analyst listened intently to an exchange on a 16th Tactical Air Army frequency between an intercept controller and the Allocator at Divisional Headquarters. The analyst was thoroughly fluent in Russian but the rapid-fire exchange was testing even his skills and the conversation had turned decidedly technical. The gist was that the progress of the NATO formation to the north and the presence of the fighters in the air lanes was causing consternation. It was at that moment that he registered the Russian word for "scramble" shortly followed by the name "Stendal". It didn't make sense. Stendal was a helicopter base and normally operated Mil-8 Hip transport and Mil-24 Hind attack helicopters. Surely they could not imagine using a Hind against the

Pembroke? Or could they? He glanced up at the tote on the operations room wall focussing on the symbol for Stendal airfield. Sure enough two plots had appeared on the display south of the airfield tracking south easterly. Their heading would take them to a point well ahead of the NATO package which was approaching Letzlinger Heide Training Area. It still didn't make sense. A scramble order had, seemingly, been issued yet these contacts must have been airborne for some minutes. He hit the button on his communications panel querying the identity of the tracks and received confirmation that the two Hind Deltas were airborne from Stendal. There was no information on their destination. The jigsaw was incomplete. He could be confident in the identification. They were, after all, receiving a direct feed from the Soviet air defence picture provided courtesy of a tap through a local telephone exchange at Neuruppin airfield, however, that was a detail that presently didn't feature high on his priority list. He scratched his head searching for inspiration.

*

The squawk box in the cabin made a noise sounding remarkably like a strangled chicken but it was enough to stimulate action as the pilots jumped to their feet and ran for the cockpits. Behind them the mechanics followed. Haring up the short ladders they dropped into the cockpits and the engines wound up as a mechanic helped them strap in. Without delay, the jets moved off the chocks making directly for the adjacent runway threshold. Maintaining the momentum they rolled down the runway turning tightly inside the airfield boundary onto a south easterly vector climbing into the blue sky. Calm once more descended over the airfield at Stendal.

*

The Battery Commander in the SA-10 control cabin watched the lead element of the NATO formation push into the corridor pondering his tactical options.

"The main force is range 30 Km and inbound along the centreline, heading east at 8,000 feet. On their present track they will pass north of our position and they will be inside our minimum range for a short time," called the surveillance operator over the intercom link from the Tin Shield radar control van.

184

"Roger copied, do you have any IFF identification?"

"Negative."

"Roger, declaring targets hostile."

As he spoke, the battery commander watched the track designations on the radar scope change, adopting a hostile tag, coincident with his actions. He scanned the formation analysing the behaviour of the disparate radar contacts, identifying the components. He could engage at any time given the all-aspect capability of his missiles. Against a medium level formation unprotected by electronic countermeasures he had total tactical freedom. He would choose his moment as they passed abeam. The slow-moving gaggle at the centre was obviously the group of fighters protecting the transport aircraft, its slow progress broadcasting its identity. Ahead and behind, two other groups were flying at tactical speeds, clearly identifying themselves as escort fighters. They were unattractive targets for the ambitious officer.

At the briefing his instructions had been made clear. If fast jets entered the corridor he was to attempt to engage at least one target in order to make a statement to the western military authorities. He had, however, been warned off engaging the airliner or transport aircraft declared as a "no strike" target by the KGB. The escorts were an easy option but something was urging him to demonstrate the prowess of his new S-300 surface-to-air missile system. Selectively picking off one of the close escorts whilst leaving the transport unharmed would give him not only satisfaction but kudos. He still had time on his side with the main element not even at the centre point of the corridor. He quickly nominated targets in each of the three elements allowing him to refine his selection at any time. As he did so, elements of the phased array of the Flap Lid tracking radar directed individual electronic beams towards the unfortunate victims monitoring their position in space. He would select only one target and if the position deteriorated he would revert to the simple option. Of one thing he was sure; not all the radar contacts presently showing on his scope would return to their base across the border after this mission.

*

Captain Jules Dubois in Renault 3 had been struggling with his reluctant Mirage and, not for the first time cursed the American flight lead for giving him the close escort role. Whilst the Phantoms were forging ahead, his element was wallowing around the slow moving Pembroke making wide, lazy turns to stay in position. The manoeuvre had not been nicknamed the "meatgrinder" for nothing. As he watched a village pass below his wingtip he made yet another turn away. The timing of the turn was critical because too gentle, and his turn radius would increase and he would infringe East German airspace; too tight and he would give the Pembroke pilot a surprise on the next pass. He hoped the Pembroke navigator was keeping to the centreline because with only 20 miles of airspace to each side of the track the margin for error was small. As he pulled into the turn, the transport drifted along his canopy centreline making slow but steady progress along the corridor but the calm in the cockpit was soon to be shattered.

*

At that moment back at Teufelsberg, the analyst watched a second contact appear overhead the airfield at Stendal and his request for identification was repeated. Two Mig-21 Fishbed Deltas deployed forward from Cochstedt came back the response. That made sense. He had watched them land yesterday. If this was a scramble order their presence at the forward base was no accident. They had to have been deployed to hold alert at the helicopter base and the proximity to the northern corridor was significant. The pieces of the jigsaw were slowly fitting together. The Fishbed was a point defence fighter without the radius of action to allow it to spend long periods of time on combat air patrol. It was launched for a reason and he was starting to think he knew what that reason might be. If the NATO plans had been compromised, with mere minutes flying time from the forward base at Stendal to the edge of the corridor, the move was logical. With pre-notification of the NATO operation the Soviet commanders would have been able to move the fighters into place. He scrabbled for his briefing sheet checking which agency was controlling the NATO fighters. With the flying time to the potential intercept point measured in minutes there was no time to go through the normal protocol using the formal notification route. The controller needed this information; and he needed it now. The analyst could already sense the harsh debriefing from his supervisor for bypassing protocol.

Alongside, his colleague who was monitoring the SAM command and control circuits looked equally disturbed.

*

The Pembroke was making slow progress and the reporting points, nominated at regular intervals along the corridor, by the formation leader, slid past, excruciatingly slowly. Out front, the US F-4Es had completed the first run to the mid way point without detecting any opposition, their radars reassuringly devoid of contacts. As they reversed, heading turning back westwards, the main element popped up on the screen, bright blips showing clearly against the background clutter. Below 10,000 feet, the American pulse radars were suffering badly from ground clutter which flooded the scope and the lead WSO constantly played with the gain controls to break out the individual formation members. He prompted his pilot to descend to position the Phantom below the package. Looking up at the formation his radar was less affected by the noise and his picture improved. A gaggle of contacts at 20 miles marked the Pembroke and its Mirage escort. Some miles behind, the British Phantoms maintained their distance scanning the flanks. He resisted the urge to lock up and make life easier knowing it would give his colleagues an anxious moment if his radar beam lit up the radar warning receivers. Instead, the F-4Es adopted a zig-zag course scanning the airspace to the north and south checking for potential intruders as they closed on the transport once more. The screen was tight and the corridor remained clear.

*

Roy South and Nick Wilson in the lead British FGR2 weaved around an easterly heading steadying up occasionally, also scanning the airspace to the north. The intelligence briefing had suggested that, if the formation was to be attacked, the likely threat axis would be from Werneuchen airfield close to Berlin, although the Mig-25 Foxbats at the base were ill equipped for interception at low level. Their own analysis was somewhat more pragmatic and private bets had been placed on an attack from the flank. Despite the reassurances, there would be no relaxing until they returned west of the Inner German Border. There were a number of eminently suitable bases ranged along the length of the corridor from which deployed Migs could operate.

The wait was short.

"Bogeys, 065 range 45, low, fast," called the navigator from the other Phantom.

"Roger, hold position and report," Roy heard from his own back seat. Normally first contact conferred tactical lead within the formation but his navigator had overruled convention. At that range, the contacts were well outside the defined boundary and their instructions were to remain within the confines of the northern corridor unless specifically cleared to leave by the Sector Controller at the Loneship control centre.

"Jinking right, roll out 150 degrees."

The reason for the turn was obvious. If they continued on their current heading they would quickly penetrate the northern boundary giving an excuse to an over-zealous air defence commander to engage. Their turn would ease them back towards the centreline and they would take another look as they re-scanned the airspace to the north. In pulse Doppler mode the friendly package containing the Pembroke was invisible but Ray had paired his air-to-air TACAN radio beacon with the lead Mirage. The range on his gauge showed that they were holding position about 15 miles behind the main formation and they could easily accelerate to give additional protection if called in. At present, the contacts to the north were the highest priority and he anticipated the turn back, eager to know if the previous contacts were still inbound. The high speed contacts were unlikely to be innocent and could be vectoring towards the Pembroke with hostile intent. The next minutes would show.

"Bentley this is Loneship, I hold contacts to the north range 40, showing hot."

The ground intercept controller was becoming equally concerned over the intentions of the rapidly approaching formation and had chosen this moment to break the tenuous radio silence.

"Showing strength two, heading 240."

"Bentley, request instructions."

"Bentley, manacle, repeat manacle," came the instant response.

"What's that mean Nick?" asked Ray anticipating a fight.

"Hold inside the corridor, switches safe," replied the harried navigator, powerless to influence events at that moment as they continued to vector away from the threat. In the back cockpit his scope was empty the radar beam pointing away from the inbound targets. Only 35 miles away and closing quickly, a formation of potentially hostile fighters threatened their flank. It took supreme discipline to hold the heading, their nerves on edge. So much for robust rules of engagement.

"Bentley, Loneship, targets identified and confirmed as truckstop, I repeat, truckstop."

The constant codewords irritated the tense crew but knowing that Soviet listening posts would be monitoring their every word, the subterfuge had a purpose.

"What the hell is truckstop?"

"Bad news, that's a Mig-21" Looks like we have company."

"Oh great. If they want us to engage these guys we'd better hope they give us engagement clearance before we hit the minimum range for the Sparrow. If we get sucked into a turning fight with a pair of Fishbeds, the outcome is bloody predictable."

"OK, to hell with it, we're south of the centreline, let's turn back and take a look. If they're still hot we need to press Loneship for clearance to engage. If they get in amongst the Mirages we've got problems. Make the heading 065."

"Coming left."

The Phantoms jinked northerly, the wingman crossing through his leaders 6 o'clock in the turn, slotting back into perfect battle formation on the left of the formation, in tight, less than a mile. The radar search resumed.

Contact 065 range 30, locking up," he announced, all attempts at radio silence dispensed with. The deliberate targeting was provocative. If the Mig pilot was equipped with a radar warner he would soon be reporting the aggression to his controller and seeking instructions. Nick checked his own radar warning receiver for a response. It remained silent, not unusual against a Soviet Mig. With its simple pulse radar and flying at low level under close control, it was unlikely whether the Soviet pilots had yet detected the Phantoms nor if they were yet using their radars. They would be relying on vectors from their ground controllers to prosecute the attack.

"Loneship this is Bentley, confirm you still hold those contacts?"

"Affirmative, targets still inbound, fast, strength two, stand by for instructions," came the urgent response.

*

At the entrance to the central corridor Razor and Flash watched as their wingman pulled towards them, the top surfaces of the Phantom showing an impressive planform against the bright blue sky, the manoeuvre prompting another orbit of the combat air patrol. Despite receiving the codeword which gave the signal that the transport aircraft was airborne, the wait seemed interminable. A further codeword was needed to unleash them from their tether.

"Come on, come on," muttered Razor tetchily.

"Shotgun 1, Shotgun 2 is Zulu Ten;" a stark message over the ether.

"Bloody hell no, not now," he muttered frustratedly. The call signalled a radar failure common with the AWG12 radar and, as usual, it had occurred at the most inopportune moment. Without the radar transmitter the other Phantom would be blind, relying on Razor and Flash to guide them into an engagement. More importantly, without the continuous wave radar to guide the semi-active missiles slung under the jet, the wingman would not be able to launch a head-on missile. With events to the north sounding increasingly ominous they needed two serviceable aircraft. Fate was cruel and timing was everything.

"At least he brings two sets of eyes and four Sidewinders to the party. I say we take him in with us," said Flash evaluating the predicament instantly. The alternative was to send the sick Phantom home. "We need to maintain

190

mutual support." His conclusion was indisputable. They could not enter hostile airspace without the support of another Phantom.

"Shotgun 2 copied. Maintain position."

Decision made.

"Shotgun 2, deep joy," he heard from the nervous wingman. He understood the sentiment excusing the unusual lapse in R/T discipline. After years of training against aggressive opponents, his wingman's first live engagement against a Fishbed would be in a neutered Phantom. They could only hope that the main formation acted as a honey pot. The plan had to work.

"Shotgun, penetrate."

It was the codeword they had anticipated.

In the central corridor the An-24 Coke droned along, its pilot oblivious to the rapidly unfolding events.

Razor nudged the throttles forward and the speed crept up to 450 knots magnified by the proximity of the ground which flashed past beneath the cockpit as he dropped the wing to "Check Six". In the back Flash screwed around in his seat peering over the tail rapidly clearing the area behind the Phantom making sure a Mig had not crept in unseen before returning his attention to the radar scope. He knew that the navigator in the other aircraft would be blind without a radar relegating the other Phantom crew to the role of observers. The wingman had become a missile carrier rather than a predator. So far the scope was empty of contacts.

Their instructions given at the briefing at Wildenrath were simple. They were to intercept a pair of transport aircraft which would takeoff from Berlin and, once alongside, provide a loose escort ensuring that the passage through the corridor was unmolested by Migs. A target appeared briefly before fading from the radar scope and Flash adjusted his heading to run tight along the northern border of the air corridor. At low level, 10 miles was more than wide enough to allow them to turn tightly around behind the transport and set up a defensive rolling escort. The radio stayed silent as instructions were passed between the jets through a series of manoeuvres rather than words. A heavy rocking of the wings rather than a radio call announced each turn as they adjusted the profile. With contact on the target re-established and happy with the intercept geometry, Flash locked up and allowed the symbology on the scope to settle into full track taking in the additional data and analysing the information rapidly. The airliner was only 15 miles away when the quiet of the frequency was broken, the static distorting the transmission from the controller many miles away in the hardened bunker at Erndtebrück.

"Shotgun this is Loneship, confirm you have a contact bearing 090 range 15?"

The call was unexpected as the briefing had stressed that minimum communications procedures were to be used unless the Phantom crews were threatened.

Shotgun 1 affirmative, 090 range 13 miles, 8000 feet, speed 280 knots," replied Flash.

"Affirmative, that's your target. Change of instructions, Shotgun 1 you are clear to engage, I repeat, you are clear to engage."

A rapid fire exchange in the cockpit underlined the gravity of the change. The airliner they had been expecting to protect had been declared hostile. It was madness.

"Shotgun 1 clear to engage, authenticate Charlie Alpha."

In the back cockpit of the lead Phantom Flash stared at the target on the radar which was approaching the optimum range for a Sparrow missile shot. His attention switched to the jumbled mass of random letters on his kneepad. Those letters, his authentication codes, were the cryptographic key to the fate of the airliner. If he received the correct response from the controller authenticating the instruction they would have no choice but to comply. Irrationally, he was willing the reply to be wrong because targeting an airliner was every fighter crew's worst nightmare.

"I authenticate Delta," replied the distant voice.

"Is that right?" queried Razor, equally anxious.

"'Afraid so old mate. Master Arm to "Arm", check Sparrow selected."

"Switches live," Razor announced over the radio, immediately alerting his wingman to the change of plan. He ran through his own weapons checks, unnecessarily, yet again.

"Coolant's on, CW's on, Interlocks out, Sparrow selected, Ready light on, LCOSS caged, Master Arm to arm."

"Camera's running in the back, ALE40 on and programmed, your dot," called Flash prompting the pilot to take up the heading for the optimum collision angle. Razor drew the bouncing steering dot towards the centre of the electronic circle in his radar repeater display, the Phantoms now tracking unerringly towards the still invisible Soviet transport.

"Range 10 miles, stand by, I'll call you in range. We'll take the shot at five miles. We'll commit two missiles."

The crew had slotted into a carefully rehearsed routine no longer questioning the morals of their instructions. Two missiles from the lead Phantom would increase the probability of kill given that the second Phantom would be unable to launch a Sparrow without a radar. Further deliberation was wasted as others far higher up the decision chain had determined the outcome of this scenario and the result was inevitable.

"Range 7, stand by."

Razor tensed, his finger poised on the trigger, monitoring the passage of the target moving rapidly towards them. The steering error circle on the radar scope grew as the simplistic weapons computer registered the increasing probability of kill increasing the latitude for manoeuvre. He made one last check of the switches. All was primed.

"Range five, Fox 1," called Flash from the back seat prompting a tightening of the pilot's trigger finger. There as a momentary pause as the electronic command was passed to the Sparrow in the semi-conformal housing under the fuselage. The pulse initiated the tiny gas grain generator, simultaneously activating a hydraulic ram to push the missile away from the underbelly into the airflow. The lanyard stretched out to its limit, eventually breaking under the strain allowing the missile motor to fire. Released from its restraints the rocket efflux powered the missile on its commanded course away from the jet, the electronics sensing the target which had been primed in its electronic memory before launch. The missile sped away following the reflected signal from the continuous wave radar still locked to the target. As its electronic brain interpreted the guidance commands from the Phantom's radar the missile corrected its course slewing, frantically, at Mach 3 towards its prey. The tracking time at such short range would be a mere 15 seconds.

*

The Russian Air Force pilot tweaked the heading bug making a fine adjustment to his navigation unaware of the incoming missile. His An-24 Coke, despite its apparent Aeroflot identity was, in reality, owned and operated by the Soviet Air Force. He was used to these covert tasks and regularly flew into western airports carrying passengers with more interest in military installations than business contracts. Without a radar warner he could have no idea that the Sparrow missile was inbound or that his lifespan could be measured in seconds. He registered the smoke trail in his peripheral vision growing rapidly and converging on his position, the missile motor still powering the Sparrow towards him. A second Sparrow followed in its wake, ready should the first missile fail but its presence was redundant. The Coke provided a perfect target. Its large radar reflection offered the missile an ideal source on which to track and the rock steady heading presented no problems to the missile autopilot which guided precisely to a point ten metres from the cockpit where the radio fuse in the rocket would sense the massive target and command a detonation. At that point and only milliseconds later the warhead burst from its tightly packaged housing and the expanding rods formed a pseudo chainsaw, ripping into the fuselage of the hapless airliner, tearing into the bright red Aeroflot lettering. With the integrity of the thin skin destroyed, the airliner broke up instantly and entered its terminal dive. The main section of the airframe plunged into a wood, the aviation fuel soaking the branches and starting fires in the dry canopy. Smaller fragments rained down littering the surrounding area turning the tranquil forest into a scene more befitting a scrap yard. After the wrenching cacophony calm returned and, very soon, all that could be heard was the brittle crackling of burning wood.

*

"These guys are fast," muttered Nick Wilson in the leading British Phantom in Bentley formation in the northern corridor.

"Battle pair, one mile spread," he heard from across the formation, his wingman monitoring the inbound targets providing a tactical air picture now that his leader had locked up. Time was becoming critical and if they were to engage they would only get one chance. Six to eight miles was the heart of the firing envelope for the Sparrow at these heights but, once the target closed inside two miles, it would be inside the minimum range. At that moment they would be committed to an air combat engagement against a formidable opponent which was much more agile than the venerable Phantom. More nerve-racking, their immediate fate was in the hands of the controller on the ground and the radio had fallen silent. The aircrew could not care less that the controller was at that very moment coordinating an engagement clearance with the battle staff in the control and reporting centre. They needed a decision so that they could dictate the tactics and they needed it instantly. With combined closing speeds of over 1,000 miles per hour time was short. It was the worst way to enter a fight. The range hit 15 miles.

"Loneship, range 15 request instructions," urged the increasingly nervous pilot.

"Bentley I'm working it, stand by," came the equally frustrated response.

Roy South had a big decision and it was not one for him alone. His navigator had an equal say in the outcome.

"Do we engage without clearance?" he asked knowing the answer as he asked the question.

"Negative," came the blunt reply. It would have been his answer to the same question.

"Agreed. OK so they will call the shots. If we blow through, they press and get in amongst the transport element. If we engage and make them turn at least it will tie them up. We'll bug out at the earliest opportunity. Happy?"

"Happy, let's do it. There's no reaction to the lock. They're still crossing ahead so they're vectoring onto Renault and the Pembroke. Bring it starboard 30 for cut off."

"Coming starboard."

"High speed, now up at 500 knots."

Loneship, instructions," harried South, the stress readily apparent in his voice despite the distortion of the UHF frequency. As he spoke the Phantom entered East German airspace. If they turned now they would present their tails to a Mig-21 with apparently hostile intent leaving themselves open to attack. If they executed a maximum rate turn, the Migs would be only a few miles behind and they would be vulnerable to the Atoll infra-red missiles. South was left with no choice. He eased the Sparrow steering dot into the centre of the aiming circle on the radar scope and pressed on towards the approaching bogeys setting up a collision course.

"Range 10," called his navigator; "Loneship instructions," he repeated over the radio by now more in hope than in expectation.

"Bentley, manacle, I repeat manacle."

Manacle was the codeword denying them clearance to engage.

"Oh great," muttered South. They had already penetrated East Germany without clearance and now they were deprived of their primary weapon. From now on, they could only fire in self defence and then only if fired upon. It was Hobson's choice.

"Looks like Plan B," he conceded. "Bentley, no shot, repeat, no shot," he called to the wingman anxious that his number two did not pre-empt the engagement.

The steering circle on the radar expanded, a prompt that he was entering the perfect launch envelope for the Sparrow but he held his trigger finger clear, reluctantly watching the circle collapse listening to the commentary from the back seat as his navigator tried to talk him into a visual acquisition. That a Mig-21 was only a few miles ahead filled him with trepidation. He stared through the cluttered windscreen moving his head around the ironwork checking the area obscured by the canopy arch, straining to see the tiny Mig a few miles away.

"Tally Ho, one o'clock range three miles, engaging."

It was his own voice. Unreal. He snatched the stick to the right simultaneously dropping the wing to keep the tiny opponent in sight. The tiny dot moved into a clear area of the canopy and he strained his eyes against the bright sunlit background to keep sight. As he presented his belly to his wingman, the other Phantom pulled hard towards, manoeuvring through his 6 o'clock, already making angles on the Mig which pressed on in a doggedly straight line towards the main formation. At that moment he broke out the second Mig.

"No reaction, bogeys extending south," he called. "Renault, heads up, bogeys inbound high speed, we're 8 miles northwest," he said checking his range from the main formation on his air-to-air TACAN. He could imaging the nervous tension in the Mirages who were wallowing in their attempts to stay with the Pembroke. He hoped his warning would allow them to pick up fighting speed before the Migs arrived.

*

To the south Razor and Flash could only watch as the airliner hit the ground exploding in a ball of flame.

"Shotgun, Loneship further contact 090 range 10 miles."

"Oh jeez, what now," muttered the chastened pilot.

"Your instructions are to intercept and shepherd the contact back to base."

"Roger Shotgun copies, shepherd to base, willco."

The surge of relief was palpable, the chastened pilot thankful that he did not have to repeat the deadly procedure. Flash locked up the contact and began to talk his pilot on. The contact was so close that there was little chance to sweeten the approach. He would have to resort to short range procedures and he would execute a hard turn in behind once they were visual.

"Visual, it's a Pembroke," he heard from the front.

Turning in, Razor initiated a 6G turn to pull around behind the lumbering commuter plane, followed by his wingman in loose fighting wing. Straining his stomach muscles ready for the manoeuvre, the G suit inflated around his legs in a vain attempt to keep the blood in his brain rather than allowing it to seep towards his toes. He felt the familiar signs of the onset of G as his peripheral vision began to narrow. A glance at the G meter registered a drift towards 7.5 and he relaxed slightly clearing his senses. His hands moved from the throttles briefly and he flipped up his clear visor, dabbing a bead of sweat from his nose with the back of his gloved hand. In the back he could hear the grunting from his navigator who was also countering the same symptoms noisily. He held the firm back pressure on the stick and the Phantoms entered a wide orbit around the Pembroke shielding it from unwanted attention. As they established the protective screen Flash knew it would be a long trek back to Wildenrath at 120 knots.

*

In the civilian air traffic control centre in Berlin frantic messages were passed as harassed controllers reacted to the loss of the secondary radar contact from the Soviet transport. Already, search and rescue services were being alerted and a helicopter was dispatched to fly along the route. A pall of smoke marked the crash site, its black tentacle reaching skywards and it would not be long before concerned witnesses reported the accident prompting even more phones to ring.

*

"Bentley, Renault this is Loneship, targets are hostile, clear engage, I authenticate November Golf."

"Check that Nick."

"That message confirmed, clear to engage, go switches live."

*

Twenty miles to the east the crews in the F-4Es listened, frustratedly, as the action occurred behind them. Resisting the urge to enter the melee the leader continued to clear the corridor ahead sticking to his brief which was that the Mirages would peel off as pairs to engage any threats which penetrated the outer screen. The remaining Mirages would continue to

198

provide close escort as his F-4Es sanitised the corridor ahead. From the increasingly frantic calls on the radio what had seemed like a sound plan in the briefing room was degenerating into chaos. As the range to the Pembroke reached 20 miles he prompted his wingman to turn, entering yet another holding orbit. For the time being he would stick to the plan.

*

Roy South cursed quietly. He nudged the throttles forward to max mil and the speed quickly increased past 600 knots as the pair of FGR2s ran down the Migs. With no reaction and the Migs still doggedly pursuing the Pembroke they had fallen behind and were over three miles away in a tailchase. They were out of range for a Sidewinder missile but, at least had been spared the ignominy of a "knife fight in a phone box" with a Fishbed. The outcome of that tussle may not have been so predictable. On his repeater display beneath his gunsight he watched as his navigator reacquired the bogeys, the two green blips showing brightly at three miles.

"They've tucked into fighting wing," he heard from the back. "I'm locking up to the trailing bogey to see if he reacts," the navigator called more in hope than expectation. The radar display in front of the pilot gyrated manically as the navigator commanded the scanner to focus its attention on the Mig-21. After more manic electronic antics the display settled and the full track symbology appeared.

"Good lock, range three miles, bogeys still running on 140 at 500 knots."

South rocked the throttles outboard into minimum afterburner watching the speed rise to 700 knots and, correspondingly, the fuel gauge begin to fall menacingly. They were a long way from Wildenrath and this engagement would need to be quick. He began to hope that, despite the navigator's belligerence, the Fishbeds did not react but what would that mean for the Pembroke? In the cockpit the noise and vibration rose in concert with the speed despite the acoustic protection from their bonedomes. They needed to close the range down to two miles before they could launch the infra-red missile.

*

"Coming left," Captain Alban heard in the cockpit of Renault 4 as his element leader turned to face the incoming threat. He had listened to the exchanges between Bentley Lead and the controller and realised that the Migs had penetrated the outer screen. If the controller had cleared the Brit Phantoms to engage this would be over now but as it was they had been put on the defensive. He rolled out and searched the sky with his Cyrano radar. Only recently graduated from the operational conversion unit and declared combat ready a mere three weeks ago, this was to have been his first NATO training exercise. It would be good experience his flight commander had told him and yet here he was facing up to a pair of Soviet Migs feeling, decidedly, unqualified for the role. He looked at the gaggle of blips on the scope and, in the absence of any guidance from his element leader, locked up the nearest contact. Beyond it, on the same azimuth, a further radar contact followed two miles behind.

"Thirty seconds to kill," he heard the call obviously coming from one of the British Phantoms, presumably in hot pursuit.

"Renault 3 and 4, steady on 330," he heard from his element leader Captain Dubois. Jeez, Renault 4 was his callsign. The pressure mounted. He watched as the weapons symbology settled in his gunsight and the firing indications illuminated on the scope. He was clear to engage. The call from the Loneship controller could not have been misinterpreted despite his relatively poor English. The controller had repeated the instructions in the clear leaving no latitude for doubt. He cross checked his switches, confirmed he had selected the Matra 530 semi-active missile and made a final check of the parameters. All looked good and he squeezed the trigger and paused. Within seconds he heard the noise of the express train from below as the missile emerged ahead of his nose, smoke erupting from the back end. It sped away towards its target.

*

"Rackets 12 o'clock", screamed the navigator in Bentley Lead struggling to digest the conflicting facts. Unbeknown to him the Mirage radar lock had transferred from the Mig to the Phantom; a cruel fluke as they had both been approaching the transport from along the same vector. The simple pulse radar had registered two vague radar responses and chosen the largest which happened to be the Phantom a couple of miles behind the tiny Mig. The navigator glanced at his radar warning receiver analysing the unexpected indications. A solid vector pulsed urgently on the tiny cathode ray tube denoting an I Band radar threat. A further pulse light glowed ominously accompanied by a forward quadrant CW threat light. It was the classic indication of an air intercept radar and it had launched a radar-guided air-to-air missile. But how could that be? The Mig-21s carried a Jaybird radar which operated in J Band. The indications were all wrong. Nevertheless, he had only one option if they were to avoid an early exit from the fight.

"Bentley, Missile break," he called on the operational frequency, unsure whether his wingman was receiving similar indications. An immediate manoeuvre acknowledged his call as the burners bit and the Phantom reefed into a spine shattering 7G break. His body was assailed by the pressure of the G forces and his head tilted forwards under the strain of his flying helmet, it's two pound weight magnified seven times. He reached his hand forward struggling against the G and settled on the control panel for the AN/ALE40 countermeasures dispenser groping for the dispense button. Punching the tiny button he released chaff into the airflow which, with any luck, would confuse the incoming missile. Still perplexed by the air picture he watched the counters in front of him wind down as the chaff bloomed in the airflow behind the Phantom, hopefully providing a false target on which the incoming missile would home. Coupled with the hard turn if the defensive response had been executed in time, it should break the missile lock. His brain struggled with the quandary. Why should anyone be shooting at them when the Migs were ahead and heading away. It was a mystery he never solved. No matter; they could do no more. The seconds counted down and the crew waited anxiously.

*

Alban watched his display waiting for the missile to time out when he noticed the closing velocity roll off. His limited experience told him that this was caused by his target executing a defensive break and it came at about the same moment as he heard the radio call from the British Phantoms reacting to a missile shot. Merde! He had targeted the wrong radar contact but how? There could be only one response and, fortunately, alert and with the help of an adrenaline shot, he made the correct decision. Grasping the radar hand controller he broke lock cutting off the guidance signals to the ill-targeted missile which immediately went ballistic starved of its electronic commands. The missile entered a tumbling spiral and headed for the ground 8,000 feet below. It was the first real test in his operational career but it seemed he had averted disaster but by a wafer thin margin. The Phantom would survive. He hoped.

The Mirage element leader faced up to the Migs checking his speed which had crept up to 350 knots. He would have liked more but the aircraft felt alive again. Peering through the gunsight, seeing nothing, a flash in his peripheral vision caught his attention. Staring at the fleck through the perspex it began to increase in size and he recognised the profile of the Mig-21. With its pointed nose radome and stubby wings it was hard to see and he struggled to keep visual contact. The Migs were moving fast and, if he turned in behind, it would be touch and go who got a shot in first. If he mistimed it, the Mig would launch against the Pembroke before he engaged the Mig. He had to catch the pilot's eye and stay between the Migs and the transport. It was too late to fire a head-on Matra 530 so he would have to intimidate his opponent if he was to close inside missile range for the Matra Magic. He pulled hard towards the tiny jet wondering where his wingman had gone just as the Mig crossed his nose reappearing in the other side of his canopy. He was pulling ahead of its nose and drove hard for a close-aboard pass hoping his wingman was following. The Mig did not react, its pilot focussed entirely on the small transport only a few miles away. As he passed beneath the Fishbed, there was a fleeting shadow as his canopy filled with the underbelly, the two jets passing feet apart at a combined closing velocity of well over 1,000 knots. There was a loud thump as his airframe was rocked in the turbulent wake but the encounter was over in milliseconds. If his intention had been to intimidate he had succeeded but had nearly died in the process. It had been too close. Dragging the stick over he dropped the wing, the planform of the lead Mig appeared on his right hand side and he pulled hard towards, holding the fighter on his canopy centreline. He snatched a quick glance over his shoulder and registered the second Mig turning away towards the north, disengaging. They were down to a single threat but an aggressive one. If this remaining Mig got in amongst the transport and its escort it might all be over quickly. He pulled the gunsight onto his target and released the infra-red seeker head of his Matra Magic into auto track. As the growl registered the heat from the Migs Tumansky jet engine, the pilot spotted the Pembroke and its remaining Mirage escort. The gap between the aggressor and the friendly contacts was narrowing and if he launched now he would have no confidence that the missile was tracking the correct target. The Magic was "fire and forget". Once launched it could not be destroyed nor could the guidance be interrupted. He cursed and held his fire. It was too risky. The possibility that he would engage the Mirage or, even worse the transport, was too high and he released his pressure on the trigger and held off. He continued to track the Mig hoping that his presence might force the pilot to respond but it pressed on, doggedly, towards the vulnerable Pembroke. The pilot was brave, he had to admit, but despite the persistence of the attack he realised that his tactics might be working. The Pembroke was shielded by a lumbering Mirage providing the final screen in close escort. As it blew into the formation the Mig could not manoeuvre into a tracking position further thwarted by the Mirage on the far side of the formation which turned towards, adding more confusion. The Mig pilot made a last ineffectual feint and flashed through maintaining 500 knots airspeed, the fleeting opportunity for a snapshot missed. It disappeared into the distance and the Mirages slotted back into their close escort positions like sheepdogs around a flock.

*

In the battery control cabin on Letzlinger Heide Training Range, the Battery Commander had watched the aborted attack from the Mig-21s. It was now his turn. He hit the direct line to the Flap Lid control cabin.

"Nominate target four. Engage with two missiles."

Huddled together in adjacent seats in the darkened cabin the engagement officers stared at the small displays as the target appeared, cued by the commander. The movement was fluid selecting auto track and double shot, allowing the computers to begin the firing sequence. Unless stopped, the launch cycle would run to its conclusion. The computer calculated the flight parameters checking and cross-checking that the target was within the permitted launch envelope. With the details confirmed, priming commands were sent to the 48N6E missiles already elevated into the firing position on the transporter erector launcher or TEL. The firing pulse followed a few seconds later and the first of the missiles emerged from the launch tube in a gout of smoke heading vertically upwards. The second missile followed moments later, the twin smoke trails marking its course towards the distant NATO formation. On the tactical display in front of the Battery Commander two electronic symbols showed the progress but at such short range the flight time was marked in seconds rather than minutes. The twin plumes arced over the apex and began to descend back towards the ground. Without advanced warning in the cockpit, the hapless victim continued in the gentle orbit unaware of the approaching threat which failed to register on the radar warning equipment. Steadying up on heading at a ponderous 200 knots the Mirage offered little challenge to the complex circuits designed to counter a testing opponent. The first missile passed close by, its proximity fuse sending a pulse to the 100 kg high explosive fragmentation warhead initiating detonation. The massive warhead fired out shards of shrapnel which ripped the wing from the Mirage in an instant. The airframe deprived of much of its lift entered a flat spin which rapidly increased in severity. Feeling that a flip was imminent and sensing rather than seeing the carnage around him, the pilot reached for the black and yellow ejection seat handle and pulled. There was a crack as the canopy separated and he was fired up the rails. Captain Jules Dubois in Renault 3 would not be making the long flight back to Wildenrath.

*

Elated at his success, the Battery Commander felt vindicated. Without jamming equipment he knew the NATO jets were entirely vulnerable to his missiles and, if he chose, he could pick off more of the formation as they tried to make their escape. With his Clam Shell radar giving low level coverage down to the surface he could track them throughout the egress. He had missiles to allocate, a Flap Lid radar which was capable and invulnerable to any countermeasures and the potential for more kills. Only his orders prevented further action. He had been instructed to make a point and he had done it surgically. He had not been instructed to start World War 3 and he suspected that the total annihilation of the fast jets might not be well received in the western capitals nor, more importantly, in Moscow. Giving the orders to stand down from full alert the personnel around him in the cabin relaxed visibly. On his surveillance screen the flight paths of the NATO jets were, as yet, unaffected by his intervention but he could imagine the confusion amongst the leaders as they worked towards the inevitable conclusion.

*

With the fuel rapidly diminishing after the high speed chase and the subsequent defensive reaction Bentley formation could help no further. Prompted by his navigator, South checked the fuel gauge which had decreased alarmingly.

"What's our recovery fuel from here?"

"Five thousand pounds staying at low level but we can save some fuel if we start a cruise climb once we're back across the border."

"Bentley is joker and RTB," he called to the mission leader pre-empting further debate. "Bentley, coming onto 300 and descending."

He turned his formation onto the exit heading retracing the track of the northerly corridor towards, Hannover still many miles distant. He considered cutting the corner because heading direct for the Inner German Border on a westerly track it would save many thousands of pounds of fuel but decided against the short cut. Although the Phantom had penetrated East German airspace to pursue the Migs he was not quite ready to run the gauntlet through the most heavily defended airspace on the planet. Following the route of the corridor, perhaps protocol and Soviet rigidity might offer a better chance of survival and, if he stayed below 100 feet, he might yet savour a pint of Dortmunder that evening. With his wingman once more in position in battle formation, the pair dived for the sanctuary of low level, the speed nudging 650 knots barely below Mach One. They could save fuel once they were back in West German airspace. For now, speed was life.

*

The mission leader's day continued to deteriorate.

"Storm Leader this is Loneship, I am receiving an emergency squawk in your area."

"Roger Sir, standby. Break-break."

The call was redundant. The strident wail of an emergency beacon on

Guard had drowned out talk in the cockpit. He adjusted his radio volume, distracted by the intrusive tone.

"Chevy, Renault, Bentley check parrots," he countered, prompting every member of the formation to check their IFF transponders. It was relatively easy in the heat of an engagement to make a simple "switch pigs" which would transmit an emergency signal to the ground radar unit. The leader had not yet assimilated the fact that a few miles away, the catastrophic impact of the Mirage was the reason for the warning. He assumed that the offending pilot was even now making notes on his kneeboard to cover his embarrassment at the debrief, chastened by his error. He was unprepared for the reality. In Chevy and Bentley formations relieved pilots realised that the mistake was not theirs and returned to their radar scopes scanning for more Migs. In Renault formation the reason was already abundantly clear and, with the leader's call redundant, the French element leader responded.

"Renault 2 remain in this area and check for a parachute. Keep me advised."

"Renault 2."

The Mission Leader finally caught on concerned not only at the loss but for the vulnerable Pembroke which was now unprotected.

"Renault Lead, Storm Lead, confirm aircraft down?"

"Affirmative, stand by."

As instructed, the wingman detached from the lumbering formation accelerating ahead and reefing into a hard turn back towards the pall of smoke that marked the crash site. As he passed the wispy column he entered a tight orbit looking down at the impact point. The Mirage had thrown up a gout of earth and debris as it had struck the ground and flash fires had started around the crater as aviation fuel splattered tinder dry scrubland setting it alight. The pilot widened his orbit scanning the sky for a 'chute but seeing nothing. In his headset the incessant bleep of the personal locator beacon pierced the silence on the emergency distress frequency, although the fact the beacon was transmitting gave him some hope that his colleague had survived. Another transmission on the tactical frequency temporarily overrode the beacon.

"Storm Lead this is Loneship, inferno, I say again inferno."

More codewords.

"Confirm that's our clearance to go hot pursuit?" the leader in the distant F-4E said to his WSO.

"Affirmative, looks like the stakes ramped up a level." One simple codeword unleashed the formation. They were clear to penetrate East German airspace and, if threatened again, would no longer be quite so compliant. Unfortunately, the clearance was too late and the indecision had cost dearly.

The Mirage pilot in Renault 4 continued to scan the countryside for the tell tale sign of a parachute canopy but to no avail.

*

The pair of Hinds hovered at the edge of a small wood, 60 Km from Berlin, their rotors kicking up a cloud of debris. Behind the tall trees they were hidden from view from the approaching NATO formation and, being stationary, were invisible on radar. The crews watched the approaching formation of camouflaged Phantoms recognising them as American, as they made a tight turn overhead and flew back westerly. On the tactical frequency the Soviet controller broadcast the progress of the element containing the transport. It seemed from the calls that further fighters were tucked in close providing a screen which the Hind crews would have to penetrate to reach their goal. Hopefully, the tactics they had briefed would leave little chance for the fighter pilots to spot their approach and they would achieve a kill before being spotted. After that it was every man for himself and survival would be the aim. The Hind attack helicopter was well suited to the guerrilla tactics.

As the range wound down inside 10 Km, the leader popped up above the tree tops and looked west. He could see the gaggle at about 3,000 metres, the Pembroke transport standing out clearly, its white fuselage bright against the blue background. Still too soon. He would wait until the formation passed overhead and remain invisible until the moment when they popped up from directly underneath the formation. The distinctive delta wing planform of a French Mirage flashed as it peeled away from the transport orbiting slowly in its defensive holding pattern. He had spotted Alban's lone Mirage and knew enough about fixed wing aircraft to be sure that the pilot was struggling with the handling at such a slow speed. It was not a limitation for his own machine and he would use that to his advantage. Easing back down to a few metres above the ground, biding his time, he waited for the precise moment.

*

The leader of Renault formation was rattled by the loss of the Mirage but there was still a job to do. He watched the F-4Es pass overhead and extend westerly, their smoking J-79 engines marking their passage. With the range to the end of the corridor winding down he expected to make one last pass towards the east before they made their exit back along the corridor. For him that moment could not come quick enough. Already he sensed his career slipping away.

*

As the NATO formation approached the overhead the lead Hind pilot made a curt call on the radio and, in unison, the pair of helicopters lifted and began an in-place turn, gaining height rapidly. The intervention of the surface-to-air missile had come as a surprise but it had worked in his favour. A smoke pall marked the crash site some miles distant and it had already drawn some of the Mirages away leaving just one in close proximity to his target. The bellies of the Mirages above were visible which meant that there was no way that the helicopters could be seen from the fighter cockpits. They climbed vertically from below as the gunners in the front cockpits trained the GSh-23 chain guns on the lumbering transport. They would have one firing opportunity before the tables were turned and they became the hunted, heavily outnumbered by the fighters. He hoped the American Phantoms did not re-commit.

*

Stunned by the loss of the Mirage and still listening to the confused exchanges on the radio, Alban in the defensive screen steadied up and dropped his wing looking back inwards towards the Pembroke clearing the airspace beyond the formation. As he stared past his charge, a flash in his peripheral vision caught his attention and he glanced downwards, stunned to see a Hind Delta attack helicopter rising rapidly towards the formation. His outward turn had shielded the approaching helicopters and, but for his clearing turn, he would not have seen them. His response was instant.

"Renault, bogeys immediately below, engaging."

He pushed the throttle forward and the engine responded immediately. The pressures and temperatures stabilised and he pushed it further into afterburner feeling an immediate effect. The engine complained, aroused from its slumber but the speed increased quickly and he dropped the nose aiming directly towards the approaching helicopter. The delta wing cut into the dense air and generated instant turn performance swinging the nose towards the aggressors. His Matra Magic seeker head remained stubbornly silent, the infra-red suppressors on the Hind engines masking the heat signature and, not realising that his missile was being inhibited by the countermeasure, he cursed and recycled the missile selector. There was still no response and the Hind begin to grow in the gunsight as the range closed.

"Switching to guns," he called to the other element which had responded to his call positioning in his 5 o'clock and following him down. Selecting auto acquisition on his Cyrano radar the scanner entered a tight raster scan locked to the centreline of the Mirage searching a narrow band of airspace around the nose. Despite the heavy ground clutter which flooded the beam a brighter blip stood out and the radar locked up. In the cockpit the pilot registered the full track guns display in the gunsight and the reticule danced as he dragged the nose onto the Hind. With the helicopter rising vertically all normal rules of aspect angles and guns pass trajectories went out of the window. Steadying the gyrations as best he could, he squeezed the trigger and hoped. Gratified to see the rounds strike home and gobbets of debris erupt from the fuselage, the helicopter's ascent was instantly arrested. He could see the fall of shot from the chain gun in the nose of the Hind as tracer rounds marked the trajectory but the target for the gunner was outside his peripheral vision. He was unable to divert his attention back to the Pembroke and all he could hope was that his attack had spoiled the gunner's aim. With the Hind growing alarmingly in his gunsight he squeezed off a second burst before throwing the stick hard to the right and beginning his breakaway manoeuvre, flashing perilously close to the spiralling machine.

Behind, Renault Lead pressed home a follow-up attack with more rounds from his Defa cannon striking home. Smoke poured from the Isotov turbines of the Hind and it began to sink back earthwards the rotors slowing noticeably as it entered auto-rotation. With damage to the tail rotor it began to rotate uncontrollably. The Mirages orbited in a descending spiral watching the helicopter fall back to earth unaware of the second threat. The excited calls registering the kill distracted the pilots at the critical time and, unseen, the second Hind which had lagged behind its leader continued its climb. The gunner dragged his sights onto the white fuselage of the Pembroke and squeezed the trigger.

The cannon shells thumped home tearing holes in the thin skin of the Pembroke, miraculously missing any of the control runs and passing harmlessly through the fuselage. Anneliese Kolber screamed as the window shattered and thousands of tiny shards of perspex rained down around her, the projectiles scattering in the turbulent wind whistling through the cabin. She curled up in her seat, her head slumped to one side as another shell thumped into the headrest, narrowly missing her head, shattering the flimsy structure and sending more pieces of shrapnel flying into the air. Miraculously the high explosive incendiary failed to detonate. She screamed as she felt a warm sensation and a red stain blossomed on her thigh. She closed her eyes and passed out.

In the cockpit of the Pembroke the crew faced an even greater challenge as the warning claxon alerted them to the problem. The fire light illuminated on the right engine and the Captain in the left hand seat quickly ran through the bold face drills feathering the propeller. The navigator in the right seat screwed around looking back at the damaged cowling immediately registering the plume of smoke trailing behind. Flames flickered.

"Fire on the right," he called pointlessly, his frantic actions emphasising the urgency.

"OK, shutting down the right. Let me know what you see."

Flicking a few more switches and dragging the throttle back to the off position killing the electrical power to the smoking nacelle, he twisted the fuel cock to the closed position.

"It's still on fire . . . . . no wait."

The fire light flicked off.

"It's out. Looking good. We should divert," he suggested to the navigator, "but screw that for a game of soldiers. How far is Gatow?"

"I make it another 40 miles."

"By the time we sort this out it'll be time to begin the recovery. We'll press for Berlin. . . . . Unless this bastard has other plans for us," he added.

*

The Mission Leader was stifling his frustration. Not only had his own formation not been involved in any of the action, he had listened in shock as the Mirage had been taken out by the SAM. Now the remaining Mirages were heavily engaged. A new column of smoke marked the latest action and joined the original plume, black against the horizon. He had considered pitching into the fight but the Mirages seemed to be coping with the helicopter if that was indeed the newest challenge. He could not know whether there was another attack imminent. So far the Soviets had coordinated attacks by Migs, a Hind and a SAM. There might be more to come and he had to be prepared. An excited call on frequency announced the kill on the Hind prompting him to call a turnabout. He pulled towards his wingman and within seconds they were bearing down on the melee. He hoped he was not adding to the confusion. The air-to-air TACAN showed 12 miles to the Pembroke and he assumed the Mirages were in close proximity. Sure enough, a group of contacts appeared on his radar as his WSO painted the formation.

"I've got a further contact bearing easterly at 6 miles coming towards," his WSO announced.

"Lock it up and call it," he snapped stating the obvious. "See if you can get an ident on TISEO."

The Northrop AN/ASX-1 Target Identification Set Electro-Optical, commonly known as TISEO was an electro-optical telescope integrated into the weapon system mounted in a bulbous housing on the wing of the F-4E. Cued by the radar, locking up to the target provided passive optical tracking. Within seconds the WSO was looking at an image of a Hind helicopter on his tactical screen.

"Jeez it's a Hind. Where did that come from? It looks like he's bugging out. He's at 5,000 feet descending."

"Confirm we've got a good lock?"

"Affirmative, good lock."

The pilot flicked the weapon selector to Sparrow, pulled the Sparrow steering dot into the centre of the radar tube and pulled the trigger. There had been no finessing an intercept. It was a snapshot.

"It's time to get one back for the good guys," he announced sounding more like a gunslinger in a bad western movie than a fighter pilot. There was a pause and the crack of the launcher rams below the fuselage pushing the missile into the turbulent airflow as the Sparrow motor fired.

*

At the All-Allied Berlin Air Safety Center in West Berlin there was total confusion. Airspace control had descended into chaos and the normal service had been totally disrupted. With the complete closure of the northern corridor due to the presence of the combat jets and the temporary restrictions on the central corridor, the only route they had been able to use for the last hour was the southerly corridor. Constrained by the need to allow 2,000 feet height separation between inbound and outbound flights and with an upper limit of 10,000 feet, the flow through the corridors to and from Berlin had been drastically reduced. The flight schedules in and out of Tempelhof and Tegel had been suspended, the phones hot with irate airline operations managers vying for priority. There was no sign of an improvement. The northern corridor was still closed and the fighter jets were being controlled by a military controller from the control and reporting centre at Erndtebrück in the west. Civilian controllers had been expecting to use the central corridor but the unexpected arrival of a pair of fighters had thrown the situation into chaos. A British Airways flight inbound to Tempelhof was still holding near Celle and was threatening to divert to Düsseldorf unless he was cleared to penetrate the central corridor within the next 10 minutes. Only the southern corridor was clear but it was a long diversion for aircraft arriving from northern European airfields and with the reduced capacity they were simply not coping. The controllers had set up rigid height blocks to separate inbound and outbound flights but the airliner captains were complaining at being held down at very low levels causing a massive increase in fuel usage. Fuel burned unnecessarily cost profits and they were not happy.

The sound of the locator beacon on the International Distress Frequency had added a new urgency and the Chief Controller pulled out the contingency plan for a crash in the corridor. To the best of his knowledge it had not been used since a Pan Am Boeing 727 had been lost in 1966. He hoped that the updates since then had been tested.

He scanned the radar display trying to make sense of events that had merged into a jumble. First the Russian flight from Schönfeld had disappeared from radar shortly after the fighters had penetrated the central corridor. Next, the squawk from one of the NATO jets had disappeared and there were reports of a distress beacon in the northern corridor. Now the Russian controller at the East Berlin Coordination Centre was reporting an aircraft down in the area adjacent to the northern corridor. How much damage could a single operation cause? He had received permission to send a search and rescue helicopter along the route of the missing An-24 but it was the only helicopter available to him. He would have to contact the Bundesgrenzschutz to ask for one of their helicopters to investigate the loss of the fighter. He would need clearance from the East Berlin Centre to penetrate the corridor without a flight plan. It was shaping up to be a long day.

*

The Mission Leader hit the transmit switch.

"Splash one bogey, bullseye 270 range 38," he called. "Chevy formation bugging out west."

He hoped the Mirages had enough fuel to see the Pembroke safely through the last few miles to Berlin as he drove for the safety of low level, his wingmen tightening up as he descended. He suddenly realised that he hadn't checked the fuel status of his other element which may have been able to cover the last few miles of the Pembroke's flight. It was too late now as the speed tickled the Mach. It was some distance to the westerly neck of the corridor and all along the edges of the air lane surface-to-air missile sites peppered the route, in all likelihood being brought to readiness at that moment. In the back cockpit the WSO pushed the button on the AN/ALQ 131 jammer putting the system into responsive mode. If a Soviet SAM decided to lock they could only hope that the programmers had come up with something to counter the threats. If not, they may yet join the Mirage pilot in an East German field. The airspeed indicator nudged 650 knots as the formation settled at 250 feet over the flat, tree covered terrain.

*

The Pembroke joined on long finals for the easterly runway at RAF Gatow, smoke still streaming from the stationary engine, its propeller windmilling gently in the airflow. From the control tower, nervous eyes watched its progress, their binoculars trained on the small aircraft. There would be anxious moments as it passed overhead the residential buildings under the flight path on short finals. Rolling to a halt on the runway the left engine coughed and spluttered to a stop. There had been no indications in the cockpit of the incendiary round that had lodged in the engine fuel feed line its lethal cargo inert for now. A few minutes more flight time and the engine would have died, in all probability along with the crew and their precious cargo. The decision not to divert had been a good one in the event but the timing had been critical. With the electrics dead they could only wait for the emergency vehicles to arrive knowing that the smoke rising from the right engine should prompt a rapid response. As they watched, red fire vehicles careered across the airfield their blue lights flashing urgently.

*

Outside the small village of Genthin, a Zil truck pulled to a halt and a platoon of heavily armed East German troops jumped from the back, their rifles clattering. With a few barked commands they fanned out and worked quickly across the field towards the Mirage pilot who was struggling with his red, white and blue panelled parachute which doggedly refused to collapse. Captain Jules Dubois unclipped the connectors from his parachute harness and, allowing it to drift away, turned towards the approaching soldiers raising his hands.

"I am a French military officer, " he said loudly, repeating the words in heavily accented English. "I wish to speak to a Soviet Officer."

He received blank stares and a rapid-fire stream of German in response.

"Sowjetischer Offizier, " he repeated receiving a nod in return. The protocol of the Four Power Allied Pact required that all contact be conducted between the Four Controlling Powers. The East German guards had no formal standing but the Mirage pilot was slowly being convinced by the waving rifles that his bargaining position at that moment was weak.

With a barrage of rifles trained on him, Dubois watched as the NCO grabbed a handset from a trooper carrying a field radio. There was more unintelligible German and he lost interest in the parachute which billowed angrily in the breeze and took off. A trooper was dispatched to chase it down as it made its bid for freedom. Dubois sat down to await the outcome of the jabbering feeling the sharp pain in his back, the result of compression fractures from his ejection. With self-preservation kicking in and anticipating a long wait, he lay down giving instant and welcome relief from the stabbing pain.

CHAPTER 32

NORDRHEIN WESTPHALIA, WEST GERMANY

A civilian twin engined plane, scheduled initially to route from Berlin to nearby Düsseldorf, had made an uneventful flight to Wildenrath diverted from its original destination, the chaos on the ground to the east masking its deviation. On arrival it was met by a Military Police convoy and its passenger was transferred to the staff car for the short trip to the Joint Headquarters at Rheindahlen.

As the groundcrew bustled around the recently arrived flight it might have been a routine movement common at the air terminal. Life continued normally at the airbase but in the command and control centres to the east it was by no means certain that conflict between the two military power blocks, ranged either side of the Inner German Border, would be avoided. The next hours would be tense.

*

Many miles away in a house in an anonymous suburb of Bonn, Meier relaxed as best he could in the rigid, hard-backed chair. He was glad to be alone for a few moments even if he knew that behind the one-way glass his every movement was being observed. Since being detained at the airport, hours had been spent in cars and vans being shuttled around. No one had volunteered any information but the distances involved had not been huge and he had wrongly assumed that he was at the military headquarters at Rheindahlen. He felt a perverse sense of importance as the team of interrogators, obviously brought in for the purpose, had set about his debriefing. These were not run-of-the-mill military types and their technique was first-rate. So far, the routine had followed the classic good guy, bad guy script. One of the pair had offered drinks and reassurances whilst the other had been aggressive and strident, threatening all manner of pain and consequences. There had been no violence nor had they resorted to drugs; yet. He suspected the latter measure might follow quite soon. A third man wearing military uniform had just arrived.

His options were limited. From his own training he recognised their methods and was ready to employ the resistance to interrogation techniques he had learned so many years before. Realistically, the grilling could go only one of three ways and each had already been hinted at as the interrogators built up their case against him. He knew that he could never be turned and act as a double agent. No offer of money would never induce him to accept that way of life and he could not live a dual existence spying on his own people whilst maintaining a veneer of normality. He was used to subterfuge but that would be courting schizophrenia. He certainly lacked the political motivation to turn capitalist and his socialist values were ingrained and unchallengeable. Money would feature somewhere in his eventual plans but not at the expense of his political values. His morals were for sale, however. Equally, he could not allow them to send him back. Once news of his detention reached his erstwhile colleagues in East Berlin he would be compromised. Even if he resisted the canny interrogators and they chose not to opt for the violent tactics or the drugs he would never be believed. The assumption would be that he had talked and plans would be changed. A compromised spymaster was worthless and he would never be trusted to run his network again for fear of duplicity. If he tried to resist the interrogation he was not sure how long he could hold out in any case. The assumptions might become the reality. That left just one viable option. He had information; in fact he had rafts of information and could string out his debriefing for months. He knew the procedures and, as soon as it was obvious that he was not going to be released, his network of contacts would be shut down. He had no loyalty to the majority of those contacts. Some would be sprung and helped to flee to the east but only the more important ones. He could think of a diplomat in Paris that would squeal at the earliest hint of risk. He would be on a plane to East Berlin or Moscow as soon as the news broke. Others would face a more uncertain future but he suspected that it might involve law courts rather than a dark alley. He also had a trump card. There was one plan of which only he and a few other highly placed Stasi officials were aware. The revelation should guarantee some interest.

Afterwards, he would need a new identity and the chance to disappear somewhere in the West. There were plenty of nice places to disappear and a quiet retirement held a few attractions. He began to craft his offer and, if the plan was to work, he needed to make sure his offer could not be refused. He had one prime candidate for compromise and this particular man deserved all that he had coming to him. His next move would seal Peter Fehler's fate.

The British military officer who had introduced himself as "Windy" Gails and seemed to be orchestrating events sat down. The military uniform seemed somehow reassuring.

"OK said Meier," pre-empting discussion. " I have a proposal."

CHAPTER 33

THE MINISTRY OF DEFENCE, WHITEHALL, LONDON

The Assistant Chief of the Air Staff leafed through the report his brow furrowed, a quiet tap breaking his concentration as his Military Assistant poked his head around the door.

"Group Captain Air Defence to see you Sir."

"Show him in Peter would you."

A grey haired staff officer appeared from the outer office.

"Sir, you asked for an update on the situation at Rheindahlen."

"Yes Nick, come in, sit down. Do you want a coffee?"

"No thanks Sir, I had one before I came upstairs."

"So what's been going on over there? Sounds like a bloody cock-up to me. How can they have got it so wrong? They've left smoking craters over half the East German countryside if this report's to be believed."

"I've literally just got off the phone to Group Captain Operations at HQ2ATAF and he's given me the latest. To be fair on the crews, the Soviets were pretty aggressive and it has all the hallmarks of a set up. There was a pretty complex ambush in play and we think they must have had advanced information to be able to choreograph it quite so effectively. He's digging into where the leak may have been but it seems like an inside job.

Someone must have passed the details of the reinforcement exercise before the mission."

"Surely it must have been tight hold, wasn't it?"

"It started as a routine exercise Sir so there were no special procedures in place. People talk and, with the French and Americans playing there was a lot of traffic across the routine communications channels. We know some of them are compromised but if it is an inside job it should be easy enough to track down the leak. Only a few people were involved in the actual mission planning so he's confident we'll catch the guilty bastard."

"This incident with the new Soviet SAM sounds worrying. I have to admit I've never heard of the darned thing. SA-10 Grumble it says in here. What do we know about it?"

"I've been checking with Defence Intelligence on that one. The answer is not much. It's the replacement for the SA-2 Guideline system, their strategic SAM, and it's only just emerged from the testing programme. It's designed as a theatre-level weapon and will probably be used to guard Moscow for the first few years as it comes into service. BRIXMIS have only recently identified it and a team out on tour got the first sighting recently. Looking at the pictures I've been sent it's an impressive beast. It looks quite similar in layout to the new American Patriot system with a phased array radar called the Flap Lid. It has track-while-scan capabilities and it's able to engage multiple targets simultaneously. The whole thing is mobile but the firings were from a training range just over the Inner German Border."

"It engaged a Mirage didn't it?"

"Yes Sir, a single engagement. It fired two missiles but we think the first one did the job. They were both targeted on the same aircraft so it wasn't his day."

"No attempt to target the rest of the formation?"

"No Sir. As you saw from the report, the Mig-21s and the Hinds were coordinated with the SAM but there's no suggestion they tried to engage any of the Phantoms. It's all very odd because the formation was well within range of the system including the pair that penetrated the central corridor."

"Is someone following up on that?"

"Yes, the intelligence staff is all over it. Teufelsberg, the listening post in Berlin, picked up some interesting electronic emissions during the firings. They've been sent for analysis already. We should hear soon."

"Make sure we share that with the French and the Americans when it comes in."

"Teufelsberg is a joint facility Sir. The data has already gone out to Washington but I'm sure it will be offered to the French given the nature of the operation. They'll be doing their own assessments."

"The report says that the tracking radar wasn't detected by any of the radar warning receivers. That's a concern."

"All over that Sir. The electronic warfare experts are on it now. Even with the old technology we have in the Phantom we should have seen or heard something. It's a mystery why we didn't. I hope the project to procure a new radar warner for the Tornado Air Defence Variant will provide a solution. It uses new technology and should be more capable. I'll chat it through with the operational requirements people but we may need to throw some money at it and bring that project forward."

"So that leaves the actual engagements. Have you had a debrief yet?"

"Not yet Sir but first impressions suggest they did everything correctly under difficult circumstances. The tactics were chosen by the American flight leader but they seem sound."

"There'll be some political fallout even if they ran everything by the book. We can't leave Soviet aircraft smoking in a field without receiving questions; or our own for that matter. I'm expecting a call over to Number Ten at any time. The Chief of the Air Staff wants to see me in 30 minutes and I suspect we'll be quizzed by the PM. The Chief was called over there first thing this morning. The Soviet Ambassador has already made a "courtesy call". He's not happy by all accounts."

"All I can say Sir is that the clearances to engage have all been checked and verified. No one went off half-cocked and they authenticated all the clearances in the air. No one fired until the Soviets had made the first moves."

"That's good. At least it proves our air-to-air weapons work. I often wondered during my time on the Phantom whether the dear old Sparrow would ever get anywhere near the target. Looks like both ours and the Americans did the business."

"Indeed Sir. I wouldn't have given good odds if I'd had to use a Red Top from a Lightning F6 under the same circumstances."

"What about all the "spook stuff" Nick; can't say that sounds healthy."

"I think we'd best leave that to the intelligence community Sir. There's a can of worms there that I think we'd best leave unopened."

"Perhaps you're right but keep your ear to the ground. Let me know if we need to tighten up any of the security procedures on the squadrons. I can have a chat with the Deputy CinC at RAF Germany if needed. Thanks for the update. I'd better get ready for the chat with the Chief. I suspect he'll have some fairly specific questions. Make sure you're around for the rest of the day. I might need you to produce some defensive briefings. Did you bring those pictures of the SA-10?"

CHAPTER 34

A SAFE HOUSE IN BONN, WEST GERMANY

"I have plenty more details to keep you interested but there is one key agent who could hold your interest for many months if you want to bring him in."

"Go on Dieter."

"If I am to go on I want your assurances that I will be taken to London immediately. We are too close to the border here and it will not take them long to work out where I am being held. What I plan to reveal will mark me as a target for life. My masters in Berlin will not take kindly to losing what I am offering."

"I'll need to check with London that they could meet your request."

"Come now, making arrangements to continue my debriefing is well within your remit. Don't forget I have experience of these things. I want that promise now before I say anything more."

"Very well, I'm sure we can deliver you to London safely. We have facilities which are ideally suited to continuing our discussions."

"And afterwards, a new identity. Trust me, once you realise the significance you will recognise that there is no way I can resume a normal life."

"I will need to discuss that step. I'm sure you realise how difficult these things can be to arrange."

"Very well, my most important contact is a politician and he is a senior member in your own Houses of Parliament. Does a new identity seem like a reasonable trade off?"

There was a flicker of alarm in the face of the hardened negotiator which Meier was quick to detect. He had sparked interest.

"He has been pivotal in the recent discussions and slowed down the political reaction at every stage. All in the name of democratic caution of course but the truth is that he has been following a carefully orchestrated script. This man has been intending to veto western intervention allowing the Soviets to close the air corridors. What he did not know is that the military officer who was calling the tactics was working to his own agenda."

"So who is he? There have only been a handful of MPs involved in this crisis. Most of the officials are from the Ministry of Defence and the Foreign Office. Even so, it shouldn't take too much to track down potential culprits."

"Of course that's true but he has covered his tracks carefully to the point where, if you start digging too deep, you may uncover false trails. As I said, it is a carefully crafted plan following all the traditional Soviet disciplines of "Maskirovka" or deception. I can save you months of effort, inevitable if you decide to search randomly. You will have his identity only once I'm safely relocated."

"I need more to go on if I'm to sell this to my masters in London."

"There is one other matter. If I said I had access to the plans for a mass defection of East German combat aircraft and attack helicopters to the West, how would your masters take that news?"

The bluster in the interrogator's response was transparent and Meier knew he had hit the spot.

"Come now, you can call up a communications aircraft at a minutes' notice. I would even be happy to take the slow ride in a Pembroke from Wildenrath if it helps," he said with a wry smile.

"Give me a few minutes," Gails replied leaving the room, his pace too fast to retain his ultra cool persona.

*

In another room back at Wildenrath a much more relaxed debriefing was taking place and coffee and sticky German pastries were abundant. The pilot and navigator of the Pembroke relaxed in deep arm chairs, although Carl Pocklington was notable by his absence. Privately they were beginning to have doubts over the fate of their colleague.

CHAPTER 35

DELTA DISPERSAL, RAF WILDENRATH

The Phantom crept slowly backwards, propelled by the small tractor hitched to the nosewheel leg. As it reached the parking marks on the floor it shuddered to a stop. With the troops bustling around the jet beginning the turnround, the crew barely noticed a green-suited body sprinting in through the open clamshell doors of the hardened aircraft shelter making directly for the cockpit. He clicked the small button inside the hinged flap in the fuselage and dropped the internal steps below Razor's cockpit climbing up the makeshift ladder. As his head appeared over the canopy rail both Razor and Flash eased their helmets away from their ears to catch his words. The whine of the external power set in the confined space made it difficult to hear and he leaned in towards the pilot.

"Boss's office now," he said without fanfare and disappeared immediately. Razor began to unstrap, trepidation rising, Flash taking the cue from the visitor's frown and the hurried gesture. In unison they stood up disentangling themselves from the webbing which had held them in the seats for the last few hours and hurried down the steps.

*

"Come in guys. Bloody hell, I said "now" but you could have dropped your flying kit off on the way through."

Razor and Flash stood to attention in front of the desk still clad in their bulky lifejackets and clutching flying helmets.

226

"Drop that stuff in the corner gents. Sit down."

Flash had decided that attack might be the best form of defence.

"Look Boss," he opened. "I know this was briefed as an escort mission but the instructions to engage came from the controller. I recognised his voice on the radio. It was the same guy who had controlled the exercise sorties; no doubt about it. We followed all the procedures to the letter and authenticated the clearance to engage. It was all done by the book."

"I know. Relax Flash. There's no suggestion you did anything wrong. I've just spent the last 15 minutes on the phone talking to Group Captain Air Intelligence and there's a lot more going on behind the scenes than we've been told before now. You know what the intelligence people are like. They always keep most of what they know to themselves and feed us the snippets they think we need rather than ask what we want. In this case there seems to be a lot of politics involved and I'm sure none of us had the full picture before the mission. I wish now that I'd led this sortie but I was too wrapped up in preparing for Decimomannu. All this QRA activity hasn't helped and the Station Commander has been on the phone every five minutes. In any event, Group Captain Air Intelligence wants to update you personally. He's called a meeting for tomorrow morning and wants you both present. He won't give me any more than the broad details until he's spoken to you both."

"Why do I get the impression that we're being hung out to dry? asked Razor.

The remark earned him a sympathetic frown.

"It doesn't help that the Chief of the Air Staff in London is taking an interest but don't worry about that. Let's run through the engagement before you go. Tell me exactly what you plan to tell him and we'll make notes. I'll decide if there are any areas you need to worry about."

Less than thrilled at the interest from London, Razor and Flash began to recount the key points from the mission but focussed on the moments after they received clearance to penetrate East German airspace. The Wing Commander scribbled notes on his pad as they spoke, his demeanour relaxed.

"OK, that sounds fine. Don't fret. I've already been through the broad details with Rheindahlen and there's nothing there that comes as a surprise. You did what you were instructed to do. Now, do you know Carl Pocklington on 60 Squadron . . . . ."

CHAPTER 36

A SAFE HOUSE IN BONN, WEST GERMANY

Looking somewhat less flustered after his return, Gails resumed the interview.

"I've asked some questions and I should have the reply within the hour. Tell me about your involvement in Portnov's plan Dieter. It's important we know as much about his intentions as possible once we begin to negotiate with the Soviets. We can't risk another episode like this. Relations are too fragile. We need to be certain that this was the action of a loner."

"I think you can be sure of that, although he seemed to secure our help rather too easily. Portnov has always been a hard-liner and he's no friend of the West which is why he is well received in some of the more radical communities in Moscow. Some of the events which have shaped his recent family history go back as far as the Great Patriotic War and I can say without fear of contradiction that he's not a fan of the Americans. Certainly not the Germans."

"So why close the corridors?"

"Simple provocation. He hoped to appeal to the traditional hard-liners in the Presidium. There is an active group which wants to demonstrate Soviet power. I think they realise that they cannot dominate Washington but as a minimum they seek parity. Fortunately, and you might be surprised at my view, they are rapidly becoming a minority. Gorbachev is winning favour with his Perestroika movement and they fear that it may lead to German reunification. The traditionalists' phobia is that reform would weaken the military and Portnov staked his all to demonstrate that only military action could maintain the status quo. If he could provoke the West into an aggressive response it might be all that would be needed to initiate a major response. He predicted the likely reactions quite well. Nevertheless, he had no interim plans; it was all or nothing. Once the armoured forces which make up the North West Front cross the Inner German Border there would be no halt before taking the Channel ports five days later. The plan works only by maintaining momentum and then only if the logistics tail can keep up the pace. Portnov wanted all out control of Western Europe. A simple desire with massive consequences."

"So how close was he to success?"

"Maybe you know the answer better than I. It would have depended on reactions during the NATO mission. Any actions seen as aggressive or provocative might have been enough to provide the catalyst. My assessment is that his plan would never have worked. There are too many rival factions in the Politburo and I think his pressure to provoke a military attack might have been opposed. There are too many reformists who want to give Perestroika a chance. That said, it would have depended on how the factions in the Politburo lined up."

"Your insight is good Dieter. As it turned out, the crews were remarkably restrained despite losing a Mirage to a surface-to-air missile. A transport aircraft was shot down but the diplomatic reaction so far has been remarkably muted."

"What of Portnov?"

"We already heard from sources at the top that he was acting alone. Short of apologising they have gone as far as we could expect at this stage. The troop build-up has been halted and the first units are heading back to barracks. Portnov was detained earlier today and we think he's on a plane back to Moscow. I'd love to be in on that debrief."

Gails hesitated realising that he was giving away too much at this formative stage.

Meier reflected on the new information, seemingly coming to a decision.

"Let me assume that what I'm about to tell you will cement our agreement. I'm prepared to offer you the intelligence coup of the decade. Have you heard of Operation Beliebig?"

"I don't believe I have. Why don't you enlighten me?"

"First I need assurances about my future. I want to be sure that I can live without looking over my shoulder every day."

"For the right information I can assure you that we can take the appropriate steps to place you into a protection programme. Your English is excellent and we can help with a new appearance. You can disappear if that is your wish."

"As I said before, Operation Beliebig is a mass defection by aircraft of the East German Air Force, albeit only certain bases would be involved."

The interrogator's attempt to feign indifference failed .

"Let me explain and you will quickly understand. Bear in mind that many people in East Germany are not doctrinally tied to communism. They live under duress, particularly the more articulate in society. The plan involves Mig-21s, Mig-23s and Hind helicopters from a number of key combat bases. We exercise procedures similar to your own to protect our assets after a NATO nuclear attack. Every serviceable aircraft on base is launched into a holding pattern; in fact, even those which are only partially serviceable would be launched providing they can fly. Operation Beliebig would be executed during this phase of a survival scramble. Although the aircraft launch individually as soon as they are available to fly, doctrine dictates that, once airborne, section leaders are nominated from the elite pilots on the Wing. They would take command of the elements once in the air and control the remainder of the sortie. Normally, they would lead their element to new combat air patrol positions close to the border. The logic is that following a nuclear strike there may be more NATO combat aircraft penetrating the border to hit follow-on targets. If armed, the jets would counter those threats. If not, they would await the call to land and would then turn round, rearm and fly another mission. This would be where Operation Beliebig diverges from routine. The section leaders would take their elements across the border and defect to a NATO base. If all the potential leaders comply, up to 200 aircraft could be involved along with their pilots."

"But how would you persuade us that this should not be perceived as an all-out attack? If I was sitting in a radar command post and saw that type of build up I would counter the incoming raid with any forces available to me."

"There is no guarantee of course but once over the IGB, the instructions are that all aircraft would adopt NATO minimum risk procedures. The pilots would lower their landing gear and fly at 250 knots in a predictable flight path. The hope is that confusion and a delay in being granted clearance to engage might prevent action by the Hawk and Nike missile batteries within the engagement zones."

"It sounds worryingly risky to me. Have these plans ever been war gamed?"

"No, only a few key personnel know the full details. Most of the pilots have been kept in the dark but, having been Soviet trained, we are certain that they would be compliant. It is ingrained in the pilots from the start of training that there can be no deviation from either the instructions from the ground controller or those from the flight leader. They are indoctrinated from the outset to comply with direction at all stages during a mission."

"Surely you would expect to lose a few aircraft to Quick Reaction Alert forces and the border missile defences? There would be utter confusion."

"Inevitably, but the majority would survive."

Which bases in West Germany would be used? Most of the combat aircraft don't have the range to penetrate beyond West German airspace."

"A few key bases were selected mostly in the hinterland because large parking areas were identified which could accommodate a mass influx. I would need to sit down with a map to remind myself of the detail but I know Geilenkirchen was one such base."

"Who knows of the plan?"

"As I say, only a few key individuals know the full plan but I can recall names."

"How would the plan be executed?"

"There is a Master Controller at an Air Direction Unit close to the border who is briefed to initiate the plan. I would need you to secure his escape as part of the deal. Clearly he is in no position to join the flyers and once he had given the execute order his position would be compromised. There can be no negotiation on this aspect."

His mind turned to the former East German Colonel still languishing in Hohenschönhausen Prison in East Berlin. He would negotiate for his release when the inevitable exchanges of prisoners began. It would be good to have an ally in London, particularly one who owed him a favour. Gails broke his train of thought.

"So the issue of a simple codeword during an exercise would be sufficient to trigger the plan?"

"As simple as that my friend but my security is that you will never have that codeword until my future and that of the controller is assured. Maybe not even then. All you have to agree is that you wish the plan to be triggered and we can begin to document the detail."

"Why should I try to sell this to my masters? The scope for cock-up is enormous."

"Think of the windfall if only a few of the combat aircraft make it through. You will have examples of the latest export versions of the major Soviet combat jets for analysis. Think of the intelligence value of exploiting those airframes. You will have combat pilots whom you can debrief giving a detailed picture of training regimes and practices. You may even acquire air-to-air and air-to-ground ordnance as some of the alert aircraft would be armed. It would be a coup. A dividend of massive proportions and I can tell you how to initiate the plan. I have contacts at each base and would be willing to coordinate on your behalf. As I say, all I need is a guarantee of safety for the ringleaders but we would need to move quickly before my departure is broadcast. Are you interested?"

"What do you think your countrymen will think if they find out that you are

233

behind the compromise?"

For the first time Meier looked a little unsure of himself.

CHAPTER 37

HEADQUARTERS RAF GERMANY, RAF RHEINDAHLEN, THE NEXT DAY

The call to the meeting at Rheindahlen had come quickly and, early the following morning, Razor and Flash bundled into a rattling old Service Mini for the short journey to the Headquarters. As they pulled into the car park a near perfect "Diamond Nine" formation, albeit with a poignant gap, flew overhead framed briefly by the Headquarters building. The box-4 of American Phantoms were flanked in the leading vic by two British FGR2s with the three remaining Mirage IIIs tucked in behind, the hole in the formation marking the loss of the French aircraft. After the flypast the formation would split and each element would make its way home.

In the outer office Razor and Flash felt slightly out of place in their green flying suits wishing, ardently, that they were back in the crewroom at Wildenrath. Around them, staff went about their normal routines wearing crisp blue Number 2 uniforms, carrying pink-jacketed Secret files and looking, disturbingly, efficient. The instructions had been clear; speed was of the essence and working dress was the order of the day. For this meeting time was more important than dress code. The hubbub of the commander's office was relentless as the PA answered yet another intrusive ring, fobbing off the latest caller with well rehearsed excuses, seeming aloof and unapproachable. Group Captain Air Intelligence was busy in an important meeting, she explained, and couldn't be disturbed. Even a call from the CinC's Outer Office had been similarly rebuffed, albeit with an offer of a return call the minute the Group Captain was free. If this was a normal day both aircrew were thankful for being able to escape into the cockpit. Razor sat on his hands to disguise the nervous twitch that threatened his credibility.

The heavy panelled door opened and Squadron Leader John Silversmith, the intelligence officer appeared, beckoning for them to enter. Donning their hats the pair followed the receding figure into the spacious office, coming to attention and saluting smartly as they entered. Two other visitors sat around the small coffee table in the corner of the room and recognition was instant. It was Razor who reacted first and he surged forward but was quickly restrained by Flash. Carl Pocklington sat at the table alongside another man, both dressed in smart business suits.

"You," he snarled. "I thought we'd got rid of you in the corridor yesterday you useless piece of shit."

"Gentlemen, please. Let's lose the hats and sit down. Would you like coffee? I think you deserve an explanation."

"Well if it wasn't him Sir, who the hell did we shoot down in the transport jet?"

They were persuaded into the easy chairs, the tense atmosphere easing slightly.

"Not that it will help but that was an East German agent called Peter Fehler. You couldn't possibly know but anyone who saw him board the aircraft in Berlin would have been reasonably impressed with the likeness to Carl here. Not that we can claim any credit for that part of the ruse. The plastic surgery was done many months before any of the recent events. Carl was never intended to leave East Germany if the Stasi had been given the choice."

"So were they planning to substitute the new bloke?"

"Yes. The switch had been carefully planned, although I'm not sure they expected Carl to drop into their laps quite so conveniently as he did. Despite extensive training to assume his new identity there might still have been holes in Fehler's story so, apparently, Carl suffered a little bang to the head during his stay which was supposed to induce an element of amnesia. All staged conveniently in front of the captured Pembroke crew before they made their own, unexpected escape. It would have explained away anomalies or inconsistencies but, I must say, it would have been good to have the chance to debrief the chap to see how thorough they had been. We know they keep extensive records on all the aircrew here in the forward area so we missed an opportunity. I'm sure he would have been convincing. Don't feel too bad about his demise, Fehler was not a nice chap."

"What were their plans?"

"Oh the handler, a certain Dieter Meier, had plans to insert the "clone" back onto 60 Squadron where he would have become a prime source of intelligence. If they could have convinced the Squadron that it was Carl, every last detail of routine events at Wildenrath would have been passed back to the Stasi through an open tap. We wouldn't have known the source of the leaks. It's always difficult to track down an insider. It might have been the perfect plan but we had begun to have suspicions about Fehler some time ago, well before this latest incident and had him under surveillance. The Soviets knew nothing of all this by the way. This was a Stasi initiative."

"It's a shame Meier wasn't aboard the Coke. It sounds like he's a problem we can do without."

"Don't worry about him. His days as a spymaster are over. Meier was picked up at Cologne/Bonn airport trying to leave the country. He was compromised by one of his own agents, Anneliese Kolber. The "clone" was compromised many months ago in Berlin. We've already begun asking Meier lots of pertinent questions and his debrief will go on for many months. I suspect we'll have a veritable treasure trove before he's finished talking."

"So how did you latch onto all this, Sir?"

"Luckily Carl came to us when he began to have suspicions about his new girlfriend. Her questions began discretely enough but she quickly pushed for him to release classified information and it was at that point he did the sensible thing."

He turned to look at Pocklington who stared fixedly at the floor.

"Her story about not being able to get papers to settle locally didn't add up. She had already settled and the only thing preventing her making it a permanent arrangement was her handler back in East Germany. We were able to link Carl up with the counter-intelligence team and when the big offer came in, we were in the driving seat. It was quickly apparent that his girlfriend was working for the opposition and she was blatant about it once she'd wheedled her way into Carl's affections. That said, she was motivated by loyalty to her family rather than political dogma. Hers is a sad story but there's more to tell."

"What happened to the other crew members from the Pembroke?"

"I must admit, their escape in the light aircraft came as something of a surprise. We had begun making diplomatic moves to secure their release when they dropped in onto the green at a golf course up in the ADIZ. It was quite a flight home from what we've heard at the debriefings. They're safe and sound and no worse off after their captivity and should be back flying soon. Incidentally, the light aircraft pilot that strayed over the border has also been released and is back with his family. Sadly his flying days are over. The consequences of his actions cannot be ignored. I suspect he will be repaying his fines for a few years to come."

"I still don't understand the plan with the transport aircraft that we were escorting," replied Flash struggling with the intricate twists of the revelations.

"Yes, somewhat convoluted wasn't it? Carl was always going to come home aboard the Pembroke from Gatow. We told the East Germans that Anneliese would be exchanged for Carl, or should that be Fehler, and she would be put aboard the An-24 when it landed at Wildenrath to be returned to Berlin. In the meantime, we made other arrangements but we had to be sure Carl was safely back at Wildenrath. Having gone to all the effort to spring our man, I'm afraid there was no way that the An-24 was ever going to arrive intact back in Berlin after its flight to Wildenrath. They had to think that Fehler, was dead and believe me they do. The plan had to end. The circuits in Berlin have been buzzing since the incident and we're collecting some fascinating traffic between Moscow and Berlin. The chaps at Teufelsberg have been on 24 hour shifts since the operation began. It seems that the KGB and the Stasi are not the best of friends at present. We have some work to do to make sure that Carl's fate is covered up after his mysterious disappearance in Berlin but that's all in hand."

"But why did we put the main effort through the Northern corridor?"

"Pure politics and that part of the operation was real. We had to make a firm statement about our rights to fly the corridors. It was all a show of strength to assert our rights. What I'm telling you now are the sub plots that few others will ever hear."

"But that statement of rights cost us a Mirage and it's pilot."

"You all know the risks you take flying in Germany, Razor. The circumstances surrounding the loss are unusual I grant you but it's not an unusual event. We lost a Jaguar and its pilot only last week as you well know. The good news is that the French pilot is safe and we'll arrange an exchange with the Soviets quite soon. We have an idea who they would like to get back. We also have assurances that Dubois is being well cared for, although the Soviet line that he is being treated for compression fractures after his ejection is a little hollow. It's merely a delaying tactic. If their apologies are genuine we'll have him back soon. I don't see a show trial helping anyone and we can all play tit-for-tat."

"Well that's good. Can we tell the blokes back at base? It's been a bit subdued back there since they landed. All we heard in the air was a PLB transmission on Guard when the Mirage went down and that SAROPS had been initiated. The rumour mill is going flat out."

"Of course, and we should have thought about that. We'll get the formal notifications out as soon as the pilot's family have been informed. We're struggling to track them down as they're on holiday but the French air staff are on it as we speak. I plan to have the exercise, or should I say operation participants briefed on a cover story as soon as they land back at their respective bases. Obviously we'll have a good reason why you were instructed to engage the An-24. You will not be criticised in any way, in fact I think the CinC might be persuaded to endorse a little thank you for you. You'll be pleased to know that the media haven't picked up on it yet but that may be a temporary blessing. The loss of both aircraft was quite public and it can only be a question of time before a sharp journalist catches on.

You should expect to be trotted out to chat to them once the story breaks but we'll have the public relations people coach you before we offer you to the wolves. It will be a carefully crafted line but you'll be allowed to describe the engagement and we'll explain why we took such drastic action."

The pair fidgeted nervously. A combat sortie was hugely preferable to a press interview.

"Will Meier be sent back?"

"Oh no. Herr Meier is going to be with us some time. He's giving us some very interesting information already. Let's say that any of his remaining contacts in the West, if they are still operating, will be carefully handled. They will not be compromised and once we've fed them some snippets, they might begin to support a useful deception plan for us. You don't need to know the rest of the details."

"So this whole scenario was a set up from the start?"

"Oh no, the politics of maintaining access to Berlin through the corridors was very real. That's why I stress that the loss of an aircraft was a cost worth paying. That's the whole reason for holding the annual exercise. West Berlin is a strategic prize. The Soviet General who orchestrated the incidents is, or hopefully was, a canny politician and he was very close to provoking a response which might have led to conflict. Had the senior leadership in Moscow not backed down the outcome might have been significantly different. We were lucky. It goes without saying that everything we've discussed today has to remain within these four walls. I wanted to say thank you personally and assure you that what you did will have a significant impact on future security. Suffice to say that the real operational plans are safe and the parts which had to be compromised for credibility will be changed."

As they spoke, there was a knock on the door and Pocklington immediately jumped to his feet. An attractive woman was ushered in. She walked hesitantly and he rushed over to embrace her, protectively. The Group Captain coughed politely.

"Gentlemen, can I introduce Anneliese Kolber."

There was a stiff exchange of greetings and eyes were averted as affection between the reunited couple overcame formality. Their whispered exchange was hard to miss.

"I'm fine darling. It's just a scratch. I was hit by flying debris but there's no permanent damage. They put me on a flight back here as soon as the Pembroke landed at Gatow."

"You're sure?"

"Yes, I'm certain. There was some damage to the aeroplane in the attack so it couldn't bring us home. The crew is fine."

Flash turned back to the Group Captain breaking an embarrassing pause.

"So what now, Sir?"

"Carl won't be rejoining the Squadron. His role has been far too public and there would be too many questions if he simply reappeared. He will assume a new role back home and we have some interesting projects for him in London working for our friends in the Old War Office."

Razor knew exactly who those friends might be. Carl Pocklington, who had disengaged himself from his embrace, moved over and shook hands with the two aircrew. A look of mutual respect passed between them before he turned and walked away accompanying his girlfriend from the room.

"That leaves us to tie up the loose ends on the operational plans. We had to allow Pocklington to take a copy of Supplan Mike with him. As you know it has most of the procedures of how we would fight a campaign in our airspace. The copy that was compromised wasn't quite all that it seemed and was doctored with inaccurate information. Sadly some of it had to be real for credibility so elements of the plans will have to change. It was due for an overhaul in any case. We'll need a new combat air patrol grid and many of our pre-surveyed hides for the Harriers will have to change. Luckily none of the nuclear plans were included nor have they been compromised as those are much more highly classified. The concepts behind the plan are still sound and I suspect they already understood those well before all of this came to light but the success of the operational plan relies on detail. It will take some hard work from the air staff but a radical overhaul will limit the loss. It will take the Soviets some months to decide whether they have good information or not and there are a number of subtle clues in there which may lead them to conclude that the whole thing is a deception plan. Either way, it will keep them guessing for some time by which stage we will have issued the new plan. Anyway, please look surprised when the revisions hit the Squadron. For most of your colleagues it will be just another routine amendment. In the meantime gentlemen I suspect you will want to celebrate."

As Razor and Flash took their leave, their puzzled looks suggested that the resumption of normality might take some time.

"Thank God we're on the flying programme this afternoon," said Flash quietly as they negotiated their escape past the harried PA.

*

Carl lay on the bed in the Officers' Mess at RAF Northolt. The HS125 had delivered them to London as soon as the meeting had broken up at Rheindahlen and they had arrived at the airbase outside the capital inside an hour. Tomorrow they would move into a new married quarter in the London suburbs, the fact that they were not yet married overlooked by the Station Families Officer who was under strict orders.

"It's all been a bit of a rush darling. Are you happy?" he asked watching her expression change as she turned away from the bedroom window.

"Of course I am," she smiled. "I can't believe we'll be living in London. It's all so sudden and it's been a childhood dream of mine to settle here. This is a beautiful old building. Are the married quarters as nice?"

"Not quite so grand, I'm afraid, but we can always look for a house locally once we settle, if you prefer."

"I'd like that. It would be nice to live out in the community again and get away from my past. What have they said about your new job in Defence Intelligence? Do you have a start date?"

"Oh let's forget that for the time being," he replied, a look of contentment creasing his face. "They've given me a few weeks to sort things out before I start. It should let us adjust to our new surroundings."

"That's good of them. Look, I just want to pop down to reception and see if I can have them post a letter. I promised to let my mother know when I arrived."

"Ask the admin officer to send it for you. They said if we needed anything just to ask. If it's addressed to Magdeburg it might be better to have them send it."

"Oh it's no trouble. I'd like a breath of fresh air anyway. I'll be back in five minutes."

Annaliese walked down the corridor towards the central foyer of the Officers' Mess, its imposing arches in the entrance hall looking out across the manicured lawns and the tennis court. She pulled the folding door of the telephone booth closed behind her after checking that the corridor was quiet. Pumping a handful of coins into the public call box she dialled, tapping her fingers, nervously, waiting for the connection. The number she had called would be unrecognisable to the normal users of this particular phone booth. It would connect with a phone on a desk in an office in the Stasi Headquarters on the Ruschestraße in East Berlin.

"Gartner."

"It's me. I'm in."

The harsh buzz as the connection was severed was all she had expected.

AUTHOR'S NOTE

With World War 2 only a recent memory the resolve of the western allies, France, Great Britain and the United States of America was to be tested for the first time. As the Soviet Union increased its stranglehold on the former eastern sector of Germany, air corridors were established to allow access to the divided city of Berlin. With rising tensions road, rail and canal access to the city was severed leaving only the links through the three Berlin Air Corridors. In 1948, with the risk of starvation real, the allies initiated the Berlin Airlift to resupply the beleaguered residents of the former capital. The operation ended officially on 30 September 1949 after fifteen months during which the allies flew in 2.3 million tons of supplies nearly two-thirds of which was coal. There were a staggering 278,228 flights into Berlin utilising a complex flow pattern through the corridors to ensure inbound and outbound flights were deconflicted.

Incidents along the Berlin Corridor were all too real during the ensuing Cold War. On 29 April 1952 an Air France Douglas C-54 airliner flying from Frankfurt to Berlin Tempelhof was attacked by a pair of Soviet Mig-15 Fagot fighters as it routed along one of the air corridors over East Germany. Badly damaged and with two of its four engines shut down the pilot made an emergency landing in Berlin. When inspected the airframe had suffered 89 hits from cannon fire but luckily there were no injuries to the crew or passengers. Typical of the Cold War rhetoric, the Soviet military authorities defended the aggression claiming the aircraft had strayed from the corridor. The only RAF aircraft which the British Government admitted had been shot down by Soviet aircraft was an Avro Lincoln from the Central Gunnery School from Leconfield in Yorkshire. On 12 March 1953, as the aircraft was entering the northerly corridor from Hamburg to Berlin, it was attacked by two Mig-15 Fagots which engaged without warning. The crippled bomber began to break up yet the Migs pressed the attack until the aircraft crashed. It was acknowledged that the Lincoln was close to the edge or even outside the corridor but its track was clearly following the path. The period was a watershed for East-West relations as the incident had been preceded by the loss of a US Air Force F-84 Thunderjet a week earlier that had also been shot down by Migs, although on that occasion the pilot was able to eject safely. Immediately after the loss of the Lincoln, a British European Airways Viking airliner was attacked by Migs on a scheduled flight. Two weeks later an American B-50 on a routine flight was attacked by more Migs but, able to respond with self defensive fire, it survived. Times were tense.

Although incidents were rare in the following years, to guard against this type of aggression and to guarantee safe passage along the Berlin corridors, reinforcement exercises were arranged by the tri-power allied nations, France, The United States and Great Britain. They were normally held at West German airbases where the Soviets could monitor the activity in the exercise area. The British bases at RAF Wildenrath and RAF Gutersloh hosted the exercises on a rotational basis.

It is history that the exercise was never employed for real but the risk was ever present. The events in Provocation are fictional but espionage activity was all too real. The Military Liaison Missions known as BRIXMIS and SOXMIS were active on both sides of the Inner German Border and were endorsed by the leadership. Ostensibly intended to build confidence through liaison they became a key means to collect intelligence against the opposition. Arguably more useful in the East where censorship and tight control of military information was the norm, the members of the missions were carefully monitored whenever they ventured from their bases. Their exploits in evading surveillance are recounted in classic tales of Cold War intrigue.

Although the registration D-EBOV is carried by a red Cessna 172, the light aircraft and its antics in the story are entirely fictional. The real Cessna is based at Leutkirsch - Unterzahl and never made an unscheduled trip to Zerbst during the Cold War. Whether it has since visited is of course entirely possible with the fall of the Wall.

Gorbachev's role in the story is also fictional but before Yuri Andropov died in 1984, he made it known that he wanted Gorbachev to succeed him as General Secretary. Despite a terminal illness, one of the old guard, Konstantin Chernenko took power but died the following year at which stage it became apparent that younger leadership was needed to guide the Soviet Union into the modern era. With his election to the position of General Secretary on 11 March 1985, Gorbachev became the youngest ever member of the Politburo at the age of 54. In 1986 Gorbachev initiated his plans for "Perestroika", or "restructuring", and the radical reforms led to the introduction of "Glasnost" in 1988 giving the Soviet citizens new freedoms including greater freedom of speech. These momentous reforms led to the breakup of the Soviet Union and the fall of the Inner German Border when East German citizens flooded across into West Berlin on 9 November 1989.

The Cold War was over but recent events question whether there is a hint of frost once more evident.

ABOUT THE AUTHOR

David Gledhill is an aviation enthusiast and aviator. Already holding a private pilot's licence at the age of 17, he was commissioned in the RAF in 1974, and after training as an air navigator, converted to the F4 Phantom in the Air Defence role. After tours in the UK and Germany, he went on to be a radar tactics instructor on the Operational Conversion Unit. After transferring to the new Tornado F2 as one of the first instructors, he eventually became the Executive Officer on the OCU. His flying career finished in the Falkland Islands where he commanded No. 1435 Flight flying the Tornado F3. During his later career he served as a staff officer in the UK Ministry of Defence and the Air Warfare Centre. He also served on exchange duties at the Joint Command and Control Center and the US. Air Force Warfare Center in the United States of America and as the Senior Operations Officer at the Balkans Combined Air Operations Centre.

GLOSSARY

AAA. Anti aircraft artillery.

ACE. Allied Command Europe.

ADIZ. Air Defence Interception Zone. Restricted airspace immediately alongside the Inner German Border.

Air-to-Air TACAN. Although the tactical air navigation system was a radio based navigation aid which gave a range and bearing to a ground station it could be operated in an air-to-air mode. The system could give a range between two cooperating aircraft if air-to-air mode was selected.

Anchor. Establish a holding pattern.

AVTUR. Aviation jet fuel.

Barrier. An arrester net stretched across the end of a runway.

Biggles. A fictional World War 1 pilot from the novels of W.E. Johns.

Blue-on-Blue. An engagement against a friendly target.

Bogey. A codeword for a hostile target.

Bold face. Initial emergency drills in the cockpit.

Bonedome. Slang for flying helmet.

Boomy. The boom operator on a US tanker.

"Brass Monkey". A radio call to warn aviators that a track is straying close to the ADIZ. On hearing the call any aircraft operating close to the border was required to turn onto a westerly heading.

BRIXMIS. The British Military Liaison Team.

Buffer Zone. An area of restricted airspace with special flight rules buffering the Air Defence Interception Zone. The combined zones prevented inadvertent incursions in to East Germany.

Bug Out. To disengage from an air combat engagement.

Bullseye. A reference point nominated by a control agency to give a reporting datum from which all contacts can be called.

Button. American terminology for a preset frequency on the radio box.

Cable. A wire stretched across the runway designed to stop a fast jet in emergency using a hook fitted to the aircraft.

CAP. Combat Air Patrol.

Chop or chopped. To switch radio frequency.

CinC. Commander in Chief; mostly CinC RAF Germany in the novel.

Clean. Not illuminated by a threat aircraft. Sometimes the term "naked" can be used.

COMAO. Combined Air Operation.

Commcen. Communications centre.

Comsec. Communications security.

Coolant. Liquid cooling to lower the temperature of an infra-red missile seeker making it more sensitive.

CW. The continuous wave radar which guided the Sparrow missile towards the target.

DCDI. Deputy Chief of Defence Intelligence.

DF. Direction finding. A means to establish a bearing to a transmission.

Many military radios are fitted with a DF function.

ECM. Electronic Countermeasures.

ELINT. Electronic Intelligence.

EWO. Electronic Warfare Officer.

FAC. Forward Air Controller.

Flight Level. A height in thousands of feet. Fight Level 250 is 25,000 feet.

Form 700. The aircraft servicing log book.

Furball. A turning engagement with multiple aircraft engaged.

GCI. Ground Controlled Interception.

Guard. The international distress frequency.

The Hard. Concrete buildings built to withstand attack by heavy weapons.

Hard Wing Phantom. The FG1 and FGR2 versions of the Phantom were not fitted with leading edge slats. Leading edge flaps that could not, officially, be used in air combat manoeuvring were fitted to the wing. Slats gave extra manoeuvrability at high angle of attack and Phantoms fitted with these devices were known as "soft wing".

HAS. Hardened Aircraft Shelter.

IFF. Identification Friend or Foe. An electronic identification system.

IFF Interrogator. An electronic system to interrogate an IFF transponder to read the transmitted codes.

IGB. Inner German Border. The border between East and West Germany, often referred to as "The Iron Curtain".

INAS. Inertial Navigation and Attack System.

Initials. A visual entry point on the runway extended centreline at 5 miles.

Interlocks. Safety circuits which prevented the launch of a missile outside set parameters.

IP. Initial Point. The start of an attack run. A reference point some miles from a target from which fine details of track and timing are set.

IRCCM. Infra-Red Counter-Countermeasures.

JAG. Judge Advocate General. The HQ legal representative.

JHQ. Joint Headquarters. A combined HQ based at Rheindahlen commanding Army and Air Force Units.

Joker. A codeword signifying an aircraft has reached recovery fuel.

Jubilee Guardsman. An IFF interrogator fitted to the Phantom weapon system.

K-Loader. A self-propelled piece of support equipment which loads heavy missiles onto aircraft.

LCOSS. Lead Computing Optical Sighting System – the gunsight.

LLADS. Low Level Air Defence System. Mobile pulse Doppler radars.

MANPADS. Man-portable air defence system. A shoulder launched surface-to-air missile.

Maskirovka. The Soviet Union's military doctrine of surprise through deception.

Max Mil. Abbreviation for maximum military power. Full power without selecting reheat.

Meaconing. The interception and rebroadcast of radio navigation signals giving false position information to confuse enemy aircrew.

Merge. The initial position of an air combat engagement when the opponents meet.

Mode Charlie. A function on the IFF system which records the height of the transponding aircraft and displays it on the controllers radar screen.

MT. Motor transport.

NATO. North Atlantic Treaty Organisation.

NCO. Non Commissioned Officer.

NOFORN. An American security caveat meaning not releasable to foreign nationals.

OCU. Operational Conversion Unit. The Phantom training squadron.

Opsec. Operational security.

ORP. Operational Readiness Platform. A dispersal close to the runway where jets can be held if waiting for takeoff.

PAN. An emergency call denoting urgency but short of a Mayday situation.

Parrot. A codeword for an IFF transponder.

PBF. Pilot's Briefing Facility.

Pk. Probability of Kill.

PLB. Personal Locator Beacon fitted in the lifejacket to provide an emergency location signal to search and rescue forces after an ejection.

Pipper. The gunsight aiming marker used for weapon aiming.

Port. Left.

PSO. Personal Staff Officer.

PVO Strany. The Russian Air Defence Command responsible for defence of the Homeland.

QFE. The pressure setting which when set on a barometric altimeter gives height above the runway threshold.

QFI. Qualified flying instructor rated on type.

QNH. The pressure setting which when set on a barometric altimeter gives height above mean sea level.

QRA. Quick Reaction Alert.

QWI. Qualified Weapons Instructor.

Rackets. A radar warning receiver alert.

Radalt. Radio altimeter which uses radio waves to measure height rather than barometric pressure.

RAFG. Royal Air Force Germany. A Command for British air forces deployed in West Germany.

RoE. Rules of Engagement.

R/T. Radio Transmission.

RTB. Return To Base.

RWR. Radar Warning Receiver.

SACEUR. Senior Allied Commander Europe. Normally an American Four Star General.

SAR. Search and Rescue.

SAROPS. Search and Rescue Operations.

Sec Def. The US Secretary of State for Defense.

SENGO. Senior Engineering Officer.

Sidetone. The background noise during a radio transmission.

SIGINT. Signals Intelligence.

Sitrep. Situation Report. A summary of the tactical situation.

Soft. Unprotected buildings made of normal construction materials.

SOXMIS. The Soviet Military Liaison Team.

Splash. An air-to-air kill.

Squawk. To transmit a selected code on the Identification Friend or Foe system.

Squawk Ident. To transmit an identification code on the Identification Friend or Foe system.

Starboard. Right.

Step. American terminology for leaving operations to crew-in to an aircraft.

Stud. A preset frequency on the radio box.

Supplan Mike. An operational plan which detailed the operational procedures for Cold War operations.

TACAN. Tactical Air Navigation System. A radio receiver in the aircraft which gives a range and bearing to a selected radio beacon.

TACEVAL. Tactical Evaluation Exercise. A NATO sponsored combat readiness evaluation.

"Tally." Short for "Tally Ho" a codeword for visual contact with the target.

UHF. Ultra High Frequency.

U/S. Unserviceable.

Visident. A visual identification. A radar controlled procedure to close in on a target.

VOR. A civilian navigation aid giving a bearing from the radio beacon.

Vul. Time. A timing reference point for an operational mission.

Weapons free. Authority to engage delegated to lower levels of command. Hostile targets could be engaged.

Weapons tight. Authority to release weapons not granted.

WSO. Abbreviated to "Wizzo". Phantom back-seaters of certain NATO air forces were known as weapons systems officers.

X Ray. A code to denote the aircraft is serviceable.

2ATAF. 2nd Allied Tactical Air Force.

COMTWOATAF. Commander 2nd Allied Tactical Air Force. A NATO appointment.

ILLUSTRATIONS

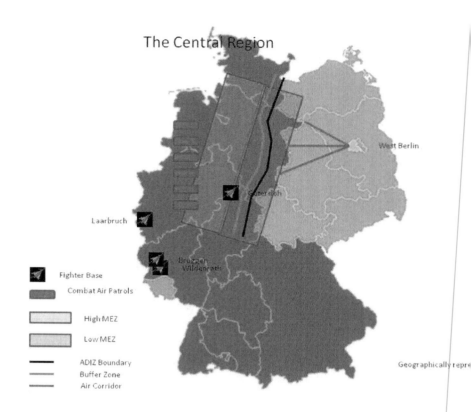

The Central Region

West Berlin

Gütersloh

Laarbruch

Brüggen
Wildenrath

Fighter Base

Combat Air Patrols

High MEZ

Low MEZ

ADIZ Boundary
Buffer Zone
Air Corridor

Geographically repre

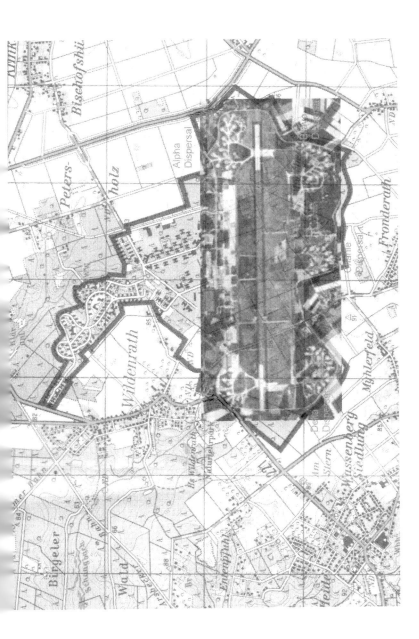

RAF Wildenrath

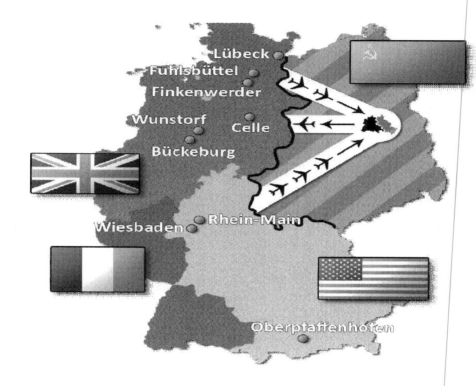

The Berlin Air Corridors

OTHER BOOKS BY THIS AUTHOR

Have you ever wondered what it was like to fly the Phantom? This is not a potted history of an aeroplane, nor is it Hollywood glamour as captured in *Top Gun*. This is the story of life on the frontline during the Cold War told in the words of a navigator who flew the iconic jet. Unique pictures, many captured from the cockpit, show the Phantom in its true environment and show why for many years the Phantom was the envy of NATO. It also tells the inside story of some of the problems which plagued the Phantom in its early days, how the aircraft developed, or was neglected, and reveals events which shaped the aircraft's history and contributed to its demise. Anecdotes capture the deep affection felt by the crews who were fortunate enough to cross paths with the Phantom during their flying careers. The nicknames the aircraft earned were not complimentary and included the 'Rhino', 'The Spook', 'Double Ugly', the 'Flying Brick' and the 'Lead Sled'. Whichever way you looked at it, you could love or hate the Phantom, but you could never ignore it.

"The Phantom in Focus: A Navigator's Eye on Britain's Cold War Warrior" - ISBN 978-178155-048-9 (print) and ASIN B00GUNIM0Q (e-book) published by Fonthill Media.

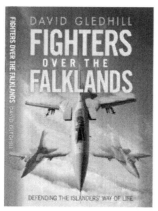

Fighters Over The Falklands: Defending the Islanders' Way of Life captures daily life using pictures taken during the author's tours of duty in the Falkland Islands. From the first detachments of Phantoms and Rapiers operating from a rapidly upgraded RAF Stanley airfield to life at RAF Mount Pleasant, see life from the author's perspective as the Commander of the Tornado F3 Flight defending the islands' airspace. Frontline fighter crews provided Quick Reaction Alert (QRA) during day to day flying operations working with the Royal Navy, Army and other air force units to defend a remote and sometimes forgotten theatre of operations. The book also examines how the islanders interacted with the forces based at Mount Pleasant and contrast high technology military operations with the lives of the original inhabitants, namely the wildlife.

"Fighters Over The Falklands – Defending the islanders Way of Life" - ISBN 978-17155-222-3 (print) and ASIN: B00H87Q7MS (e book) published by Fonthill Media.

The Tornado F2 had a troubled introduction to service. Unwanted by its crews and procured as a political imperative, it was blighted by failures in the acquisition system. Adapted from a multi-national design and planned by committee, it was developed to counter a threat which disappeared. Modified rapidly before it could be sent to war, the Tornado F3 eventually matured into a capable weapons system but despite datalinks and new air to air weapons, its poor reputation sealed its fate. The author, a former Tornado F3 navigator, tells the story from an insider's perspective from the early days as one of the first instructors on the Operational Conversion Unit, through its development and operational testing, to its demise. He reflects on its capabilities and deficiencies and analyses why the aircraft was mostly under-estimated by opponents. Although many books have already described the Tornado F3, the author's involvement in its development will provide a unique insight into this complex and misunderstood aircraft programme and dispel some of the myths. This is the author's 3rd book and, like the others, captures the story in pictures taken in the cockpit and around the squadron.

"Tornado F3 In Focus – A Navigator's Eye on Britain's Last Interceptor" - ISBN 978-178155-307-7 (print) and ASIN B00TM7A80E (e book) published by Fonthill Media.

The Panavia Tornado was designed as a multi-role combat aircraft to meet the needs of Germany Italy and the United Kingdom. Since the prototype flew in 1974, nearly 1000 Tornados have been produced in a number of variants serving as a fighter-bomber, a fighter and in the reconnaissance and electronic suppression roles. Deployed operationally in numerous theatres throughout the world, the Tornado has proved to be exceptionally capable and flexible. From its early Cold War roles it adapted to the rigours of expeditionary warfare from The Gulf to Kosovo to Afghanistan. The early "dumb" bombs were replaced by laser-guided weapons and cruise missiles and in the air-to-air arena fitted with the AMRAAM and ASRAAM missiles.

In this book David Gledhill explores the range of capabilities and, having flown the Tornado F2 and F3 Air Defence Variant, offers an insight into life in the cockpit of the Tornado. Lavishly illustrated, Darren Willmin's superb photographs capture the essence of the machine both from the ground and in the air. This unique collection including some of David Gledhill's own air-to-air pictures of the Tornado F2 and F3 will appeal to everyone with an interest in this iconic aircraft.

"Tornado In Pictures _ The Multi Role Legend" - ISBN 978-1781554630 *(print) published by Fonthill Media.*

.

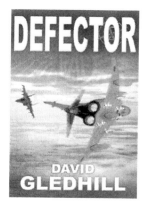

Colonel Yuri Andrenev, a respected test pilot is trusted to evaluate the latest Soviet fighter, the Sukhoi Su27 "Flanker", from a secret test facility near Moscow. Surely he is above suspicion? With thoughts of defection in his mind, and flying close to the Inner German Border, could he be tempted to make a daring escape across the most heavily defended airspace in the world? A flight test against a Mig fighter begins a sequence of events that forces his hand and after an unexpected air-to-air encounter he crosses the border with the help of British Phantom crews. How will Western Intelligence use this unexpected windfall? Are Soviet efforts to recover the advanced fighter as devious as they seem or could more sinister motives be in play? Defector is a pacy thriller which reflects the intrigue of The Cold War. It takes you into the cockpit of the Phantom fighter jet with the realism that can only come from an author who has flown operationally in the NATO Central Region.

"Defector" - ISBN 978-1-49356-759-1 (print) and ASIN B00EUYEUDK (e book) published by DeeGee Media.

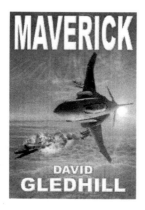

Combat veteran Major Pablo Carmendez holds a grudge against his former adversaries. Diverting his armed Skyhawk fighter-bomber from a firepower demonstration he flies eastwards towards the Falkland Islands intent on revenge. What is his target and will he survive the defences alerted of his intentions? Crucially, will his plan wreck delicate negotiations between Britain and Argentina designed to mend strained relations? Are Government officials charged with protecting the islanders' interests worthy of that trust or are more sinister motives in play? Maverick is an aviation thriller set in the remote outpost in the South Atlantic Ocean that takes you into the cockpits of the Phantom fighters based on the Islands where you will experience the thrills of air combat as the conspiracy unfolds.

"Maverick" - ISBN 978-1507801895 (print) and ASIN B00S9ULA30 (e book) published by DeeGee Media.

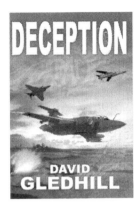

When a hostage is snatched from the streets of Beirut by Hezbollah terrorists it sets in train a series of events from the UK to the Middle East that end in the corridors of power. A combined air operation is mounted from a base in Cyprus to release the agent from his enforced captivity. Phantom and Buccaneer crews help a special forces team to mount a daring raid, the like of which has not been attempted since Operation Jericho during World War 2. With Syrian forces ranged against them and Israeli and American friends seemingly bent on thwarting them, the outcome is by no means certain. As in his other novels David Gledhill takes you into the cockpit in this fast paced Cold War tale of intrigue and deception.

"Deception" - *ISBN* 978-1508762096 *(print) and ASIN* B00V8JTE40 *(e book)* published by *DeeGee Media.*

Printed in Great Britain
by Amazon